THE SIXTH SEAL

To W.S.

THE
SIXTH
SEAL

MARY WESLEY

And I beheld when he had opened the
sixth seal, and, lo, there was a great
earthquake; and the sun became black
as sackcloth of hair, and the moon became as blood.

Revelation vi.12

THE OVERLOOK PRESS
WOODSTOCK • NEW YORK

First published in 1993 by
The Overlook Press
Lewis Hollow Road
Woodstock, New York 12498

Library of Congress Cataloging-in-Publication Data

Wesley, Mary
The sixth seal / Mary Wesley.
p.cm.
Summary: After a mysterious apocalypse destroys the world, the
few survivors must learn how to coexist in desperate times.
[1. Survival–Fiction. 2. Disasters–Fiction.]
I. Title
PZ7.W5SI 1993
[Fic]–dc 20
93-25783
CIP
AC

Originally published in Great Britain by J.M. Dent,
a division of The Orion Publishing Group.

ISBN: 0-87951-506-6

1

'Mama?'

Sam's quiet voice, which he'd affected since he was at Oxford, murmured in her ear.

'Oh, hullo darling, where are you?'

'In London with John Kelly.'

'Coming home?'

'Well, not immediately. We're going to Germany for a trip.'

'What fun for you. Whereabouts?'

'Just to look. You know it's all this pink snow and green stuff we want to see. Then we want to come home. Can I bring John?'

'Of course you can. Give him my love. When will you be back?'

'We don't know, but I'll telephone. We are motoring.'

Another affectation.

'Enjoy yourselves. Have you got enough money?'

'Yes, thank you. Goodbye Mama.'

'Goodbye, darling. Goodbye.'

Click. A dead line. How lonely she felt. John, Germany, coloured snow in July. Lonely sterile telephone. She banged down the receiver.

'Mum? Mum? Where are you?'

'Here, darling. Here, by the telephone.'

'Who was it?'

'Sam.'

'Is he coming home?'

'Presently. He's just going to Germany to look at that pink and green snow.'

'But it's in East Germany.'

'Oh.'

'Yes, it said near Dresden. That's East. How is he going to get there?'

'They get visas I think.'

'Paul, Paul, come on. It's nearly ready. Do buck up.'

'Okay. 'Bye, Mum.' Paul tore off to join the voice in the garden, leaving all the doors open as he ran.

Lonely. Silly. She had the two boys. Thirteen is a nice age she thought to herself as she laid tea on a tray. Nice to be thirteen and innocent. Sam was nineteen: John twenty-two and American.

The dogs followed her as she carried the tray up the garden to the extraordinary encampment the children had made. Her back ached.

'Mum, we can sleep here tonight, can't we?' Pleading.

'If you promise to come in if it rains.'

'We will. The rain would make an awful noise on the corrugated iron.'

'Pink snow wouldn't.'

'Stupid, it won't fall here, it's in Germany.'

'Blue then.'

'No snow. It's warm.'

'Oh, well.' Henry shrugged. 'England's dull.'

Henry looked so like Paul; dressed alike, hair alike, altogether the same colouring. Henry had done all the work of the camp, laying corrugated iron sheets found round about the farm across the brick-sided pond, which never had held water even when it was just built in the early nineteen hundreds as a small lily pond of all things. Dry it had always been, drier than the whole garden. Muriel looked with amusement at the iron covering, the mattresses and sleeping bags ready laid for the night.

'Mrs Wake, won't you join us!' Henry had a courteous old-fashioned way of speaking which he had picked out of some book. Muriel wondered which, as his mode of speech varied from month to month.

'Thank you very much, but I think not.' Muriel could see Paul's look of relief. He wanted his friend to himself. 'You see I have the dogs and cat sleeping with me. It would make rather a crowd.'

Paul said, 'Oh, couldn't they come?'

'Well, I might snore and keep you awake.'

'Henry snores. He sleeps on his back with his mouth open.'

Henry laughed. 'Let's have tea.'

They ate sitting by the camp and looking down over the moors to the valleys beyond.

'Pink snow.' Paul was jealous. 'How soon will we be able to travel alone—just to ring you up and say we are going?'

'Not long—about sixteen. That's when Sam started travelling on his own.'

'Where shall we go to first?' said Henry. He left big decisions to Paul sometimes.

'To wherever it's snowing or doing something out of context.'

Out of context, thought Muriel, pouring out tea and handing round buns. Where did that come from?

'Think of the floods in China.'

'Dreamy.'

'Those earthquakes in Africa.'

'Super.'

'Those pestilences in America.'

'Fab.'

'Plagues of Egypt,' said Muriel lightly. 'Listen to the Abbey bells. It must be a south-west wind.'

'Yes.' The two boys munched and held out their mugs for more tea.

'Look, Peg is dribbling.'

'Give her a bun.'

Peg ate daintily with an apologetic look at Muriel.

'When are her puppies due?'

'Oh, any day now.'

'And Charlie's kittens? I hope they have moustaches too.'

'Quite soon by the look of her.'

Muriel gathered up the tea things and sat for a moment looking down at the house, a grey stone hollow E, with the sun on it; the centre to live in, the east wing barns and lofts and stables, and the west wing garages with more lofts above them. Too large really, she thought, as she idly watched Charlie disappear up the steps into one of the lofts above the stable.

'She's made her nest below ground in the cellar,' said Paul, following her eyes.

'Well, so long as they aren't all born in my bed. Peg has her eye on that.' Muriel picked up the tray and carried it back to the house, hearing an argument break out between the two boys as she went. The house was quiet. She could hear a mouse in the wainscot, and the clocks. She washed up.

'Tidy, tidy, so tidy, oh God.' She wandered from room to room, 'It could have been heaven,' she muttered. 'Self-pity,' she said aloud, picking up a photograph of a man, the man she had loved, Paul's father, and putting it on the log fire which

3

burnt winter and summer in the drawing-room. 'If you are dead I'd rather not see you.'

Sam had given her no address. It was stupid not to have asked him. She wandered back through the hall and picked up a pile of letters, the morning's post which she had not bothered to look at. 'Heavens, what a lot of bills.' Just like Julian to put in oil-fired central heating and get enough oil for three years stored up here, and coal too, logs and coke for the Aga and oil for the electric plant. 'You never know,' he had said, and Muriel agreed one did not. He was killed three months ago now, she thought. Mustn't think of it.

The telephone again. 'Oh, hullo, Susan.'

'We are just leaving London, darling. Is Henry all right?'

'Oh yes.'

'Not being a nuisance?'

'You know I adore having him.'

Susan talked on about people, plays, films, clothes she had bought, Spain where she was going. Muriel hardly heard or listened.

'Yes, darling, yes, I'll see he gets to bed early. Yes, of course, not overdo things. Treat him as my own. Goodbye, Susan, have a good time, goodbye.'

Muriel went back towards the kitchen thinking it would be nice to have supper there, then watch the news on TV and that serial she liked, silly and unrealistic as it was, then an early bed with lots of pills to bring sleep so that she would not hear the shriek of brakes then the silence which underlay every waking moment.

She went across to the farm to fetch eggs and cream from Mrs Perryman who was preparing a colossal meal for her husband and son to eat after milking. She listened to the account of the birth of three new calves the night before, two heifers and a little bull. She enquired after the family, the hens, the sheep, the lambs, the ponies, the expected illegitimate babies in the village five miles away, and then, followed by Peg whose extended stomach swung rhythmically as she walked, she went back to the house and switched on the news and sat watching.

The announcer gave a lurid account of the road accidents on the A30 and A38: the traffic at a standstill for five hours on the Exeter by-pass; three more bank robberies in the City of London; the birth of triplets to a lady in Camborne; the unsuc-

4

cessful search for the missing yachtsman off the north Devon coast; the weather forecast. 'Sunny and glorious, ever victorious,' muttered Muriel.

'More pinkish-red snow is reported from East Germany and our reporter from West Germany says there are reports of heavy falls of green snow in the Bavarian Alps. From Stockholm there are unconfirmed reports of black snow in Finland and Russia...' Muriel switched off. Disasters, she thought, but what about me? She went to the telephone and dialled the Abbey.

'Can I speak to Father Richard?'

A distant sighing voice said, 'Father Richard has taken the novices potholing. Can I give a message? It's Mrs Wake isn't it?'

'No, thank you. I'll try later.' I can't tell him I'm in a state of despair very well. Muriel laughed in the empty house.

'Mum! Mum! When is supper?'

'As soon as I can get it.'

'Come on, Henry, it's now. Then we can see Whirligig before we settle down.'

The children helped her with supper then sat rapt (watching a futuristic film of extreme violence) before disappearing in the dusk to their camp. Muriel let Peg out for a run, visited the camp and shouted, 'Are you all right?'

'Yes, it's wonderful. Cover us over will you, Mum?'

Muriel covered the last gap between the corrugated sheets with a board, called out goodnight and went back to the house. As she went in the stout figure of Charlie joined her from under a bush and together with the dog and cat she went up to her room.

Pills. Three perhaps. Muriel swallowed three. She undressed, put on her nightdress and got into bed. The dog and the cat settled themselves on the bed with her, so arranging themselves that either she had to lie curved like the letter S, or flat on her back with her legs apart. She listened to the noises of the night; the sheep on the moor, the ponies and cattle giving an occasional neigh or low, the owls from the barn crying as they set about their night's work.

Muriel sat up suddenly. 'What the hell does he want to go potholing for when I want spiritual advice?' She grabbed the telephone by the bed and heard it ringing unanswered for a long time in the hall by those ugly parlours. 'No answer. Of course, it's after Compline, they can't speak.' Muriel lay down and heard the clatter of horses' hooves and a man's Devonshire voice calling urgently. A woman's voice answered and, sleepily, she thought she heard Paul's and Henry's unbroken piping joining in.

'Curse it!' Muriel sat up and switched the radio on. Yehudi Menuhin was playing his violin, wailing, consoling, demanding. Suddenly he was interrupted. 'This is a News Flash. There has been a heavy fall of black snow in the mountains of Scotland and our correspondent from our northern studio reports yellow and green snowfalls in parts of Northumberland and Durham with heavy drifting. There are gale warnings all round the coast of England, Scotland and the Irish Channel.' Muriel switched off. 'Neapolitan ices—quite mad.' She curled up, taking sudden advantage of Peg changing position, and slept.

'If your mother heard that would she worry?' Henry propped up on an elbow, tried to see Paul in the dark. Between them was a small transistor radio.

'I expect she's asleep. There was no light in her window when we got back.'

'Do you think the animals have gone mad?'

'I can't think. Anyway we shut the ponies in and they can't run off and Mr Perryman has shut in those three cows and their calves and those five sheep with their lambs. He couldn't round up any others.'

'Perhaps he will in the morning.'

'Well, they've all gone to bed now. Lights out in the farm.'

'I wish your mother was here with us.'

'She's got enough worries.'

'I forgot.'

'My father killed—bills, bills, bills, no money. I don't think Sam ought to have gone off just like that. She was expecting him tomorrow.'

'Grown-ups are odd.'

'Not really. D'you know I found out a lot by reading her letters?'

'Paul!'

'Don't pretend to be shocked. I bet you read all your family's.'

'They lock them up usually.'

'There you are. You would if you could.'

6

Henry giggled. 'I listen outside doors.'

'Everyone does that.'

'One has to keep abreast. It's like not being told about sex and birth control.'

'Oh, I know all that but it's frightfully dull.'

'Well, all their plans, and "don't let's tell the children until we've made up our minds": that sort of stuff.'

'I can't hear anything now.'

'Let's listen.'

The two boys listened.

'Oh blast!'

'What's that?'

'Not very interesting. I'll tell you some time. Blow your nose and then you won't snuffle and we might hear something.' Henry blew. They listened.

'Absolutely nothing, and it said gales. Not even a breeze.'

'Paul.'

'Yes.'

'I'm frightened.' There was a long pause. Then Paul whispered, 'So am I.'

'What shall we do?'

'I'm going to put on a jersey.' They both put on jerseys and lay down again. The jerseys were prickly and the night very silent. Paul struggled out of his sleeping bag and stood up. The brick-sided pit was a good twelve feet deep and up one side they had a ladder. Without a word to Paul, Henry began tiptoeing up the ladder. Paul followed and held his breath while Henry cautiously slid open the corrugated iron trap door. They climbed out and stood listening. Not a sound. Not a breath of air.

'Damn all,' said Henry.

'Damn all,' said Paul.

'I'm going to see if Mrs Wake is all right.'

'I'm coming. I'm just as frightened as you.' They crept down the garden to the house and slipped in at the back door. Warmth from the Aga in the kitchen and the sound of Chap's tail wagging gently in greeting.

'Does he always sleep here?'

'Yes. He likes it.'

Both boys jumped as the cuckoo clock began to strike midnight, echoed by the Abbey bells in the distance.

'Will she be furious?'

'No, she's too unhappy.'

Chap got up and followed as the two boys crept up stairs. Paul opened his mother's door. 'Mum.'

From deep sleep Muriel came up slowly. She heard the shriek of brakes and silence, then her son's voice. 'Yes, darling? I was asleep.'

'Mum we're frightened.'

'Oh dear.'

'Could you come to the pit, Mrs Wake? And bring Charlie and Peg. Chap is here.'

Muriel switched on her bedside light. 'Okay,' she said matter-of-factly. 'Lead on.' Henry led.

Chap and Charlie got down the ladder by themselves. Peg made rather a fuss though appearing anxious to get down. Muriel and the animals settled on the mattress between the two boys.

'All the Perrymans' animals have run away.'

'So that's what I heard.'

'All except our ponies. Henry and I caught them and a few cows and sheep. It said snow was falling in England.'

'Yes, I heard it too, and Yehudi Menuhin.'

'Culture! Listen, planes.'

'Yes, going fast. It's the night run to Africa.'

'Mum.'

'Yes?'

'Listen to Henry snoring.'

'I'll come closer. Father Richard went potholing.'

'Crackers!'

'Let's sleep.'

'I can't.'

'Why?'

'My jersey tickles.'

'Take the damn thing off, it's as hot as the Black Hole of Calcutta now we're all down here.'

'Mum.'

'Let's talk a bit. I don't feel sleepy.'

'What about?'

'There are some more planes. Shall I switch on the radio? We might hear something.'

'We'd wake Henry.'

'Not Henry. There's Radio Albatross about now.'

'That's why you're always so hard to wake in the morning.'

'Shall I?'

'All right, but quietly. My watch says it's after one o'clock.'

'Listen.'

Radio Albatross said, 'If your mother seems worried and cross give her Super-white Everdry—washes whiter than snow, whiter than white—'

'Snow's green and pink now.'

'Whiter than the whites of a baby's eyes.'

Paul made a slight retching sound.

'And now the News. Our latest information is that all Europe is blanketed in snow, not only pink and green as previously reported, but in many varying colours. The resorts in the Alps are already overwhelmed with telephone calls for hotel bookings by winter sports enthusiasts. The floods in China appear to be unabated and the earthquakes in India, the Far East and the Middle East are continuing. The plague in America—'

'Plague!'

'—is spreading from the East to the West Coast and is reported as far north as Alaska and as far south as Mexico City. We have no further news of missing shipping.'

'No news!'

The news died away. Muriel fiddled with the controls of the small transistor but no more came. Paul was asleep. Henry snored in the dark. The three animals fitted themselves snugly to the curve of the human bodies. Charlie snarled under her breath. Peg sighed as her unborn puppies moved in her belly. Muriel felt, though she could not see, that Chap had his ears pricked. She slept.

2

Henry woke and in the twilight of the pit was aware of two things: an overwhelming desire to go to the lavatory and a glaring expression in the cat's eyes. She hissed at him.

'Puss, puss, Charlie.' Another hiss. Her whiskers bristled, her back was up, her white moustache seemed to flare at him against her black coat and the dim background of the pit.

'Oh, I *see*.' Henry saw slight humping heaving movements against her flank. He climbed out of his bag and, keeping well away from the cat and the recumbent forms of Paul and Muriel — both asleep with their mouths open, he was glad to see — pulled on a shirt and his jeans and climbed out of the pit. Chap whined. Henry held the trap-door open while the dog scrambled after him. Once up, he opened his flies and in companionship with the dog watered an azalea. Much relieved, he stood thoughtfully looking about him.

Gorgeously quiet, thought Henry. He turned a somersault from sheer joy. Nobody nags here. He was hungry. He peeped down into the pit. Everyone was asleep except Peg who opened one eye and then buried her nose deeper into a rug.

Henry danced down the path to the house and went in at the back door. The clock was striking and died unwound with a gasp. Henry pulled up the chains with the metal fir cones on them and set the pendulum swinging. It cuckooed twice more. 'Must be dawn. You hungry too?'

Henry and the dog went to the larder. 'Ah, bacon and eggs!' Henry helped himself and fetched a frying-pan. The Aga! Hastily he riddled it and poured in fuel. He fried eggs and bacon and sat down to eat it out of the pan thinking of his mother. She'd have a fit, he thought happily. He scraped up the last of the egg and fat with a bit of bread and caught Chap's eye. 'Oh Lord!' In the larder he found dog meat and biscuits and watched while the dog ate. 'I bet Charlie needs

10

something, and Peg.' Henry filled the bowl again with biscuit and meat, and filled another bowl with milk. Carefully he threaded his way in the sun to the pit.

'Still asleep. Gosh!'

Henry climbed down the ladder carefully with the bowl of dog food. Peg ate quietly, still lying down. Charlie glared.

'Oh, well—'

Henry climbed up the ladder again and fetched the milk. The cat drank ungratefully. 'Cats!'

Mrs Wake and Paul, the transistor between them, were snoring.

'Snubs!'

Henry went up the ladder again, replaced the trap-door and stood listening. Not a thing to be heard. He set off towards the farm. The farmhouse door was shut; he tried it, to find it locked. The Perrymans, he supposed, had gone off to round up their animals who had disappeared in that curious stampede last night. 'Oh well, they'll be back soon.'

Henry walked round the sheds to the silo pit. From the bottom of the pit three cows and three calves stared up at him, one cow in particular. The night before, he and Paul and the Perrymans' son had made a high wall of hay bales to keep them in, but they had no water. Henry remembered Mr Perryman saying, 'We'll let them get at the trough in the yard in the morning.'

'Forgotten I suppose.'

Henry dragged away the top bale and struggled with the others until he had made a narrow exit through which the cows and their calves pushed their way and rushed to the trough to drink deeply, then stared at him sighing, with water running out of their mouths as their calves nudged and jostled to get at their teats.

Henry remembered the sheep. 'Gosh, I need Paul's assistance.' He raced to the pit and whispered, 'Paul, wake up.'

Paul woke.

'The sheep.'

'The ponies.' Paul was struggling into his jeans.

'The cows are all right but the Perrymans must have forgotten them; they've gone out and locked the door.'

The boys ran together. The night before, so panic-striken had been the sheep and lambs that they had fallen down the chute into the coal cellar. 'Let un be,' Perryman had said. 'They won't

11

hurt. We'll get them out in the morning.' And he had slammed down the trap-door on them.

'They are there,' said Paul, 'but we need Mother.'

'Why?'

'Ever tried lifting one of these black-faced sheep alone? It takes a strong man.'

'I thought Mr Perryman beastly to leave them there.'

'Not really. They are quite safe and he was tired.'

'What about the ponies?'

'Let's look.' Paul led the way. 'You're very interested in animals suddenly. I thought all you Chelsea lot only liked them in their proper place and all that lark.'

'I like animals really. It's my family who don't. Besides a coal cellar can't be the proper place for sheep; even my town up-bringing tells me that.'

'Sure.' Paul unbolted the top door of the first loose box and a delicate whinny greeted them. 'One is all right anyway, but do look at that.'

Both boys stared at a heap of bay horsehair lying in the rough shape of a horse, mane hair then long tail hairs.

'Christ!'

'Let's look at the others.'

In all six loose boxes the same pattern was repeated with variations: heaps of horse hair near the box doors and, standing looking at them, one or more ponies.

'How macabre. Let's let them out.' In all, five ponies came out where ten had been shut in. They hurried to the horse trough then stood in a group looking around them.

'Don't let them out of the yard yet. There's plenty of hay.'

Paul went back to the loose boxes. With the hair lay horse-shoes, four to each heap of hair. He shut the doors.

'What about the hens? What could have made them all panic?' Henry, the boy from Chelsea who swore daily at cock-crow, remembered them. The boys walked, rather white-faced, to the the barn where Mrs Perryman kept her large flock of free-ranging hens.

'Nothing but feathers,' whispered Paul. Then suddenly, 'Mummy, Mummy!' and he raced away from his friend, tore open the trap-door covering the pit, clambered down into it and gripped his sleeping mother.

'Mummy, Mummy, there's nothing but fur and feathers, fur and feathers, oh, oh,' he wept hysterically.

12

'Hi, what is all this?' Muriel surged up out of her deep sleep.

'Fur and feathers.'

'What?'

'It's true, Mrs Wake, at least almost true, and the Perrymans are out.'

Muriel got up, cramped, and Peg stood up beside her. 'Good heavens, Charlie has had her kittens and somebody's fed her.'

'Yes, I did,' said Henry. 'We found the cows and their calves and some of the ponies are alive but the others are gone. There are just heaps of fur and hair and horse-shoes left and the sheep we caught last night are in the coal cellar, that's why we came for you.'

'I'm coming. Help me with Peg.'

All three struggled to get the large bitch up the ladder. Muriel looked about her and up into the sky. Funny, she thought, no planes.

'Has the post come?'

'I don't know, but I've made up the Aga and fed Charlie and Peg and Chap.'

'Oh, thank you, Henry.' Muriel yawned.

'And wound up the clock and cooked myself breakfast. I hope you don't mind.'

'Splendid. Why should I? Where have the Perrymans gone, Paul?'

'To find their stock I suppose. They locked their door.'

'Let's look.'

Muriel, in her nightdress and slippers and Marks and Spencer dressing-gown, ran across the garden and up towards the farm. The boys showed her the cows with their calves and the five ponies, the heaps of feathers, the fur in the stables, the silent sheep standing with their lambs in the cellar, their yellow eyes blinking up at them.

'We'll have a game getting those out. I must put on some clothes.' In the house Muriel tore off her nightdress and put on jeans and a shirt.

'First the Perrymans,' she said. The farm door was locked. 'A ladder. Their window is open.'

'I'll go up.'

'No, Paul, I think I will. I'm quite spry.'

Muriel climbed the ladder and squeezed in by the Perrymans' bathroom window. 'Mrs Perryman? Mrs Perryman?' She opened the first bedroom door.

'Oh!'

On the pillow lay Mrs Perryman's red, too tightly home-permed hair, beside it Fred's dark straight hair; on each side of the bed false teeth in a glass of water on a small table. Forcing herself, she shut the door and crossing the landing went into Abner's room. Here too the bedclothes were flat, the pillow dented, but just holding Abner's rather too long hair; at his feet a heap of rough, short, white hair. 'Nell.'

'Mum, can you find anyone?'

'No, I'm coming out.' Muriel climbed down the ladder again.

'Why didn't you come out by the door?'

'I didn't think.'

'Are they dead?'

'I suppose so.'

'They must be one thing or the other. Be logical,' said Henry rudely.

'It isn't logical. There's nothing there but their hair and false teeth.'

Paul began to laugh wildly.

'Paul, you need your breakfast. The sheep must wait.'

They hurried to the house and Muriel, quick at the best of times, rushed breakfast on to the table.

'Lunch really,' said Henry, as the clock struck.

'Yes, lunch.' Muriel drank coffee watching the boys eat. 'Now the sheep. We know they are alive.' They went up again to the farm.

'Jack is dead,' said Paul as they passed a ruffled heap of black and white hair beside a dog collar at the end of a chain tied to a barrel kennel.

Muriel forced herself up the ladder again and opened the door downstairs to the boys. 'Best get them out through the house.'

Half an hour later the sheep and their lambs were grazing in the orchard. Henry was covered in coal dust and Paul had a black eye. Muriel felt drained.

'Dial 999,' said Henry. Muriel went to the telephone.

'The line is dead. We'll have to walk down to Roberts and report it.'

'He has false teeth too, and Mrs Roberts.'

'Oh, Henry!'

'Well, we'd better be sensible about it, hadn't we?'

14

'Bags I break in.' Henry ran ahead, found a ladder, and by the time Muriel and Paul reached the Roberts' cottage he was climbing in.

'Sleep with their windows shut,' said Paul.

Henry jabbed his elbow neatly at a pane of glass and, carefully sliding his small hand through the jagged hole, opened the window and climbed in.

Two minutes later he emerged quickly from the front door, shutting it behind him. 'Two lots of grey hair and two sets of false teeth.' Then he was sick. 'Sorry,' he said.

'We'll get used to it, won't we, Mum?'

Muriel looked at the boys bleakly. 'I think we should go to the village and report the telephone and see the police.'

'Yes.'

'All together in the Landrover and take the dogs.'

3

Before leaving the house they made a tour. Everything seemed as usual, the kitchen and larder, the dining-room, the large beautiful library lined with books from floor to ceiling.

'What colour are the curtains going to be?' asked Henry.

'White, very extravagant velvet.'

'Mourning colour in the East.'

'Yes.'

'Have you got the stuff?'

'Yes, and for all the chairs and sofas.'

'What colour?'

'Green and pink and red.'

'Same as the snow,' said Paul.

'Any yellow?' Henry loved colour.

'Well, just this little button chair.'

'Beautiful.'

'Yes. Come on.'

They looked in at the drawing-room. 'That must have been a mouse.' Soft, short, silky fur on the rug. Muriel looked away.

'We can Hoover it up. Does the electricity work?' Paul tried a switch and the lights lit up pale in the sunshine.

'That's something. And we have our own water.'

'Why?' said Henry.

'So far from any mains here. We have everything on our own.'

They climbed up the stairs and looked into all the bedrooms and bathrooms.

'Lots of mice,' said Henry.

'Oh, look, bats!' Paul pointed at a transparent outline near the window.

'They squeaked.'

'I like bats, their teeth are soft.'

Muriel tried a tap. The water ran normally. The tank in the hot cupboard was hot. 'We can all have baths when we get back.'

'I suppose we had better leave the door open in case anyone comes, and leave Charlie in charge.'

'Yes.'

'We shall meet anyone coming on the road; it ends here.'

They climbed into the Landrover and sat three abreast with the two dogs behind and drove quickly down the drive, past the Roberts's silent cottage, on to the road over the moor, which dipped after half a mile into the valley and led down to the village.

'No sheep, ponies or anything about,' said Paul. 'The Perrymans' stock must have run miles.'

The road led past the huge reservoir like a lake which drained off to supply the coastal towns.

'Stop a minute, Mum, by the moor gate.'

Muriel stopped at the gate which Paul held open for her, and she and Henry watched as he ran down to the dam and stood staring into the water. Presently he ran up the slope, shouting something which they could not hear.

'What?'

'Fish, masses of them, alive,' Paul gasped joyfully as he climbed in.

'Oh Happy Living Things!' exclaimed Henry.

'Culture!' Paul gave him a friendly jog and they all laughed as Muriel let in the clutch and they drove on down into the valley.

'Here's old Courtier's farm. Shall we just see if he's all right?'

'Yes. His telephone may be working. It often is when ours goes wrong.'

They stopped at the farm. The door was locked.

'I know where he keeps his key.' Paul felt under a stone. 'It's locked from the inside.'

'Oh.'

They looked at each other.

'You two look round the farm. I'll climb in,' said Muriel. The two boys went off to the yard and shippens, while Muriel waited before scrambling up a step ladder at the back of the house to squeeze in by a half-open window. Five minutes later she came out of the front door and met the boys.

'Nothing but fur, wool and feathers,' they said.

'Only hair,' said Muriel.

'No teeth?' asked Henry.

'He had his own.'

'All the better to bite you with.' Henry seemed to be feeling rather cheerful.

'What's that?' asked Muriel, looking at Paul's wrist. Paul held out his arm.

'The bull's nose-ring. D'you remember when he chased Mrs Perryman?'

'The telephone is dead in there too.' Muriel climbed crossly into the Landrover. 'Come on. I can't think why they are so slipshod about it.' They drove on.

'Nothing on the road,' said Paul.

'Never is much traffic.' Muriel braked violently as they rounded a blind corner. 'Old Bartlett's car in the ditch.' Paul jumped out and ran to look, peering in at the old car's side windows.

'Just teeth and a terrific smell of whisky,' he said· when he climbed back into the Landrover.

Muriel squeezed past the wrecked car, scraping the wings of the Landrover, and drove on slowly without speaking.

As they came down into the village nobody spoke. Muriel parked the car in the square and looked up at the Church tower.

'Nearly four o'clock.'

'Nobody about.'

'No.'

'Where shall we go first?'

'The Post Office.'

17

'It's shut. I can see from here.'

'The Police.'

'Yes.'

They walked, with the dogs close on their heels, to Constable Halstead's house and banged on the door.

'No answer. Look.' Paul pointed at a heap of fur near the door. 'His cat. And I've seen several others.'

'And Foss was the name of his cat.'

'Shut up.'

'Let's try the telephone box.'

They walked back to the square and Muriel went into the box, taking money out of her pocket as she went.

'Annie loves George,' read Paul.

'Bugger off you,' read Henry.

'There's my mother looking green.'

'She is too.'

'No answer.' Muriel stepped out of the box. The boys were writing their names on the dusty glass panes with their forefingers.

'I don't think anyone will answer,' said Henry.

'Don't be absurd,' said Muriel.

'Well, there isn't anyone about here is there?'

'No.' Muriel looked round the village square. 'It isn't early closing is it?'

'Mum, you can't put it off.'

'No.'

'Well?'

The church clock struck four cheerfully but with dignity.

'I wonder how it's wound?'

'Why?'

'Well, it will run down.'

'Oh.'

'It lasts for a week. The sexton winds it on Sunday.'

'Why not Saturday?'

'I don't know. I'm hungry,' said Paul suddenly.

'So am I,' said Henry.

'We've brought nothing with us.' Muriel looked guilty.

'Let's help ourselves.' Henry suddenly smashed the fruit shop window and handed Paul a bunch of bananas. 'We had better load the Landrover,' he said.

Muriel looked curiously at the two boys.

'Dog and cat food,' said Paul. 'Mum starts all her lists with

18

that. Then tea, coffee, sugar, soap, fruit, vegetables—except that we grow our own—meat, eggs—and we have our own eggs—'

'Not now,' said Henry.

'Okay then, eggs, butter, tinned fruit and so on and on and on until she gets to chemist and writes Disprin and s. pills. That's sleeping pills. Where shall we start?'

'That grocer.' Henry pointed.

'We don't go to that one. We go to the other one.'

'What does it matter now?'

'Nothing.'

'I must fill up with petrol,' said Muriel.

'The pumps will be locked,' said Henry. 'I'll come with you, Mrs Wake.'

'Thank you.' Muriel got into the Landrover.

'You start,' shouted Henry to Paul.

'Right.'

As Muriel drove out of the square to the garage she heard the sound of breaking glass.

'Here's the garage.'

'Nobody about.' Henry jumped down and looked round him. 'This will do.' He picked up a large spanner lying beside the pump and with great deftness smashed the lock off the nearest petrol pump. 'I'll fill her right up. There's a hand-pump.'

Muriel watched Henry filling the Landrover's tank with petrol, testing the oil and water and peering into the battery. 'Okay,' he said, wiping his hands on his behind. 'If you go back and help Paul I'll join you, Mrs Wake.'

'Ever courteous,' muttered Muriel, driving off.

In the square she found Paul surrounded by a vast heap of groceries. 'Ah, here you are, Mum. This is fun. We shan't get more than this lot in, allowing room for the dogs. Give us a hand.'

Muriel found herself hard at work loading boxes of dog food, cat food, tea and sugar, coffee, soap and an apparently endless stream of groceries.

'Have you made a list?' she asked.

'No, why?'

'We must pay.'

'Pay who? There's only Mr and Mrs Barnes' hair and teeth in the flat above the shop. I looked.'

'Dear God!'

'You're always telling me not to blaspheme. Listen!'

'A car.'

'It is. I swear it is. There *is* someone.'

Round the corner of the square rocked an Austin Mini, drawing up beside them.

'It's Henry!'

'I didn't know you could drive.'

'We Londoners—' Henry got out of the Mini rather self-consciously. 'Let's load this too. I've filled her up.'

'It belongs to Mr Collins.'

'Well, he isn't here to say so.'

'You are too young to drive. You will get had up.'

'By whom?'

'Is there another for me?'

'Yes, several.'

'Come on then.' The boys raced off on foot. Muriel stood watching, feeling very tired.

'Curse it,' said Muriel. 'I need a drink.' She walked across to the Pig and Whistle, raised her elbow as she had seen Henry do, smashed in a pane of glass in the door and reached in for the handle. Behind the bar she helped herself to a double Vat 69 and sat drinking it until she heard the sound of another car. Looking through the door she watched her son drive happily into the square and draw up behind the first Mini.

'That belongs to Mrs Carlisle,' she called.

The boys laughed and waved and then started loading the two small vans with tinned food. Presently they joined her.

'Drinking out of licensing hours,' said Paul complacently.

'Coke?' enquired Henry.

'Yes, please.'

'Before we leave I must wind the church clock.'

'I must see if the poor parson is all right.'

Henry shook his head gently. 'This is his.' He drew from his pocket a glass eye.

4

The wind rose to a gale as the three cars went back from the village on to the moor. They squeezed past the wrecked car, and Muriel admired the dexterity of the children's driving. Paul struggled to hold the moor gate open as his mother and Henry drove through, stopped and waited for him. Wind which had not existed that morning, or even at lunch, shrieked as it hurled itself up the valley. The moor gate fought to slam shut like a live thing, and Muriel drove Paul's Mini through for him as both boys held the gate open together. Driven by the wind came bunches of fleece, fur and feathers which stuck to their clothes. The lea of the tor gave a little shelter as they drove over the moor and up the drive. Muriel drove straight into the garage and got out and watched. The two children followed her in. All together they shut the heavy doors and ran to the house and stood gasping for breath.

'We must shut up the animals.'

Paul ran to the camp in the dried-up pond. All the corrugated iron sheets had been whipped away by the wind. Even in the sheltered bottom of the dry pond the sleeping bags and blankets were driven into a corner. Frantically he searched for Charlie and her kittens but found no sign. 'She must be here, she must,' he screamed, but she was not. He ran back to the house.

'Charlie is gone.'

'We must gather up the other animals; no time to lose.'

Leaning against the gale they held hands and walked slowly into the wind to the meadow where they had put the sheep. Chap crept under the gate but there was no need for his skill. No sooner was the gate a quarter open than the five sheep and their lambs, seeming to float on the gale, streamed past into the farmyard and into the shippen.

'Have they got water?'

'Yes.'

Muriel dragged the heavy door shut.

21

The cows and ponies were together by the gate and, as they watched, the weight of the animals pressing against it broke it down and the ponies, whinnying wildly, raced into the stables. Muriel and the two children fought the wind to get the doors shut on them, and then climbed over to fill buckets of water from the stable tap. Paul let hay down from the loft above and they turned without speaking to look for the cows. They found one calf penned by the wind against the yard wall, its mother, a huge Devon Brown, lowing beside it. Muriel and Paul dragged it protesting towards the silage pit where the remainder of the cows sheltered uneasily.

'If we build a wall of bales and fill the trough they'll be all right.' Paul's voice was carried away, but his mother and Henry understood.

The wind rose every minute and when they turned to get back to the house none of them could stand. They were penned against the yard wall. The fifty yards separating them from the house seemed enormous, a huge flood of railing wind. Muriel, her eyes filled with fear, looked at the two boys beaten against the wall. Suddenly Paul grinned. Inch by inch the dogs, flat on their bellies, were crawling across the yard, eyes half shut, snarling, their ears and tails streaming in the wind. Muriel and the children dropped on their stomachs and followed. Viciously the wind clawed at them, spitefully it filled their eyes and mouths with dust, but at what seemed long last they reached the back door porch and joined the dogs, crouching out of the wind. Muriel opened the door and they all rushed into the kitchen together, slamming, locking and bolting the door behind them.

'The windows.' Muriel could hear the gale leaping at the front of the house. They forced their exhausted bodies into action and scattered through the house, shutting windows, bolting them, nipping their fingers in their haste, moving from room to room, upstairs and down, until the air in the house was quiet behind the shutters. Standing at bay in the hall, their faces tear-streaked, their eyes full of grit, their clothes covered with sticky bits of wool and bramble, they listened.

'Charlie must have been blown away. Look at that.' Paul pointed at an angle through the library door and they watched through the window the great beech tree at the bottom of the garden heel over and crash like a capsizing frigate.

'She must have been blown miles.'

'Don't think of it. Come on, I'm going to get something to eat and then we can all have baths.'

'I couldn't eat.'

'Hot tea then.' Muriel boiled the kettle and made tea in the kitchen. They all drank.

'Thank you, Mum.' Paul was trying not to cry.

'Look at that!' Muriel stared out of the window which had grown dark.

'It's snowing or hailing.'

'The doors clapped to.The pane was blind with showers—'

Paul lashed out at Henry. 'Oh, shut up!'

'All right, sorry,' Henry muttered.

'Baths now,' said Muriel, 'and bed. It seems quite late.'

'Oh, just let me see the news.' Paul ran out of the room to the drawing-room where they kept the television set.

'No wonder it's dark. The snow is—yes, navy blue.'

'Henry.'

'Yes, Mrs Wake? Rather smart really.'

'Henry.'

'Yes?'

'Oh, nothing. Let's all have a bath.'

'Mummy, the television is dead.' Paul came back to the kitchen. 'But the lights work.'

'That's having our own plant.' Muriel switched the lights on and off in an irritated way.

'The refrigerator is working too. Listen to it humming.'

'Yes, it would. It runs off the plant. Try the telephone.'

Muriel tried it. 'Still dead.'

'Nobody could get to mend it in this gale.'

'No.'

'As for the television,' said Henry lightly, 'I don't suppose there is anyone left to broadcast.' He left the room.

Muriel and Paul stood looking at each other.

'Henry's parents,' said Paul flatly.

'We seem to be facing rather a lot of things at once,' said Muriel, looking out at the driving snow.

'Look, it's changing colour.'

'Yellow.'

'Getting dark too.'

Muriel absently wound up the cuckoo clock and made up the Aga, tipping the ashes into a large bucket. They walked upstairs together, followed by the dogs.

'I feel filthy.'

Muriel saw the dogs climb on to her bed and lie down sighing. They watched her undress, their noses on their paws. She opened her door and called down the passage to where the boys were undressing. 'Wash your heads.'

The roar of the wind outside and the sound of hail on the windows drowned her voice so she put on her dressing-gown and went to them. Paul was standing looking out of his bedroom window, and Henry was lying sunk in the bath with only his nose above water.

'Wash your heads.' She took a bottle of shampoo off the shelf.

'All those kittens too.'

'Stop it, Paul.'

'Four of them.'

'Stop it, Paul.'

Paul undressed and stepped into the bath companionably beside his friend.

'Lovely shiner you've got. Does it hurt?' They were all shouting to make themselves heard above the rage of the wind.

'No. I'm all right.'

Muriel wondered whether those were tears for Charlie or water from the sponge. She went back to her bathroom. In the bath her body felt beaten, scratched, bruised and empty. She forced herself to wash, wash her hair, and let the bath water out.

'Ugh, how filthy!' As she came back to her room Henry looked in.

'I'm going to get us all a hot drink,' he shouted and disappeared.

Muriel rubbed her hair with a towel and combed it through then stood, uncertainly, thinking of Henry.

The two boys arrived together with a tray. They wore pyjamas and were clean and neat.

'Ovaltine,' shouted Henry. He handed her a large glass.

'Sleeping pills,' shouted Paul.

Muriel shouted, 'Thank you', but shook her head.

'What's that?'

Through the door left ajar by the boys slipped a very small black cat with a white moustache carrying a tiny blind kitten.

'Charlie!'

Paul spilt his Ovaltine.

Charlie jumped on the armchair where Muriel had flung her clothes, gave them a derisory kick and push, deposited the kitten and vanished. Three times they watched her return and each time she placed a kitten on the growing pile. Then she licked them all, arranged them neatly and deigned to drink some Ovaltine out of the top of Henry's glass. She blinked twice, then placed her chin on the faintly stirring heap of kittens and composed herself for sleep.

Henry looked at Paul. Paul looked away.

'Mrs Wake,' Henry shouted.

'Yes.'

'Mrs Wake, we feel it would be ungallant to leave you alone.'

'He means we are damn frightened,' shouted Paul.

Muriel laughed. The two boys slippped into bed, one on each side of her, the dogs shifted their positions, and Muriel switched off the light. Outside the wind hit the house with great whumps of air and the noise echoed down the chimneys.

'Harsh winds do shake—' began Henry in a cheerful shout. 'Sleep I can get none for thinking of my dearie.' Henry turned suddenly towards Muriel and she took his hand. Beside her she could feel his body shaking with sobs. Her eyes filled with tears.

Paul switched on the beside lamp. 'Let's all have a good cry,' he said, looking at his mother and friend, and tears began to spurt from his eyes.

'Handkerchiefs.' Muriel struggled out of the bed and snatched a box of paper handkerchiefs off her dressing table. They all three sat in a row in the bed and wept.

'Look at the animals,' sniffed Paul and his tears turned to laughter. Both dogs were staring at the three of them with amazement, while Charlie glared from her chair.

'Oh, I feel better.' Muriel mopped her eyes.

'I'm so hungry.' Paul wiped his tear-streaked face.

'We have none of us had a proper meal since it began.'

'The dogs and Charlie have.'

'They have more sense.'

'Come on.'

Muriel got up and led the boys down to the kitchen. The dogs followed patiently.

'Something hot,' said Muriel.

'Porridge,' said Paul.

'Why not? Everything is odd and porridge is easy.'

Muriel made porridge while Paul and Henry found sugar and opened a tin of Nestlé's milk. They sat down round the kitchen table to eat in silence.

'We shall have to milk the cows tomorrow.'

'I suppose so.'

'Gosh, we're *talking* not shouting.'

'So we are.'

All three listened. Outside the windows the wind was dying down, they could hear the cuckoo clock ticking and the grandfather clock in the hall chiming.

'What's the time?'

'A quarter to two.'

'Just about twenty-four hours since it started.' Henry looked at the clock. 'Open the shutters, Paul.'

They peered out of the window into the backyard.

'What piles of snow.'

Muriel opened the window a fraction. 'I must see if those poor beasts are all right.' She put on gumboots in the hall and took a torch from a chair where it was lying with a collection of letters, dog leads and a torn windcheater of Paul's.

'No, don't come,' she said to the two boys as she let herself out into the yard.

'Is she all right?'

'Oh yes, I think so. Quick, Henry, while she is out.'

'What?'

Henry followed Paul and watched him sweep the pile of letters off the chair, run into the library and snatch many more from the pigeon holes in the desk, seize a box of matches and set fire to the whole lot in the grate, cover them with sticks and nurse the fire alight until it caught enough to lay logs on.

'One thing less for her to worry about.'

'It smells good.'

'Apple wood.'

Outside in the snow Muriel went to the stables. The ponies blinked at her and one of them whinnied. The others were munching hay. The sheep in the shippen sprang to their feet and glared at her, their eyes green in the torchlight. The cows seemed peaceful enough. Muriel turned back to the house, her feet sloshing now in the snow. All around her was the sound of running water; water running down drains and gullies, dripping off eaves, snow melting away as fast as it had come.

'Mum?'

'Yes.'

'Henry and I have made a fire.'

'How gorgeous.'

The smell of woodsmoke against the ticking clocks. The silence of the night. 'I honestly think we should sleep.'

'Okay.'

Paul stopped fiddling with the dead television set and followed his mother and Henry up the stairs.

'Still want to sleep with me?'

'Just for tonight.' Paul lay down in the bed and instantly fell asleep.

'You all right, Henry?'

'Mrs Wake, I hated my parents.'

'Henry!'

'It's marvellous really. I shall never see them again, like you and your bills.'

'What do you mean?'

'We burnt them all, you won't ever see them again, nor will I see my beastly father and quite vile mother.'

'Really, Henry—'

'Well, it's true, Mrs Wake.'

'The telephone is dead. It went click.'

'When?'

'When Susan rang off.'

'Ah.' Henry took her hand and held it. 'Go to sleep Mrs Wake.'

Paul and Muriel slept while Henry listened with the acute ear of a child to their breathing and the occasional sigh of a dog or sniff from the cat.

'But when night is on the hills, and the great voices roll in from the sea, by starlight and by dreamlight.'

Henry yawned and slept.

5

Paul woke first and wondered why his right elbow was sore. Remembering the day and night before, he lay very still and listened to the quiet. He wondered whether any of it had happened, wondered what Henry had done with the parson's glass eye, remembered the parson, a nice man, a retired naval chaplain. Paul smiled to himself. That eye. 'Not lost in some naval engagement but at an engagement party,' he could hear the parson's amused voice explaining. The sudden attack of a champagne cork, at his daughter's engagement party, resulting in the total loss of his eye. He hoped Henry had the eye safe; he must remember to ask him. Meanwhile he enjoyed the silence, the sound of clocks ticking, his mother and Henry breathing, and the bells in the distance striking.

'Tag rag merry derry, periwig and...'

Paul leant across his mother and poked Henry. Henry smiled broadly and finished, 'Hic hoc horum Gerritivo!'

'Wake up, Mum.'

'Well!' Muriel looked surprised and pleased. They all scrambled out of bed and dressed.

'Can you feed the animals while I get the breakfast?'

'Of course.'

Muriel flung open her windows to look at the blue summer morning. She frowned at the fallen beech tree and examined the view. She could see nothing move nor hear anything except the boys' high voices as they worked up in the yard. The view from her window was subtly changed. She looked closer, peering into the morning light, murmuring to herself, 'No sheep, no cattle, nothing moving.' Several tall trees besides the fallen beech were blown down, gates hung askew, and gaps which had not been there before showed in walls and hedges. Muriel dressed and went to the kitchen.

'Oh damn! No milk.' She picked up a jug and walked out into the yard. Paul saw her and called, 'Shall we let the sheep out?'

'Yes, they won't go very far. I'm going to try and milk a cow.'

'Try Muriel,' called Paul.

'Why Muriel?' asked Henry.

'Meant as a compliment,' said Paul. 'The Perrymans loved my mother.'

'Pity there are no eggs.'

'There may be a few laid in the barn. Let's look.'

Muriel found a bucket and approached her namesake firmly. A brief tussle ensued, but Muriel was victorious and succeeded in getting half a pail of milk from Muriel the cow.

'If we keep the calves in the cows won't go far.'

'True.'

Muriel went back to lay and cook the breakfast.

'Breakfast at lunchtime, breakfast at two in the morning, breakfast again, very nice.' Henry washed his hands and sat down to eat.

'What shall we do first?'

'Don't talk with your mouth full, Paul.'

'Okay, Mum.'

'The village again?' Henry seemed dubious.

'No, let's ride somewhere.' Paul looked eager.

'Why ride? We've got the Minis.'

'Yes, but trees will be down. If we ride we can see how far we can get.'

'That sounds sensible, let's do that. I'll wash up while you put the saddles on.'

Muriel listened to her oddly normal voice. The boys went out and she washed up. She picked up the telephone and wiggled it, listened and laid it back in its cradle, sighing.

'We'd better leave a note,' she said as the boys returned.

'Who for?' Henry looked at her.

'Well, just in case—' Muriel's voice trailed away. The boys looked at each other with raised eyebrows as she wrote in pencil on a large sheet of paper— 'Gone out. Back Soon.' Weighing it down with the electric torch, she left it on the kitchen table.

'I'm leaving food for Charlie, and the window open,' said Henry.

'All right.' Muriel stood undecided.

'Come on, Mum.'

They mounted the ponies and rode slowly across the moor down into the valley in the bright sun.

'I think we must explore the village again.'

'Why?'

'Well, there must be someone...'

'As you please.' Paul shrugged.

'No moor gate,' said Henry. 'Blown away, and just look at the wood!'

The wind seemed to have cut swathes through the wood, but the trees had fallen in all directions, some uphill, some down.

'Must have been a whirlwind.'

'Mrs Wake.'

'Yes?'

'Very quiet, isn't it?'

'What do you mean?'

'Well, no planes, no helicopters, no traffic, nothing, only us.'

'Yes.'

They rode on down hill into the valley. Here and there a tree had fallen across the lane. The ponies either jumped over or the small party found a way round.

'We can bring the chain saw and clear the road.'

'Can you work it?' Muriel was doubtful.

'Oh yes, we know how.'

The village when they reached it looked wildly untidy: rubbish scattered in the streets, tiles strewn across the road and broken milk bottles from the stacks outside the dairy. Apart from the signs of the wind, the village was not changed in any way since their visit the day before.

'We should go separately and meet in a hour,' said Paul. 'Can I take Chap?'

'Yes, of course. Do you want Peg, Henry?'

'I think I would rather be alone, Mrs Wake.'

Muriel rode out of the village square to the council estate which was eerily quiet, empty cars, paper, fluff, cellophane, milk bottles, tins lying about the road, no sign of life from the houses. Her heart failed her. She rode back to the village where she could hear the boys' voices calling.

'Anybody there?'

'Only me.'

'Anybody there?'

'Only me.'

The echo threw back, 'There? There? There?'

Back in the square she found the boys together.

'It's too weird alone,' said Henry. 'There isn't anybody, Mrs Wake.'

30

'I'm going to ring the church bells,' said Paul suddenly. 'I've always wanted to ring out wild bells.'

'Ring out wild bells across the snow.'

'It's melted, stupid. Come on.'

The boys ran to the church, old, solid, beautiful, its clock with hands pointing to letters which spelt out, 'My dear mother', instead of numerals. Muriel walked across the churchyard to the vicarage, wondering how Henry had got in the day before. The back door swung on squeaking hinges. She went in. 'Anybody there?' As she searched the rooms, empty of life, she heard the bells begin to clang and clatter. Finding nothing, she went back to the church and in at the side door which was always open. At the foot of the tower, swinging on the bell ropes, she found the two boys. Muriel took a third rope and began to pull on it. Presently they stopped, breathless.

'Pouff! How far can these bells be heard, Mum?'

'It depends on the wind. Quite a long way I think. We hear the Abbey bells three miles across country.'

'We haven't heard the Abbey bells.'

'No. Oh dear!'

'We'd better leave a note here and ride over there and look.'

Muriel found the fly-leaf of a hymn book and wrote: 'We are alive at Brendon' and signed it 'Muriel Wake'. They took a pin from a notice which said: 'Choir Practice will be at 6.30 p.m. on Wednesday instead of 6 p.m.' in the Vicar's neat script and pinned the note to the outer door.

'How will they know how to find Brendon and know it's us?'

'It's marked on the AA map.'

'Like throwing a bottle overboard,' remarked Henry as he mounted his pony.

'Well, there's no post.'

'No, no nothing and no anybody.'

Muriel rode ahead not wanting to hear.

Across country to the Abbey was comparatively easy going. The gates were mostly blown down and the gaps made in the hedges convenient. They went carefully but steadily. She heard the boys talking ahead of her but her thoughts were far away. Sam. Where was Sam? And how queer, she thought, this morning she had woken for the first time from a dreamless sleep, no shriek of brakes, no silence. She had just woken to feel rested and peaceful, amused to hear the two boys talking across her as she lay dozing.

At the bottom of the valley, where the track joined the lane which led to the main road from Exeter to Plymouth, was a small pub, The Fisherman's Arms. The boys reined in their ponies and waited for Muriel.

'Shall we look?' Paul was already off his pony, handing the reins to Henry.

'We had better.' Muriel got off her pony and looked up at the quiet little country pub. 'About the only one I know which manages not to be folksy.' Julian's easy deep voice came into her mind from a long time ago. Three months perhaps?

The pub sat sleepy in the sunlight, its upper window half open, the sign of a leaping salmon hanging quite straight above the door which was closed. The boys went round into the backyard and came back carrying a ladder between them. Already, thought Muriel, we know better than to try the doors.

Henry climbed the ladder followed by Paul. Muriel waited, listening to the ponies breathing and the sound of the river across the field racing towards the sea. The boys looked out of a bedroom window together and waved.

'The usual,' said Henry.

'Oh.'

'Coming in a minute,' Paul called and vanished. Henry went on leaning out of the window, looking down at Muriel gravely.

'Got it all in a basket. Can you help?' Paul reappeared and the boys came down the ladder together carrying a large basket.

'What's that?' Muriel peered at the basket.

'Brandy, whisky, peanuts, crisps, olives and coke for us.'

'And an opener. You are practical.'

'We may find someone at the Abbey.' Paul did not sound hopeful.

'Yes, of course we will.' Henry looked at Muriel and she looked away.

'Give me the basket and you ride on,' said Muriel.

The boys trotted ahead.

'That was a lapse.' Paul apologised for his mother to his friend.

'Oh, it's natural. It's a habit.'

'What's a habit?'

'Lying to children.'

'Yes.' Paul stroked his pony's neck. 'She hasn't lost hope. It's mortal sin. She tries to avoid them.'

'Faith, Hope and Charity and all that?'

32

'Yes.'

'What does she hope for at the Abbey?'

'She hopes to find the Abbey standing as it was last Sunday full of monks, and in particular she wants Father Richard.'

'Why?'

'To confess and get spiritual help and advice.'

'Confess what?'

'How should I know? But she was ringing up the Abbey the night before it happened. I heard when I slipped into the house to get those biscuits and she was asking for Father Richard. That means she wants advice, confession, etcetera.'

'I wish I could get it.'

'Well, you aren't a Catholic like us, but old Father Richard would fix you up in a jiffy.'

'Old?'

'Not really. He is young. I meant old affectionately.'

'Oh. Not old.' Henry meditated. 'Paul, I feel great affection for your ma.'

'Good.'

'She was awfully funny when we all cried.'

'She can't help being funny. My father used to roar.'

'He was nice too. What is Sam like?'

'What *was* Sam like you should say. Now *you've* lapsed.'

'Yes. Sorry.'

The lane turned several hairpin bends and reached the main road.

'Heavens!'

For a mile in each direction a dual carriageway. All along it, as far as the boys could see, heavy lorries, vans, cars and all forms of transport had either run into each other or off the road and into the ditches, and the giant machines now rested silent. Muriel came up to the boys and gazed with them.

'All the night traffic,' she said. 'The police must have got those jams moving from the Exeter by-pass.'

'Nothing could get along it now.'

'Impossible. We shall be stuck in the lanes.'

Paul's face fell. 'I was so looking forward to racing in my Mini.'

'Mrs Carlisle's—'

'Yes, but—oh well, shall we look, Mum?'

'No, let's go back and get to the Abbey by the river path and the woods.' Muriel turned her pony's head and led the way.

'She didn't lapse that time.' Paul looked at his friend.

'No.'

'The woods are very quiet.'

'No birds.'

'And no birds sang,' Paul shouted suddenly at Henry.

'That's a ham one. It's the ones everyone doesn't know that count.'

'I only know the clichés.'

'I know. Come on, let's catch up with your mother and get to the bare ruined choirs.'

Muriel smiled when the two boys joined her and they trotted along the track through the wood.

'There's the tower.' All together, for no particular reason, they hurried their ponies into a canter and raced across the last field by the river to the Abbey.

'The clock is going—it's midday.'

'Then there should be the Angelus—listen.'

They got off their ponies and stood listening.

'Nothing,' said Paul. 'How do we get in? The great gates are locked at night.'

'Let's try them.' Henry rode up to the gates and shook them. 'Locked all right.'

'We can climb over quite easily.' They tied the ponies to the gate and climbed over.

'Quite easy really,' said Muriel, puffing. 'Let's try the doors.'

All the doors were locked. Muriel banged on the side door with her fist.

'No good, Mum. Let's make a tour.'

They began walking round the Abbey, calling out at intervals, 'Anybody there? Anybody there?' There was no answer. No jackdaws were startled from the tower, no swallows wheeled, no sparrows chattered, no starlings shone. They made the tour of the Church and Monastery and came back to where they had started.

'I'm going to look at the bees.' Paul raced across the Abbey lawns into an orchard. Muriel and Henry followed.

'No bees,' called Paul.

'It will be the same everywhere. Have a peanut, Mrs Wake.'

'Thank you.' Muriel accepted the peanuts and looked at Henry. He looked old.

'We'd better look at their farm.' Paul looked anxious.

'You look.' Henry sat down.

Paul looked undecided, then turned away from his mother and friend and walked away. They watched him cross two fields and reach the farm and saw him moving in and out among the buildings.

'Now he's lapsed,' said Henry.

'What do you mean?'

'Well, he won't and you won't believe what's under your noses. Nothing is left alive except us. You go on and on hoping.' Henry's voice rose to a scream. 'You two with your Faith, Hope and Charity. It's ridiculous.' Henry began to cry. 'I wish I had it.'

'I think you have.'

'It was taken away from me or never taught me.'

'Here's a handkerchief.'

'Thank you. I'm sorry, Mrs Wake.'

Paul rejoined them looking dejected. Neither his mother nor Henry asked him any questions.

'Let's go home.'

'I suppose so. We can't break in here, and if we did—' Muriel looked away.

'Come on.'

Laboriously they climbed over the great gates and remounted their ponies.

'Let's go back past the quarry and home over the moor.'

'Very well.'

The track leading to the quarry led sharply uphill from the Abbey. 'It's a scandal really.'

'What's a scandal?'

'A scandal that they let these people go on quarrying into the hill, making it hideous and incidentally destroying the caves. They should have done something to stop them. They are so slow round here.' Muriel was talking to Henry, using an educative, explanatory tone of voice. 'If they are allowed to go on there will be no caves left. They are prehistoric and terribly interesting, natural caves enlarged and lived in, and they let them quarry away.'

Henry burst out laughing. '"They" and "them" aren't here any more. No more "they", no more "them", only "us".' Henry began to chant, 'No more Them, no more They, only Us,' to the tune of 'God Save the Queen'. Laughing, Paul joined in, and the boys broke into a canter up the track, singing at the top of their voices. Muriel followed, the basket full of loot from

The Fisherman's Arms over her arm and the two dogs trotting by her. Peg looked rather too large for long expeditions and Muriel made a mental note that in future she must be left in the house until she had her puppies. When Chap stopped to sniff in the quarry at a lump of mud, and Muriel's pony shied, she nearly fell off. 'Steady,' she said to the pony, and then began to shriek. The mud was moving.

Muriel flung herself off her pony and ran towards the dog who was eagerly licking a man's face.

'Father Richard!'

'Oh, it's you, Mrs Wake. What are you doing here? Picnicking?'

'Potholing!' shouted Muriel furiously. 'You were potholing,' she accused.

'Yes, yes, we were. And I'm afraid brothers John and Peter are still in there.' Father Richard choked and spat. 'Sorry, Mrs Wake. It's the mud. There was a rock fall and we got lost.'

'Here, drink this.' Muriel, her hands shaking, uncorked a brandy flask.

'Oh, oh thank you, Mrs Wake. I was coming to get help. Father Abbot will be anxious—' Father Richard sat up. 'That's much better, thank you. Do you always carry brandy like a St Bernard?'

'Father—'

'Yes?'

Muriel's voice was drowned by the clatter of hooves.

'Mum, what on earth?'

'Is it alive?' Henry approached cautiously.

'Very much alive.' Father Richard sounded tart.

'But nobody *is*.'

'I don't know what you are talking about, but brother John and brother Peter are in that cave and I must get help to get them out.'

'Alive?'

'Naturally.'

The boys looked at each other across Father Richard. Paul winked.

'Where are they?'

'Jammed in a crevice, a crack really. It's not the proper way out, but as I was telling your mother there was a fall of rock and we got lost and somehow by a miracle we found a way out. Now that's interesting. This way out must be quite a new way—quite a discovery.'

'Have an olive,' said Henry.

'Thank you. I'm afraid I'm spoiling your picnic, but could you, could one of you fetch help. You see they are in there and rather exhausted. It must be the day before yesterday—'

'How far in?' Paul spoke urgently.

'Not far, not far at all, but they got jammed. I am small, you see, so—'

'We'll get them. Come on Henry. Chap, quick! Will you tell him, Mum?'

'Yes.'

'Don't you think some of the stronger brothers—'

'No, Father. Here, have another swig and some peanuts.'

'Thank you.'

'Father, there are no other brothers, only us—'

'Only us?'

Sitting beside the exhausted little monk, Muriel told him all she knew. When she had finished he was silent for a long time.

'When we get brother John and brother Peter out, we must get to the Abbey.'

'We will help you.'

'Mum, Mum, got the brandy?' Paul came leaping down the quarry. 'We've got them out. We made them take off their clothes and squeeze.'

'Here.' Muriel handed Paul the flask. 'Are they hurt?'

'Oh, none of us is hurt.' Father Richard laughed. 'Here they come.'

Henry came down the slope of the quarry ahead of two tall young men smothered in mud from head to foot.

'Look, you three get on to the ponies. We'll take you back. Can any of you ride?'

'Sort of.'

The children held the ponies while Muriel helped the three muddy men to mount and then, each leading a pony and supporting its rider, they wound their way down to the Abbey.

'And the earth shall be filled with the glory of God, As the waters cover the sea,' sang Henry.

'He was brought up an atheist,' said Muriel dryly to Father Richard.

6

During the long summer afternoon Muriel waited outside the Abbey. At intervals either Henry or Paul came out to see her.

'They have washed, changed and eaten.'

'We have gone all round the place with them.'

'They went potholing as a sort of treat. It's crazy.'

'Nobody else left. Just the usual.'

'We are all coming out to have tea on the grass with you.'

'A council, I think,' said the monk, sitting down beside her. 'I suggest that we all meet tomorrow. You have food and a few animals at Brendon. We have food here.'

'You should have half our animals,' interrupted Paul.

'That would be nice, but we only need a cow, if that.'

'You have two cows and their calves, and we will keep the other. Tell you what, Henry and I can drive them over tomorrow.'

'Thank you. Then, Mrs Wake, we really should find out what is happening in Exeter and Plymouth, or go to meet the search parties from those centres.'

'Do you think there will be search parties?'

'Surely.'

'We don't,' said Henry. 'There have been no planes or helicopters and nothing can get along the roads. You and your two novices are just freaks.'

The monks laughed.

'I didn't mean to be rude.'

'I know. But I still think we should go and look. Now suppose two of us ride to Plymouth and two to Exeter while one person stays at Brendon and one here. How would that be?'

'Bags I Plymouth,' said Paul.

'Very well, Paul. You go to Plymouth with John, and Henry can go to Exeter with Peter. I will stay here. I feel I must. And your mother must stay at Brendon.'

'Why?' said Muriel mutinously. 'I feel left out.'

'Of course, but you can milk and so can I, so we must stay in those two places.'

'I shall jolly well see that Henry learns, at least as much as Paul.'

'Yes, but later.' The little monk looked very small beside his two tall novices.

'All right. This doesn't seem much of a council.'

'No, but everything is so simplified.'

'Probably only temporarily,' said Henry.

Muriel stood up uneasily. 'Come on boys, early start tomorrow then—'

The three men came to the great gates and waved goodbye and called out their thanks.

'Mind you ring the bells,' shouted Paul as he rode away.

'They are very hospitable, aren't they,' said Henry.

'They would have you to stay if you wanted to.'

'Would they?'

'Yes, of course.'

'Then I will stay with them one day. I want a long talk.'

'They don't talk after eight-thirty.'

'It's nearly six now. Let's hurry. Early start tomorrow.'

Muriel kicked her pony into a canter and sped across the moor for home. Then slowed up quickly, remembering Peg's condition.

'You go ahead,' she said, and watched the two boys and Chap diminish as they rode on over the moor. When she arrived half an hour later she found Henry smiling at her from a loft. 'I've found some eggs.'

'Good.'

'Do you think we could hatch any? We shall miss them.'

'I don't know the right temperature but put six in a box in the hot cupboard for luck. Where is Paul?'

'Seeing to the cows and sheep. He says we must take Diana and Flo to the monks tomorrow.'

'Very good. You do that.'

'And he says we had better winter all the cows at the Abbey.'

'You do look ahead.'

'I think we should. So does Paul.'

Muriel took the eggs. 'Would you like an omelette?'

'Yes, please.'

Supper that evening was quite convivial. All their spirits

39

were high and Henry voiced their feelings. 'I feel fine now we know we have three friendly men only three miles away.'

They washed up and went to see that the animals were safe. The cows and ponies were grazing peacefully in the pasture, and the five sheep lying in a corner with their lambs.

'Is it safe to leave them out?' asked Paul.

'Yes, somehow I feel it is. None of them looks scared or restless as they did last night, and we shall hear if anything goes wrong. We can have our windows open and the dogs would bark.'

'Perchance my dog shall bark.'

'Henry, if you will stop quoting at us, so will we,' said Paul irritably.

'All right. Joke over.'

'You go to bed,' said Muriel.

The boys went into the house and Muriel walked slowly round the house, checking on the stables, the cowsheds, the electric engine, the garages. Everything seemed in order. She sighed, looking up at the quiet sky. 'Oh, well.' She went upstairs and into Paul's room.

'Good-night, my love.'

'Good-night, Mum. Don't worry.'

'Did you clean your teeth?'

'Yup, and I'll bring back all the toothbrushes I can from the big bad town.'

'Good-night, Henry.'

Henry was lying on his back with his arms behind his head. He put them up to kiss her and suddenly hugged her.

'I'm so sorry about your husband and Sam.'

'And I'm sorry about your parents.'

'I'm not, but I promise I'll tell you why. Not now though. I told that monk.'

'Goodness, did you?'

'Yes, he was extraordinary. He said my feelings were natural enough but I wasn't the only one and to look forward not back, or something like that, and I said wasn't I terribly wicked, and he said, "O, bless you no." I like him. I'll tell you all about it some day.'

'Yes, some day.'

'You know we may be gone more than a day, don't you?'

'Oh, no!' Muriel choked with dismay.

'Oh, yes. Think. Both lots of us have to ride twenty miles at least to get to Plymouth and Exeter. You must *not* expect us back in one day, Mrs Wake. Give us several, and don't worry. After all, we are each going with a large monk.'

'Henry, you sound fatherly.'

'Seems to me you need one—no offence meant.' Henry giggled.

'All right. I'll come with you two and the cows in the morning and we'll have a quick council and decide how long before we feel we should send out search parties.'

'You do that.' Henry snuggled into his pillow.

Muriel went to her room, undressed, got into bed and fell asleep almost immediately. The cat left her kittens, jumped on to the bed and, avoiding the dogs, came close to Muriel's face on the pillow. She twitched her whiskers, hesitated, and then went back to lie watchfully by her kittens.

Dawn was breaking as they drove the cows with their calves across the moor. They made a leisurely procession, stopping to let the animals drink at small streams. At the highest point of the moor, before the track turned downhill to the Abbey, they stopped.

'Look, the sea.' Paul pointed.

'No ships,' said Henry. 'I suppose they are drifting on the current.'

'Why?'

'Well, no *things* have disappeared, only people and animals. A ship with no crew will drift.'

'Gloomy.'

'Well, there will be lots tied up in Plymouth. Lucky you.'

'Our own private battleship,' said Paul. 'That would be fun.'

'But the Navy—' began Muriel, and as she caught the boys looking at each other, she finished, 'No, I suppose not the Navy.'

They rode on down to the Abbey. Father Richard, wearing grey flannel trousers and a shirt, met them and they drove the cows into a field.

'Brother Peter was saying just now that motor scooters would be far quicker than ponies,' he said. 'He and Brother Paul have gone to the garage on the road to look for some.'

'How silly of us not to think of that. We can wind our way in and out of the debris.' Henry sounded delighted.

'Oh yes, let's go and meet them.' Paul and Henry darted off towards the main road.

'The children think they may be gone longer than a day.' Muriel looked at Father Richard.

'Oh, sure to be,' he saw she was anxious. 'Don't worry. If you leave a pony here with me, I can get over to you quickly if there is any news of them.'

'Oh dear, how long will they be?'

'It depends on the state of the roads and streets. It depends on what they find.'

'I don't like it.'

'Those novices are large and responsible.'

'I suppose so.' Muriel was doubtful now of the whole project.

'They must go. It is our duty to find out.'

'Very well. But I was just beginning to feel safe at Brendon.'

'Would you like to stay here?'

'No. I'll go back. I must. I must. Only I hope they won't be long. I wish we had the telephone.'

'Not even homing pigeons or the proverbial dove. I promise I'll come over to you and you must come to me if you are worried. Listen.'

From the direction of the main road came the popping sound of motor scooters, shouts and laughter, and soon they saw the two monks and the boys ride into the forecourt of the Abbey. They all looked happy and pleased.

'Ready to go?' Father Richard was brisk.

'Yes, yes.'

'Then go now, find out all you can, do not stay away too long because your mother will be anxious, and be careful.' He raised his hand.

'Come,' he said to Muriel. 'If we climb the tower we can watch them for their first two miles.'

Muriel kissed the children and watched them all ride their scooters out on to the road, then hurried up the narrow tower steps after the monk. When they reached the top of the tower the scooter party was already on the road. Muriel watched them part and begin weaving in and out of the wrecked vehicles on their separate ways, west and east.

'But whose scooters were they?'

'One of the brothers remembered the Scooter Club.'

'Oh.'

'Look, Brother Peter nearly fell off.'

'As long as it's only nearly—'

'There's quite a long stretch there with nothing to hinder them. With any luck there will be a lot of those.'

'You sound as if it were all a jolly adventure.'

'In some ways it is. The boys are enjoying it and the novices may have such fun they will lose their vocations.'

'I feel I may lose my reason.'

'Oh no you won't. Come on down now. They are all out of sight. You must have some hope and faith and keep yourself busy.'

'You too.' Muriel was rueful.

'Yes.'

When Muriel rode away up the hill she was thoughtful. 'This is going to be hard,' she addressed the dog. Then, 'Clothes' she said to herself, and wondered whether she could somehow get the Landrover down to the village and stock up with clothes from the elegant shop called 'Hawkers' by the boys, but in truth 'Hawk', where they sold beautiful sweaters and sports clothes which she could never afford. As soon as she got back to the house she checked quickly that all was well, that the bitch and cat had food and drink, and went out again with Chap to the Landrover.

Later Muriel had to admit that she had enjoyed herself. For one thing, the ground was dry and the Landrover made easy detours from the road when it was blocked by fallen trees, and for another she enjoyed being alone. She wound her way in and out of fields back on to the lane, downhill to the village, only almost giving up hope when she reached the river, but even the river could not stop her for long when she followed its banks to a ford, crossed it and zigzagged back to the village.

The village was empty and sad as it had been two days ago, but curiously Muriel felt no horror. She smashed in the door of Hawk's and spent a useful hour collecting clothes for herself and for the boys, also for the boys to grow into. 'They will grow tall,' she said to the dog, 'and their feet will grow.' She moved the Landrover to the shoe shop and chose a variety of gum-boots, sandals and slippers, also a large collection of socks. Then she walked slowly round the village looking at every shop intently. The butcher's was bare, so were the fishmonger's and dairy. From the baker's she collected huge sacks of flour, almost too heavy to lift, thinking that *she* must learn to bake bread. The vegetable shop looked sad; most of the vegetables were withering and the fruit rotting. She picked

43

about until she found a bunch of bananas and then sat on the shop step eating them and some figs and dates from boxes. Chap snoozed at her feet in the sun. The church clock struck three. Muriel got up, went to the church and wound the clock as Paul had shown her. Her notice was still on the door, 'Alive at Brendon—' She wondered whether the grass would grow tall and unkempt over the graves, and smiled because Sam had called them 'All the RIP's. Makes them sound like PTO or MFH or OMH or VIP or any old thing in this age of initials.' She wiped a tear from her eye. 'Goodbye, Mama,' he had said, and she had let him go when she so urgently wanted to see him.

'Hell!' shouted Muriel, 'Hell!' And then laughed because Henry would not have been able to resist adding, 'Knows no fury etcetera'. She pottered round the churchyard thinking of Sam. Sam, tall and dark, her first child, Sam who was nineteen and so beautiful. Sam who had spent hours in this very churchyard when he was thirteen and emerged at last triumphant with the answer as to why this village so hated the next. 'These were Cavaliers—they were Roundheads,' which the vicar had corroborated. Six years since then. Three months since—

'Oh, Hell!' Muriel yelled. 'Hell, Hell, Hell!' Her voice echoed round the village, ''ell, 'ell, 'ell.'

'Who's that?'

From somewhere near came a disturbed croaking voice. Muriel jumped and stood still. Chap was standing over a freshly dug grave wagging his tail, peering down. Muriel tiptoed across the grass to join the dog.

'Oh!'

'Morning, Mrs Wake. This isn't your pitch. You belong to that new Abbey over the hill, not here.'

'It's rebuilt on the old foundations.' Muriel spoke automatically. Then, 'Mr Perdue! What on earth are you doing here?'

'Here, give us a hand, I don't feel quite myself somehow.'

Muriel knelt and reached down to the old man struggling to his feet from under a clutter of boards and spades, earth and sacking.

'I can't reach you.'

'Not surprised. This is a double grave, extra deep you know. That Mrs Willis, she's going to be buried on top of poor old Ned. Same in death as in life. She wants to be top. Now don't tell anyone I said so.'

'There isn't anyone.'

'What's that? Where's my ladder?'

'Blown away I expect.'

'Them boys more like. They were larking about horrible, so I laid down to have a little nap.' The old man looked up at Muriel as he dusted his clothes.

'There's some steps in the vestry. I'll fetch them.'

'Don't let nobody see you.'

'There is nobody.'

'What's that?'

Muriel ran to the church and, finding a pair of steps in the vestry, carried them back and lowered them into the grave. The old man climbed up shakily.

'You need a drink,' she said.

'I don't drink,' the old man said huffily. Then, catching Muriel's eye, added, 'Only now and again when Fred Bartlett come to give me a hand with a big job like this. He was here last night.'

'Not last night. Three nights ago.'

'What's that? Never!'

'Yes.'

The old man muttered, 'My wife, she would have been proper angry.' Then he smiled. 'But she died. She won't be buried on top of me like Mrs Willis on top of Ned.'

'I think you had better come to the pub and I'll get you some food.'

'Never go inside the place. It's people like you who do such things, and football pools and horses and incense.'

'Let's leave the incense out for a minute, Mr Perdue. Come on.' Muriel led the old man across the churchyard to the inn.

'Where is everybody?' he asked. 'Blown away or what?'

'Blown away I think.'

'It isn't reasonable.'

'No. Will you sit here, Mr Perdue, drink this, eat that, and listen to me.' Muriel opened a bottle of beer, poured it into a tankard and handed the old man a packet of peanuts and a banana.

'Funny sort of breakfast,' he said.

'It's four o'clock. Now will you listen, Mr Perdue?'

'I'm listening. Don't hold with women in bars.'

'Mr Perdue, please.'

'All right, no offence, but it's laxity, that's what it is, incense and laxity. They go together.'

'Mr Perdue, will you shut up and listen? I have a lot to tell you.'

'If it's going to take long we'd better have another bottle.'

Muriel went behind the bar and poured out a whisky for herself and another beer for the old man.

'What's happened to the parrot?' He was peering into a large cage which had a notice, 'Please do not feed the parrot' wired on to it. 'Nothing but feathers.'

'That's what I want to tell you.'

Muriel began her story slowly, trying to remember the sequence of events, frowning, her eyes half shut. The old man listened without interrupting until she came to the bell-ringing, when he exclaimed, 'Ah! I thought they was rung all wrong, like that scare in the 1939 war. Now that was something. Rung them all wrong they did, and it was a false alarm.'

'Let me finish.'

'All right.' He took a swig of beer sulkily. 'Women! They always interrupt.'

Muriel finished her story and said, 'Then you spoke from that grave.'

The old man burst into a roar of laughter. 'Hah! Hahahaha! Arrh!' He clutched his head in pain.

'Hangover,' said Muriel. 'Never!'

7

Mr Perdue stood up. 'I must see the Vicar and Mrs Willis.'

'You won't, Mr Perdue. I've told you there is nobody left.'

'Like to see for myself. They call me grumpy, but I'm thorough.'

'Just as you like.'

Muriel followed the old man across the square to the vicarage, up the stairs, and waited while Mr Perdue knocked at the Vicar's bedroom door and, getting no answer, went into the room. She heard him walk round it and then watched him come out scratching his head.

'Gone,' said Mr Perdue. 'Clean as a whistle. Only his pyjamas in the bed, and his glass eye is gone too.'

'It's the same everywhere,' said Muriel hastily.

'Won't be with Mrs Willis. She wanted the grave hand-dug, she did. "No modern machine for me," she said. I have a proper good suction digger for graves, but she's old-fashioned, she is. That's why old Bartlett and I was digging so long. Ridiculous.'

Muriel followed Mr Perdue across the road and down a side lane to a row of pretty cottages.

'Here we are.' Mr Perdue knocked at the first door. 'Anyone up?' He raised his voice.

'We break in,' said Muriel. The old man looked shocked. 'I told you about it.'

'Yes, so you did. Housebreaking.'

Muriel shrugged her shoulders.

'Oh, all right.' Mr Perdue picked up a stone and smashed a front window. 'You nip in, Mrs Wake, and let me in.'

Muriel climbed in at the window and opened the door for the old man.

'I'm strong,' he said, 'for seventy-five, but not so nimble as I was.'

They walked upstairs. Muriel opened the door of the back bedroom. The bed was ruffled and on the pillow lay a mat of grey hair and curlers. The teeth, which were now becoming so commonplace, reposed in a glass beside the bed.

'She won't want any burying.' Mr Perdue stared. 'The coffin is in here. The funeral is today.'

Muriel did not bother to correct him but watched as the old man lifted the lid and peered in.

'His teeth, his hair, his wedding ring, nothing else but his clothes. She made the poor chap wear that ring even in death. She had her clamps on him and there was no need. He never looked at women, gardening was what he liked.' Mr Perdue replaced the coffin lid. 'Won't need burying now. All that heavy digging for nothing.'

They left the cottage and Muriel said quietly, 'Come up to Brendon with me, Mr Perdue, we would love to have you and we've masses of food and it's warm and light.'

'No, thank you all the same, I have my own house. There it is.' Mr Perdue pointed. 'Very comfortable it is and I have my cat and dog. I don't need anything else.'

'Let's go and look.' Muriel turned back up the road towards the sexton's house where Mr Perdue lived.

'Quiet,' said Mr Perdue. 'It's very quiet. My dog and cat won't be long in coming to meet me. My dog, he's old like me but he's company, and my cat she's good company too, better in some ways than the dog.' Mr Perdue hastened his steps and, fishing in his pockets for a key, went into the little house calling, 'Nip, Nip, where are you boy? Puss, come here, you must be hungry.'

There was a long silence. Muriel heard the old man moving about and clicking light switches and muttering. Waiting, she watched Chap scratching himself indulgently and listened to the silence of the street. The church clock struck five and Mr Perdue came out and sat down beside her. In his hand he held a dog collar and a bunch of fur.

'She was a tortoiseshell,' he said.

They sat together for a long time saying nothing.

At last Muriel broke the silence. 'At Brendon we have a cat with four kittens, Mr Perdue. Their father was a Siamese. He was killed in the accident which killed my husband.'

'I always said taking a cat in a car weren't natural.'

'And my dog is having puppies any day,' Muriel went on. 'Don't you think you could come up there for a while and give me a hand?'

'It wouldn't be proper.' Mr Perdue pursed his lips.

Muriel smiled and went on. 'The cows and calves, ponies and sheep need attending to too. It's rather a lot for me alone.'

'Nothing seems to work in my house,' said the old man. 'The power is gone, no light, no heat. It's mad, that's what it is, it's mad.'

'We have light and heat. We have our own plant.'

'Very old-fashioned.' Mr Perdue looked disapproving.

'My husband liked it. That way he said we were independent.'

'Nothing wrong with independence,' Mr Perdue conceded.

'We have fuel and oil for three years.'

'Have you now?' Mr Perdue looked obstinate. 'Isn't paid for I bet.'

'No, not yet. It's a big worry.'

'Don't see why it should worry you now.' Old Perdue stood up. 'Those kittens and that bitch shouldn't be left alone too long.' They walked towards the Landrover and got in. Muriel drove slowly out of the square.

'See that?' Mr Perdue was pointing.

'What?'

'The bank. Now's the time to rob it, no one about.' He laughed, adding, 'I still got my own teeth.'

'How lovely for you, so have I.'

'Well,' he leant back in the seat beside her. 'T'isn't decent, just blowing off and leaving things like that.'

Muriel said nothing but concentrated on her driving. She negotiated the ford and, changing into higher gear, set off up the hill. They passed the overturned car. Mr Perdue looked at it with one eyebrow raised. 'Poor chap!' he shouted in her ear. 'He drank. Steady on, look at that now.'

Ahead of the car in the evening light waddled a large female badger. She glanced over her shoulder and then vanished into the undergrowth of the wood.

'How queer.' Muriel stopped the car. Chap's eyes were bulging out of his head. She laid a restraining hand on his collar.

'Badgers!'

'They survive everything,' said Mr Perdue. 'Nice to see her though.'

Muriel drove on up over the edge of the moor to the house. Walking to meet them, her tail straight in the air, came the cat who at once began to wind herself in and out of the old man's legs, pressing herself against him. Mindful of Mr Perdue's feelings, Muriel went into the house and upstairs to the hot cupboard. The hot water tank gave a welcoming rumble as she took out clean sheets and pillowcases and went to the far end of the corridor past the boys' rooms to what had once, long ago, been called the bachelor wing, now two spare rooms which, with a communicating door, could be entirely separate from the rest of the house. She made up the bed, looked quickly in the chest of drawers and cupboard to see that they were clean and empty and went downstairs again. Mr Perdue was sitting steaming in front of the Aga.

'Heavens, Mr Perdue, you are soaking! I never noticed. You must have been snowed on.'

'Don't notice much, women don't. Now the cat, she did. Wouldn't sit on my knee.'

'I'm so sorry. You should have a hot bath and change, otherwise you'll get rheumatism.'

'Ain't got nothing to change into.' The old man looked not only cross but exhausted.

'I have masses of spare clothes.'

49

'Don't want women's clothes.' Muriel knew he was being annoying on purpose.

'Men's clothes,' she said firmly. 'Come and choose.'

Sulkily Mr Perdue followed her to her husband's room.

'Dusty in here,' he said.

'Well, I've not been in it for some time.'

'Not since he was killed I suppose. Were you driving?'

Mr Perdue looked through the drawers, picking out a shirt, underwear, a bright orange sweater, muttering as he did so, 'I like bright colours', a red neck scarf and green corduroy trousers, unworn and given to his father as a joke the previous Christmas by Sam.

Muriel steered the old man to his room.

'Here you are.'

'Does it lock?' He tried the door.

'Yes, of course. Now I'll get supper while you have a bath.'

She left him and went downstairs. In the library she threw some sticks on to the smouldering ashes and knelt while the fire kindled before she laid on logs. Among the ashes she saw a scrap of paper, rather charred. 'To account rendered' she read and smiled, putting the last trace of the bill on to the fire. In the kitchen she riddled the Aga, laid the table for two, fetched a can of soup from the store cupboard, and began to prepare supper thoughtfully.

After a few minutes she said loudly to herself, 'I will *not* be bullied,' and leaving the pans to simmer, she ran down to the cellar. As she came up carrying a bottle of claret she met Mr Perdue coming down the stairs wearing the dry clothes. 'You look wonderful,' she said, 'and you will feel better after a proper meal.'

Mr Perdue did not answer her but sat down at the table. Muriel gave him a bowl of soup and poured him a glass of wine. He made no comment. They ate silently and Muriel from the corner of her eye saw Mr Perdue sip his wine, hesitate, then drink. He smiled at her.

'That cat needs fresh food,' he said. 'She needs fish.'

'She's had masses out of the tins, and milk.'

'Not enough. She's nursing them kittens. They drain her strength.'

'Paul said there were fish in the lake—alive.'

'Did he now? Then tomorrow when I've seen to the farm I'll go fishing. That suit you, puss?' Mr Perdue and the cat exchanged an enigmatic look. 'Fishing is nice and quiet. A man gets away from all that jaw, jaw, jaw.'

'Then while you are fishing and looking after the place, I shall ride over to the Abbey and see whether there is any news of the boys.'

'And see that monk?'

'Yes.'

'Has he got a fish pond?'

'As a matter of fact there is one.'

'Ah.'

'And they are independent too. They get their electricity from the river.'

'Very old-fashioned.' Mr Perdue pursed his lips.

'Well, it works and none of the mains work, do they?'

'I grant you that, Mrs Wake. I was brought up differently, that's all. My mother liked everything modern and so do I. I like my mechanical grave-digger. I like cars and engines. I like the telephone and the telly.'

'Alas, they aren't working either.'

'Let's try un now.' Mr Perdue sprang to his feet, disturbing the cat. 'My cat was very fond of those nature programmes.'

Muriel led the way to the telephone.

'Try it yourself.' She stood by it watching the old man lift the receiver and jiggle the instrument.

'It's no good,' he said.

'Try the television too.'

'No, but I want to know why.' Mr Perdue sounded irritated.

'So do I,' said Muriel crossly. 'You think it out while you are fishing tomorrow.'

'I'll try,' he said, and went slowly away up the stairs.

51

8

In the morning, as she rode away over the hill, Muriel could see Mr Perdue sitting in a boat near the shore casting his line out where the breeze ruffled the water. Anxious now for Paul and Henry, she cantered quickly across the moor and down the valley to the Abbey. She turned her pony loose in the orchard to graze and went into the church to be met by the sound of a Hoover. Up by the great altar Father Richard was standing on a ladder directing the nozzle of the Hoover at the curtains round the altar.

'Good morning, Mrs Wake. It's all terribly dusty.'

'Don't you think, Father, that you should leave some spiders' webs for posterity? The time may come when people will not know what a spider was.'

'That's interesting.' Father Richard came down the ladder.

'I haven't seen any insects, but there are fish in our reservoir.'

'Are there? The fish are all right in our pond too.'

'We saw a badger yesterday evening.'

'We?'

'I must tell you. I found the village gravedigger lying at the bottom of a double grave in the churchyard.'

'Did you?'

'Yes, he'd fallen asleep drunk and knew nothing about anything. He's at Brendon now.'

'Well, that almost proves—' Father Richard wrinkled his brow.

'Proves what?'

'I'm not sure yet so I won't say, but I'm beginning to think, to puzzle out a theory.' Father Richard looked at his watch. 'Time to ring the Angelus.'

'May I come up the tower with you?'

'Of course. When I have rung it we can look out and see if we can see any sign of the boys and the novices.'

'That's what I meant.'

Father Richard rang the bell energetically. 'One must keep some semblance of continuity,' he said when he stopped.

'Some symbol,' said Muriel. 'That awful old man has gone out fishing. He wants quiet.'

'He will get plenty of that.' Father Richard climbed ahead of Muriel up the stairs and opened the door at the top. They came out into the sun together.

'I should have brought field glasses.' Muriel shaded her eyes, gazing down the road towards Plymouth. 'I can't see anything, only the wrecks.'

'In this stillness we would hear rather than see first,' said the little monk.

'I suppose so. Can I help you? I don't want to wait up here.'

'No, there is no point in that, and there is plenty to do.'

'At the farm?'

'Yes, at the farm, in the gardens and in the Abbey.' They climbed down the tower again.

'Who is this boy Henry?' asked Father Richard.

'He is Paul's best friend at school.'

'I thought it was term time.'

'It is but they are home as the school closed because of that odd disease so many children got. It didn't seem to hurt them, but some of the parents got panicky and of course the children were only too delighted to come home.'

'He told me he came from London.'

'He does, but his family have gone abroad.'

'I wonder if they will ever come back.'

'Father Richard, you really think—' Muriel paused.

'Yes, I do. The last news was of odd happenings in Europe, very queer things in America and South America and floods all over Asia.'

'Sam went to look.' Muriel spoke flatly.

'Come and give me a hand with those cows,' said the little monk. 'If we are careful we can build up quite a herd.'

'Did Paul show you his bull-ring?' Muriel asked.

'Yes, he did, and one of the calves you brought over is a bull.'

'So he is. I must see which of our lambs is a ram, mustn't I, so that we can build up a flock. The boys want to bring all the animals down to you for the winter. They look ahead too. I wish—'

'Yes, you wish they would come back. So in a way do I, but they will not come today. Go back now, Mrs Wake, to your old man and see that all is in order at Brendon.'

'He's such a hypocrite,' exclaimed Muriel. 'The drunken old creature.'

'If he had not been drunk he might not have survived.' Father Richard spoke cheerfully.

'You speak as though his getting pickled was a virtue. He is disagreeable too.'

'I daresay he will mellow, and the pickling was a pre-servative.'

'The boys and I were not drunk, nor the cat or the dogs, nor the sheep, cows and ponies. What preservative had we?'

'We shall find out.' Father Richard looked at his watch again. 'Must do some work in the monastery I'm afraid.'

'Can't I help?' Muriel was loath to leave.

'Not in this.' He spoke gently. Muriel watched him go into the monastery and close the door. She called her pony and rode home, hoping that perhaps the boys had reached Brendon along the other road, the A30. How surprised and amused they would be to find old Mr Perdue in the house.

But there were no boys, only Mr Perdue, flushed from the sun, sitting by the Aga watching Charlie eating.

'Ah,' he said when she came in. 'I told you she needed fish.'

'How clever of you, Mr Perdue.'

'Not clever, just quiet I was. There are plenty for us too.'

'Mr Perdue, you *are* clever.'

'The one who is being clever is being clever all over your drawing-room sofa,' said the old man.

'Who?'

'Your bitch.'

Muriel ran to the drawing-room to find Peg lying blissfully quiet with four blind squealing puppies at her side.

'Torn the cover she has.' Mr Perdue had followed her.

'Oh, it doesn't matter. The boys will be thrilled.'

'Maybe, but if you'd had a proper modern sofa instead of this 'ere thing it wouldn't have got torn.'

'We like old things. She is hungry.'

'I'll get her some milk.' The old man went off.

Muriel sat stroking her dog, who lapped thirstily when Mr Perdue brought her a bowl of milk.

'Two dogs and two bitches,' said Muriel.

'Call them John, George, Ringo and Paul.'

'Why?'

'You remember, they was Top of the Pops.'

'Of course,' said Muriel vaguely, 'very nice names.'

Mr Perdue looked disappointed, so Muriel said quickly, 'How do you like your trout cooked?'

'I like 'em grilled, but with this old Aga thing you can't grill.'

'Yes, I can.' Muriel stood up. 'Did you milk the cows, Mr Perdue?'

'Yes, and I saw to the sheep and ponies too. Tomorrow I'll give your kitchen garden a look-see.'

Muriel thanked him and set to work cooking their supper.

'I enjoyed myself,' said the old man grudgingly.

Muriel smiled. 'If you did, I'll go over to the Abbey again tomorrow. The boys will turn up some time.'

'Don't fret.' Mr Perdue took the plate of fish Muriel handed him. Sitting at the table in his bright sweater, eating, Mr Perdue reminded Muriel of other times and other places.

'You look like an Augustus John,' she said.

'Who's 'e?'

'Or a Picasso.'

'What?'

'It's the bright colours. They were painters who loved bright colours and food.'

'Well, I like bright colours and food, but I never heard of them. My old mother she brought us up to be modern, contemporary she called it.'

'I wish I had known her.'

'Well, she'd be old-fashioned now, I daresay, but she'd never hold with what you've got here.'

'What do you mean, Mr Perdue?'

'All those chairs and sofas that's unwashable, that Aga thing and your own electricity, milking those poor cows by hand, and not even giving them no music, not having your own spin dryer, only cars and horses, ridiculous she'd have called it.'

'We liked it that way, and you must admit, Mr Perdue, it works.' Muriel felt rather annoyed.

'Works, I daresay, but tomorrow morning before I see to the garden, I'm going to fix the cows up with a bit of music. They'll give much more milk with a bit of music. No science 'ere at all.'

'No music either. The radio and television are dead. You will have to sing to them, Mr Perdue.

'Sing?'

'Well, if you want some music for the cows, you will have to sing to them.'

'What I want is a bit of quiet away from all this chattering.'

'Then go fishing. I'm going to the Abbey again to see if the boys have come back.'

'They won't, not for weeks, not them boys.'

'How can you tell?'

'I know boys, they lark about and shatter the peace and quiet. Yes, I'll go fishing.'

Muriel looked with distaste at the old man, thinking how terrible it would be to be alone with him for long.

'Mr Perdue,' she said, 'I'm going now. Can you keep an eye on the animals? There's a full moon. The boys might come back.'

Mr Perdue made a contemptuous noise. 'You go,' he said. 'There's a record player in your library. I'm going to take it to the cowshed. Lots of old records too. Old-fashioned, but the cows won't know. Remind me of my old mother if I play them a bit of John, George and Ringo, a bit of Twist and Shout and they will milk lovely. Yeh! Yeh! Yeh!' he sang at her.

Muriel hesitated.

'You go,' said the old man more kindly. 'I'll see to things here.'

Still Muriel hesitated, thinking of Charlie and the kittens.

'I'll see to them.' The old man read her thoughts. 'They like a bit of quiet like me.'

Muriel left the house, feeling thoroughly unwanted, followed by Chap. She saddled a pony and rode slowly over the moor by the light of the moon. By the reservoir she paused to let the pony drink and looked around her. She saw Chap prick his ears and watch something up on the moor behind her.

'Sit quiet, Chap.'

The dog sat still watching, and Muriel strained her eyes. The pony raised his head and stood still with water dribbling out of his mouth. Turned in her saddle away from the water, Muriel tried to follow the dog's pointing nose. After a minute she was rewarded by the sight of a pair of foxes, silhouetted against the moon, trotting along the crest of the hill. She followed them with her eyes until they dropped out of sight behind the hill.

'Foxes and badgers,' she said cheerfully to the dog and proceeded on her way over the moor and downhill to the Abbey.

As she got near the Abbey Muriel began to feel rather ridiculous. She had, after all, only left it that evening, and here she was again coming back in the early hours of the morning, over-anxious about her son and Henry who were, she told herself, quite safe, each accompanied by one of the novices. The Abbey door was open so she went in. Chap, ignoring the notice pinned on the door: 'No Dogs Allowed', followed her quietly. Up at the high altar Father Richard was kneeling by what looked like a biscuit tin on a stand draped with a violet cloth. Muriel knelt too. Presently Father Richard rose and came down to join her.

'How good of you to come,' he said. 'This is Sunday and I am going to say a Requiem Mass and bury—' he hesitated.

'Bury the bits,' said a voice behind her.

'Henry!' Muriel spun round. Henry was smiling at her.

'The others will be here soon,' he said.

'What others?'

'That novice chap and the people we found in Exeter.'

'We never heard you coming.'

'I don't suppose you did. We are on skates.'

'Skates?'

'Yes, roller skates. We got them in Exeter and simply buzzed along the main road. Ann and June are fearfully good on them, much better than us. They will be here in a minute. What's going on?'

'Father Richard is going to say Mass and bury—'

'Oh goodoh! Then we are just in time. Can I toll the bell, Father? Here they come.'

Henry appeared to be in high spirits and ran down the aisle to meet Peter and two girls who were standing in the porch taking off their roller skates. They all smiled at Muriel, and the novice hurried up to Father Richard and began to talk to him. The two girls put their skates down and shook hands with Muriel.

'Nice to meet you,' they said in chorus. 'What's going on? This is Ann and I am June.'

'Well, Father Richard is going to say Mass and then bury—' Muriel looked helplessly at the girls who, she could see in the half light, were wearing track suits and were bareheaded. One seemed dark, the other fair.

'Well, there wouldn't be enough to fill a coffin, would there?' said the girl called June practically.

'Yes, it would be silly to have a coffin,' agreed the other girl. 'I'm Church of England myself.'

'Even the Church of England wouldn't fill a coffin, things being as they are,' said June. 'Henry told us about you, Mrs Wake. How can we help?'

'By just being here I think.'

Muriel looked up towards the altar where Father Richard was talking to Henry, who presently hurried off towards the Bell Tower, and within minutes the funeral bell began its tolling. Father Richard was joined by his novice in a surplice and began the Mass. The two strange girls knelt beside Muriel and copied her movements, and all three slowly followed the little procession, made up of Father Richard, the novice and Henry, to the cemetery.

'Nice smell,' whispered June.

'That's incense. What's he doing now?' asked Ann.

'Sprinkling holy water.'

'Oh.'

They followed Father Richard back to the Abbey. 'You must be hungry,' he said. 'We will bring you breakfast in the parlour. Henry, will you help?'

Muriel led the two girls to the parlour. 'Please tell me—' she began.

'Well,' said Ann, 'seems much the same thing happened in Exeter as it did to you, from what Henry told us. Snow and wind and that. June and I were staying in a basement flat. We were frightened and when we thought it was all over, the storm you know, we came out from under the bedclothes and we went out to look for other people.'

'But there were no other people,' said June.

'No, nobody,' went on Ann. 'Well, we stole food from shops and places, and we started shouting, but nobody came.'

'Not until Henry.'

'No, not until Henry. We don't know Exeter very well, you see. We are skating champions for the South West and we'd only come down for the contest.'

'What contest?'

'Oh, the championship contest.'

'I see.' Muriel did not see but wanted to hear more.

'Well, we couldn't find anything but messed up cars, lorries and trains, and we were in a fair state of nerves when yesterday we heard somebody shouting, "Anybody there? Anybody there?" so we screamed.'

'Then what?' Muriel bent forward on her elbows, looking at the two young faces with joy.

'Well, Henry and that novice chap came round a corner and we fell into their arms. It was lovely.' Both girls looked happily reminiscent.

At this moment the little monk and Henry came in carrying trays of breakfast and the story was continued by Henry.

'We hunted the whole city, the University, everywhere, but the whole caboodle is blown away and there's an awful mess.'

'Really nobody left?'

'Not that we could find. We thought you would be getting anxious so we came back. It was Ann and June who thought about skating here. It's even easier than the scooters.'

'Once you have learnt,' said the young novice with a grin.

'And I have found Mr Perdue and there are foxes and badgers alive.' Muriel told her story.

'You two girls must come to Brendon.'

'We'd love to,' they said.

'We'll get another Landrover off the road somehow,' said Henry. 'The moor is very dry. I'm sure I could get one across country.'

'If you can roller-skate from Exeter I'm sure you can.'

'Oh, I brought you a present.' Henry left the room.

'We each brought a pack of clothes,' said June. 'Just in case.'

Henry came back grinning. 'This is it.' He placed a large jar of caviar in Muriel's lap.

'Henry! Where did you get it?'

'I broke into that posh hotel.'

'Well, it's gorgeous.'

'I brought this.' The novice opened his knapsack. 'We broke into the hospitals and I took all the drugs I know which I could find.'

'That was sensible.'

'Nothing makes sense.'

'It depends what you mean by sense.'

'Sense and sensibility.'

'Nonsense, sense is. Well, sense makes nonsense.'

They were all laughing and talking together, glad of company, glad to be six people together and not just one or two.

'By the way,' said Peter when they paused for breath. 'The Exe has changed its course and this part of England is completely cut off. As far as we could see, the sea has come right inland and flooded out all the low lying country.'

'So we can't get to London?'

'Not unless we fly or get a boat across and then try.'

'We shall have to soon.'

'I come from Australia,' said June suddenly. 'I wonder what has happened there.'

'The last news,' began Muriel, then added, 'well, I suppose we all heard the last news.'

They all looked at one another and then at their plates.

'Is it the end of the world?' Henry's voice was quiet.

'Oh, no, I don't think so, Henry.' Father Richard's voice sounded very normal. 'After all, we are here. Something abnormal has happened, that's all. We shall find out in time what it is.'

'Our parents thought it was the end of the world in 1939,' said Muriel.

'1939?' Henry blinked. 'Oh, *that* war. How silly of them.'

'Then everybody thought it would be the end of the world if there were another war,' said Peter.

'My parents were CND,' said June, 'before they went to Australia.'

'Henry says you are absolutely self-sufficient, got all your own electricity, water, the lot, he says. Is it true?'

'Yes,' said Muriel. 'It's lucky really that my husband was so old-fashioned. He wanted to keep our house as it had once been. One can't, but he tried.'

'Henry says it's marvellous.' Ann turned to the little monk. 'What do you think, if it isn't the end of the world? Do you think it's a war?' She sounded incredulous.

'Oh no, some sort of accident or natural upheaval like an earthquake or something of that sort. I expect we shall find out.'

'Let's go and find a Landrover. I saw one not far off down the road.' Henry was impatient. The girls got up and set off with him.

Muriel went outside and stood chatting to the monk and his novice.

'I'll take those two girls home. Will you be all right here?'

'Oh, yes,' he said. 'We have plenty to do and Paul will be

60

coming back here with John. They may have gleaned some more news in Plymouth than the others did in Exeter. I think it's only a matter of waiting.'

'I have no patience,' Muriel exclaimed. 'I want to know what has happened to Sam. I want to know about Henry's family. Waiting is not my forte.'

The men said nothing and they stood in the early sunshine looking about them at the blue sky, green grass, the grey stone buildings.

'I miss the birds,' said Peter.

'Look what a straight line those moles are making.' Muriel pointed at a line of mole hills erupting across the orchard grass.

'Moles!' The little monk looked eager. 'Moles. Those are fresh today. Moles—and you say you have seen badgers and foxes?'

'We saw rabbits too as we came along,' said Peter.

'Then—I think I am right.'

'What do you mean?' Muriel looked at the eager face.

'I cannot be sure yet. Ah, here they come.'

Ann drove a slightly battered Landrover into the courtyard. The girls and Henry loaded their packs into it, slung in their skates, said goodbye to the monks and set off up the lane to the moor. Muriel, too, said goodbye and rode off after them, thinking as she went that Father Richard's explanation of their present predicament as an accident was quite a remarkable understatement.

9

During the days that followed the people at Brendon fell into a comfortable routine. The two girls helped Muriel in the house, while Henry and Mr Perdue made expeditions down to the village to collect all the food, clothes and fuel and any household items they could find. These were all stored and stacked in the attics and lofts. Henry and the old man also brought loads of hay, cow cake, corn and veterinary medicines for the animals. They all wasted a lot of time playing with the kittens

61

and puppies and just sitting in the incredible sun chatting and dozing.

'I've never known a summer like this.'

'It's like Australia.'

'Tell us about Australia.'

Muriel watched the young people lying easily relaxed in the sun, and the old man out on the lake fishing, and wondered why Paul had not come back and where Sam was. She envied them their ease.

'We have enough stores for years,' she said, interrupting the description of a duck-billed platypus.

'Yes, and they have at the Abbey too.'

'Are you worrying?' Henry looked at Muriel.

'Yes, and I can't bear it much longer.'

'You may have to.' Henry's eyes were on her.

'Sam—I can understand that Sam may never come back, but Paul should be back by now. It's nearly three weeks, Henry, since you went off to Exeter and he to Plymouth.'

'I know. Tell you what, let's go for a ride.' Henry was anxious to distract her.

'All right.' Muriel heard herself sounding ungracious and added quickly, 'Where shall we go?'

'Let's go to the holiday camp. It isn't far.'

'Why there? I always have thought it the height of bad taste to build a holiday camp just there near the prison.'

'Oh well, it makes an objective.' Henry picked up two saddles and bridles. 'No need to go inside,' he added.

'Inside used to have a sinister ring.'

'I know, but the camp is quite jolly now or was.' Henry caught two ponies and saddled and bridled them.

'Do you know the way across country?'

'Yes, I used to visit a man there years ago, in the prison.'

'Did you? How thrilling. What was it like? What had he done?'

'He was a burglar of sorts. It wasn't really interesting, Henry, only sad.'

'We are all burglars now I suppose.' Henry trotted beside her looking cheerful.

'Henry, you look very cheerful.' Henry laughed.

'I am cheerful. I'm enjoying all this, whatever it is. I like you, I like old Perdue, I like those two girls, I like this life.'

'So do I, except that I fret about Sam and Paul.'

62

'Paul will be all right.' Muriel noticed that Henry made no mention of Sam.

'What makes you so sure?'

'Well Paul has John with him and he was dead keen on going to Plymouth. I think he's found something there to amuse him.'

'I should go and look,' said Muriel. 'We are all being so apathetic in a way, storing everything at Brendon and not going far afield, only to the village and to rob farms of their food stores and to the Abbey.'

'Well,' Henry said soothingly, 'we are going somewhere now aren't we? We may find something. Let's go faster.'

Muriel cantered after Henry for a couple of miles across the heather until they stopped at the top of a hill.

'There it is. The holiday camp and the prison.'

They looked down at the ugly shape of the prison, the terror of all criminals. It stood huge, star-shaped, near a dark wood of fir. Near it was the little town where the holiday camp provided rooms or houses during the summer months.

'It does look grim. Whoever thought of turning this into a holiday resort can have had no sensibility at all.' Muriel spoke with disgust.

'Some of us like that sort of thing.' Henry looked at her sidelong. They rode down into the little town and Henry raised his voice to cry—'Anybody there? Anybody here?' His voice came back to them mockingly—'Here, here, here.'

Henry got off his pony and handed the reins to Muriel. He ran ahead of her in and out of garden gates, peering into windows, looking into cars parked outside houses, vanishing suddenly into a house where the ground floor window had been left open. Muriel watched him as she rode slowly up towards the holiday camp.

'It's all "the usual",' Henry called from an upper window of a small house, 'except this. This is the first I've found.'

'First what?'

'First National Health wig.' Henry sounded pleased. 'Can't be too squeamish,' he added, joining her. 'Come on, let's get to the main gates. I've read about it but never seen it.' He loped ahead of her to the huge building.

Muriel rode up the little street seeing the now so familiar tufts of hair and fur blown into corners, the deserted cars, the empty windows. She wondered whether she liked Henry.

'Look, they left the gate open.' Henry opened the small door in the main gate. 'I wonder why?'

Muriel looked up at what had once been a terrible prison. She remembered the time not so long ago when she and her husband had tried so hard to get this place demolished, but had failed, and seen instead a tremendous tourist boom take place and a holiday camp built with flatlets with every modern convenience, with tennis courts and a cinema, with a swimming pool and a crêche for babies; 'No need to leave the premises during your stay' had been a nauseating sentence in the brochure of the camp. Muriel sat on her pony, looking at it with disgust. Inside the camp she heard Henry calling, 'Anybody here? Anybody there?' his voice bouncing back at him from the buildings like a squash ball, then dying away. She got off her pony and, slipping the stirrup leather through the rein, left it to graze by the road, did the same to Henry's and went in through the little gate by the main gate to find Henry.

Inside the main gate was a courtyard and across it another door. Henry had left the door open. She noticed that the gravel paths and intensely geometrical flowerbeds were the same as long ago, and the silence. Far away she heard Henry shriek. Muriel stood stock still wishing she had brought Chap with her.

'Henry!' she shouted. 'Henry,' the stone walls answered her on all sides. Henry did not shriek again or answer her.

'Henry! Henry!' Muriel began to run round the outside of the prison block and down the road to the camp nearby. 'Henry! Henry!' She ran on past another block of buildings and found herself standing by a large quiet swimming pool. 'Henry!'

'It's all right, Mrs Wake, we're here.' Henry emerged from a doorway followed by a very short, fat, middle-aged woman with a kind, wrinkled face who advanced to meet her holding out a welcoming hand.

'Very glad to meet you,' said the woman. 'I gave poor Henry here quite a fright.'

'Who are you?' Muriel took the warm friendly hand which was being held out to her.

'I'm Mrs Luard.'

'Mrs Luard?'

'Yes, dear. I'm here on my holiday. I'm an upholsterer from London.'

10

Muriel and Henry sat by the pool staring at Mrs Luard in silence while she smiled at them. After a long time Henry, who had been very white in the face, recovered and asked, 'Could you tell us?'

'Of course I can. Well now, there was a dreadful storm of wind and a lot of snow but it didn't worry me much because I was down in the basement watching the chicks hatch.'

'The what?'

'The chicks. Mr Linton who runs this place has a battery of hens in the basement and his chicks hatch regular as clockwork or they did do until the electricity went. He had, I should say, because I can't find any trace of him or anybody else and you can't say I haven't looked because I have. Nobody could say I haven't looked. I'm nosy by nature and this time I've had enough nosying to last me a lifetime I have.' She looked at Henry who was beginning to giggle and smiled. 'I've looked all over the place and there was nothing left but—'

'We know,' said Muriel.

'Well, there are the chicks—those I could save. I've always wanted to see chicks hatch out of their eggs and except on the television I never saw it. But Mr Linton, who was really kind, said if I liked I could sit in the basement and watch the little things hatch so that's what I was doing all that night. It was wonderfully interesting until all the lights went out and I had a terrible time getting upstairs. All I could hear was a cheep or two and when daylight came all the little dears were dead except for four of them and I put them inside my blouse and here they are.'

Mrs Luard paused, produced a box and brought forth four active chicks. 'I fed them on the chick mash I found,' she said proudly, 'and I keep them warm like a broody hen. That's how they were reared in the old days,' she added informatively, 'by a hen.' Mrs Luard put the four chicks beside her on the grass, smiling maternally. 'I'm going to bring them up to be free range chickens, the modern way,' she said proudly.

'We have, or had free range chickens,' said Muriel.

'Aylesbury ducks?' enquired Mrs Luard.

'All our poultry have vanished.'

'Then I can show you some.' Mrs Luard jumped up and with surprising agility ran into the prison block to emerge two minutes later with another box. 'Five ducklings,' she said with pride. 'Mr Linton had a battery for ducks, too, for us all to eat you know, only now there is nobody. I found an oil stove of course.'

'Has Henry told you about us?'

'I haven't had time,' said Henry.

'Mrs Luard, would you and your poultry like to come and live with us? There are five of us and I'm expecting, hoping, for my son to come back.'

Mrs Luard eyed her thoughtfully. 'I'm very independent,' she said. 'But maybe you've got a pond for the ducks?'

'We have a pond and everything for the chicks. You could have a room to yourself, Mrs Luard. Do come.'

'I've kind of got used to it here, but it's London I must get back to. My holiday is over and I must get back to my work. There are very few upholsterers left you know.'

'We don't know what has happened in London,' said Henry. 'Devon has become an island.'

'Has it indeed?' Mrs Luard did not seem particularly surprised. 'How can I get to your place anyway? I am fat.' Which was indeed true.

'I'll go home and get one of the Landrovers.' Henry jumped up.

'You are to young to drive.'

'The children seem to have grown up overnight,' said Muriel.

'All right then. You wait with me.' Mrs Luard laid a protective hand on Muriel's knee.

'Will you be all right?' Henry looked at the two women.

'Of course.'

Henry left them and presently they heard him clatter off on his pony and the sound died away in the still air.

Mrs Luard clucked and the young chickens and ducks gathered round her. 'They've been company,' she said, and a slow fat tear ran down her cheek.

Muriel felt it her turn to pat Mrs Luard's hand and did so. 'I think you were quite wonderful saving their lives,' she said.

'I never had anything to do with young birds before.' Mrs Luard looked happier. 'They need warmth, I could see that, so I lit the paraffin stove and kept it by my bed.'

'Mrs Luard, are you and the birds really the only people left?'

'Oh yes, I looked all right. I couldn't make it out at first, finding nobody, it didn't make sense. Then I thought it was some joke and then I just waited with my chicks. I don't mind waiting, that's what I'm used to. First my mum and I waited for my dad. He was inside here ten years. Then my old man was inside twice, first for eight years and then for five. He's dead now and when I got my holiday I thought to myself, well now, Norah—that's my name—you go and have a holiday at that camp, a kind of pilgrimage it was, but I didn't expect this to happen. Seems silly.'

'More than silly.'

'All a matter of proportion.' Mrs Luard patted Muriel's hand again. Muriel absently patted Mrs Luard's.

'When we can we must get to London. Henry's parents should be back.'

'They won't be. If they was they would have come to look for him wouldn't they?'

'They went to Spain for their holiday and left him with us.'

'Can't get back I daresay. You know,' Mrs Luard leant close to Muriel, 'there's been no post since that night, there's been no television, no aeroplanes, that means no communications. What an opportunity!' she exclaimed.

'Opportunity?'

'Yes. My dad and my old man they would have called this heaven-sent and made us all millionaires in a week.'

'We have been stealing food and clothes,' said Muriel.

'Ah, but think of the gold and diamonds, the fortunes that must be lying about for the taking. Not that I go in for the game myself, it was the men in our family who did that.'

Muriel hastily patted Mrs Luard's hand again to get in first.

'Ah, they were great thieves,' Mrs Luard said proudly. 'My grandad was a cat burglar. Did you ever hear of them?'

'I've read about them.'

'Well, my dad he specialised in safes in banks. He was very particular who he stole from.'

'I see.'

'My old man, now, he liked gold and diamonds but he lost his touch after we was married. I don't know why, and he was inside so much I had to take to upholstering. Now there's an *art*.'

'Old Mr Perdue who is living with us thinks it's very old-fashioned. He likes modern things.'

'Pah! It's antiques which are lovely. I love antiques.'

'So do I.'

'Got any antiques at this house of yours?'

'Yes, a great many.'

'Then I'll like that, make me feel at home. I like collections of all kinds, antiques, pictures, furniture, jewellery. Nice lot of things I have in London. Hope they're all right.'

'I'm sure they will be, Mrs Luard. It isn't the things which have gone, it's the people.'

'Well, I have nobody to miss. I have me ducks and chicks now.' Mrs Luard clucked and the little birds gathered round her, bright-eyed. 'Time for their tea.' Mrs Luard waddled off into the house behind the pool and came back carrying two bowls of food.

'Ducks,' she said. 'I feed them wet and the chicks dry.'

Muriel lay back in the sun listening to Mrs Luard's clucking noises and the small cheeps from the young birds. She wondered how long Henry would be getting to them in the Landrover and whether he would bring one of the girls with him. Presently she slept.

When Mrs Luard jogged Muriel's elbow she woke.

'Sounds like Henry.' Mrs Luard was listening. Muriel sat up.

'Yes, that's Henry crashing gears.' They went to the gate and found Henry with both the girls getting out of the Landrover. Muriel introduced June and Ann while Henry busied himself packing Mrs Luard and her chicks into the Landrover where she occupied the whole of the front seat, spreading her substantial thighs wide and clasping the box of small birds protectively to her huge breast. With Henry driving and the two girls walking beside Muriel on her pony, they wound their way slowly across the moor to Brendon. As they got near to the house Henry accelerated and, leaving Muriel behind with the girls, drove ahead into the yard tooting his horn. Muriel and the girls laughed as they heard the dogs bark in greeting and Henry shouting for Mr Perdue.

'I hope Mrs Luard and Mr Perdue will get on,' said Muriel.

'That's not very likely from what Henry told us.'

'Why not?'

'Well, Mr Perdue is so terribly virtuous and from what Henry said about Mrs Luard,' June hesitated, 'well, she seems more Henry's sort than old Perdue's.'

'Let's hurry and find out. She'll be dying for a cup of tea and company.' Ann broke into a run.

'I wonder whether she will.' Muriel turned her pony loose and walked towards the house with June. In the quiet of the warm summer evening they could hear voices coming from the house which suddenly rose to a crescendo of bass and contralto raised in argument.

'Oh dear!'

'It's sacrilege,' Mrs Luard was saying in a high voice.

'Not on that old thing. Ought to be thrown out it did.'

'What do you know about it, ignorant old man.'

'My old mother, she wouldn't have had such things near her, she was modern.'

'Collectors' pieces.'

'Now, Mrs Luard,' Henry's voice piped in.

'Get off it—look what they're doing—chewing it.'

Muriel ran into the house and hurried to the drawing-room where she heard the voices. Mrs Luard was standing glaring at Mr Perdue across the button sofa where Peg lay complacently surrounded by her puppies.

'Old philistine!' shouted Mrs Luard. 'Can't get these for love or money, let alone steal.'

'Mrs Luard!' bawled Henry as Muriel came in. 'There are yards and yards and yards of velvet to cover them just waiting for you.'

'Ah!' Mrs Luard stopped with her mouth open. 'And for the chairs too?' Her eyes were suspicious.

'Yes, yes, and curtains.'

'Then everything's all right. But that dog must get off. A job for an artist,' she murmured, 'and that artist is me.' Lovingly she stroked the chairs and the sofa.

11

Muriel settled Mrs Luard in the best spare room with a bathroom to herself. Mrs Luard prowled round the room, picking up objects and putting them down again, giving the impression of a suspicious goose being slowly mollified.

'Nice things you have here,' she said at last. 'Will you show me the whole house?'

'I would love to, but do settle in first and we will have supper. Come down when you are ready.'

'All right, dear.' Mrs Luard laid down a small piece of china she was examining and looked out of the window. 'Very quiet here,' she observed.

'Yes, that's why we live here. My husband and I loved it.'

'Is he dead then?'

'Yes, a car accident.' Muriel found she could speak quite naturally and without hearing the shriek of brakes and the silence after which had so haunted her.

'Was he the collector or was it you?'

'Oh, both of us, and a lot of things have been in the house for ever.'

'Cars shouldn't be allowed. Flying is much safer.'

'Yes, but this is a Nature Reserve. That's why we ride and have cars.'

'Nasty things horses. They give you such looks.'

Muriel laughed. 'You should meet my son Sam. He hates them. Or,' she corrected herself, 'he hated them.'

Mrs Luard advanced to pat Muriel. 'I'll soon fix those chairs and sofas,' she said kindly. 'It will be a pleasure, a real joy. Your dog can sleep somewhere else, can't she? I didn't mean to hurt your feelings but that old man was so rude.' Mrs Luard's hackles seemed to be rising again, 'No appreciation of good things.'

'He is all right really.' Muriel felt bound to defend Mr Perdue. 'He's been very good to us and he does like to be modern.'

'Not with me.' Mrs Luard was firm.

Muriel went downstairs deep in thought and into the kitchen where she found Henry and the two girls in a frenzy of activity.

'Here, try this.' Henry thrust an icy glass into her hand. Muriel sipped.

'Henry, it's marvellous!'

'It's to pacify.' Henry and both girls beamed. 'We mixed it for a treat. We just have to get one, just one, into old Perdue and Mrs Luard and all will be well.'

June laughed and said, 'Come and see what we've done.' She led Muriel into the dining-room which was in darkness and switched on the light. The table was laid for six with fine silver and glass, and candelabra waiting to be lit.

'The menu is clear iced soup, ham with mushrooms and Christmas pudding. Will you choose some wine, Mrs Wake?'

'How lovely! Of course I will. But what is old Perdue doing?'

'Getting a suitable box to put the little birds in by the Aga. He isn't so bad. We love your sofa and chairs too, you know, and I'm sure that gorgeous fat old thing will make a good job of them. Her eyes fairly shone when she saw them.'

'Where's a can of tomato juice, quick?' Henry was laughing and eager.

'Here's one ready cold in the ice-box.' June swiftly snatched a can from the refrigerator and opened it.

'Here comes Mr Perdue.' Ann wandered to the back door. 'Oh, Mr Perdue, can I help you?'

'No, you can't. You don't know nothing about young birds. You girls are just townspeople and that fat old geezer is another.'

'Well, Mr Perdue, she did keep them alive.' June spoke soothingly as she watched the old man put down a coop by the Aga.

'There, they'll be just right there. You get them a dish of water, girl. Alive by her bed! T'isn't sanitary. My old mother would turn in her grave. Disgusting, she'd call it.'

'Here's a dish.' Ann handed him a flat dish of water and the little birds began to drink from it.

'I expect you are thirsty too, Mr Perdue.' Henry advanced on the old man offering a large glass of tomato juice.

'What's this?'

'Tomato juice.'

'Tastes funny.'

'Well, speaking from a purely academic point of view, everything has been funny lately.' Henry sipped from his own glass which he took off the dresser.

'What's that you're drinking?' Mr Perdue looked at Henry with righteous suspicion.

'Oh, just a mild little drink Ann and June made for Mrs Wake and Mrs Luard. We are celebrating the arrival of Mrs Luard and her birds in the dining-room. High time we had a party.'

Mr Perdue finished his drink. 'Birds and parties used to mean something quite different in my day.' He laughed heartily and suddenly smacked June's behind.

'Henry, what did you give him?' Muriel pulled Henry into the passage.

'Three quarters vodka, one quarter tomato juice. Here comes Mrs Luard.'

Mrs Luard swept downstairs wearing a clean dress.

'Where are my chicks?'

'Safe by the Aga. Mr Perdue put them there in a coop. Have a drink, Mrs Luard.' Ann thrust a glass into Mrs Luard's hand. 'Coo, that's good! Now, where's me chicks?'

'Here, safe and sound. Got more room to move around than they had before.' Mr Perdue crouched by the coop holding an empty glass. 'Not that they was badly off before.' He eyed Mrs Luard gallantly.

'Let's have dinner as soon as we can. I'm starving.' June took Muriel's arm. 'Henry, for heaven's sake bring the food.'

Henry obeyed, sweeping into the dining-room carrying plates and dishes, while Ann lit the candles and put out the light. They all sat down except Henry, who toured the table filling wine glasses to the brim before taking his place beside Mrs Luard.

'My discovery!' Henry raised his glass and gazed up into Mrs Luard's face. Intently they drank a toast and then Mrs Luard whispered something to Henry who shouted with laughter and cried out, 'Oh, we will. Yes, let's.'

Muriel watched Mr Perdue refill his glass and drink gallantly to June. Then she turned to Ann. 'You had the right idea,' she said. 'I wish Paul and Sam were here to enjoy this.'

'Eat and drink,' said Ann. 'We have our lives to live.'

Muriel looked at Ann, at June, at Henry and at Mr Perdue eating and drinking and laughing together, and suddenly she no longer felt hungry, only tired. 'Excuse me a moment.' She slipped almost unnoticed out of the room. She passed the telephone, giving it a glance of hate, looked into the drawing-room where Peg lay comfortably with her puppies, and then walked out into the quiet night, leaving the sound of revelry behind her. Chap joined her, and in his silent company she walked down the hill to the reservoir, or lake as she and Julian had always called it, and sat down by the water to think. The water was very still except for the occasional plop of a trout rising. The woods across the water stood silent and enigmatic. Far away she heard a fox bark and Chap pricked his ears. It was very warm and Muriel wondered when it would rain.

'I can't think, I can't think.' She clutched her head.

'None of us dares.' Henry, who had followed her, sat down beside her. Chap wagged his tail.

'Henry!'

'Yes.'

'Henry, I can't think.'

'I can but I prefer not to.'

'Henry, what is all this about?'

'I've no idea.' Henry sounded cross.

'Are they all right back at the house?'

'Oh, yes. The girls are clearing up and old Perdue and Mrs Luard are bosom friends. Hail vodka!'

'The vodka was a good idea.'

'Yes.'

'Have I been here long?'

'About two hours.'

'It's so warm, it isn't natural.'

'Nothing is.'

'Henry, you don't think Paul has gone for good?'

'Oh no, of course I don't. He's too fond of you and of his home.'

'Henry, you can stay here for ever you know.'

'Thank you.' Henry put his arms around Muriel and kissed her. 'They found those six eggs I put in the hot cupboard had hatched,' he said. 'That's really what I came to tell you.'

'What eggs?'

'Don't you remember? I found some eggs in the loft and you said to put them in a box in the hot cupboard. Well, they've hatched. June spilt a lot of wine and went to get a clean cloth and she found them. Mrs Luard is drooling over them and so is old Perdue. It's been a funny evening.'

'Have they gone to bed?'

'I think so. The girls and I cleared up and Mrs Luard and Mr Perdue squabbled about the new chicks. She wanted them in her room but they settled them near the Aga. It's lucky you have the Aga.'

'Well, you know why.'

'Not really.'

'Sam and Julian decided we must be absolutely self-sufficient.'

'Why?'

'Well, in case of war. They said that if we kept our own power and warmth and lived here where it's isolated we should have more chance of survival. We have survived. Father Richard thinks it's accidental.'

'So do I. I bet my parents are blown away.'

'Poor Henry.'

'I didn't like them, you know I didn't.'

Muriel said nothing.

'I don't mind if they have been blown away.'

'Henry, you are drunk.'

'Not particularly. I love you and Paul and I like those girls and old Perdue and Mrs Luard and those chaps at the Abbey, but nothing could make me like my parents.' Henry paused. 'Look,' he said. 'There's something else left—otters.'

Muriel followed his pointing finger to where along the edge of the lake a pair of otters were playing in and out of the water. Henry was holding Chap's collar.

'Otters, foxes, rabbits, moles. You see, it proves what Father Richard thinks.'

'I don't see anything proved. Why do you hate your parents? I always rather liked them.'

'My mother loathes me because I am not her child and my father because I am not his.'

'Is this true?'

'Yes, I found out by listening at keyholes and reading letters.'

'I never knew.' Muriel was bewildered.

'They adopted me and then they found me a bore and I couldn't like the things they liked.'

'But that's normal between parents and children.'

'Yes, if you are parents and children, but we were not. You see, they are or were mad about politics. I adored literature. They said it was waste of time and intellect. They loved sport.

I'm afraid of it. They loved travelling. Well, I'm like old Perdue's mother. I'm modern but not over-modern. Nothing would ever make them like me or me them. They are or were *inhuman*, Mrs Wake.'

'I suppose you know.'

'Yes, I do know. If they were here now they would be rushing round knowing what had happened, expounding theories as to why it had happened. They wouldn't have gone into a state of shock like you.'

'Is that what I'm in?'

'Yes. You were in a state of shock already over your husband's death. If you hadn't been you would be much worse than you are now.'

'Worse?' Muriel was indignant.

'Screaming worse.' Henry laughed. 'Come home to bed, Mrs Wake.' He took her hand and pulled her to her feet and then led her up from the lake to the house which stood very still and quiet in the moonlight. Henry led Muriel upstairs to her room and Chap followed.

'I moved Peg and her family up here before I came to fetch you.'

Muriel looked round her room at the cat and her kittens in the only comfortable chair, and at Peg and her family lying in a large basket. Peg thumped her tail in greeting. Muriel stroked her head. Chap jumped on to the bed and watched Muriel undress. Henry had gone.

'I can't think,' Muriel was muttering to herself. 'I can't think.'

'Far better not to.' Henry had come back wearing his pyjamas.

'You are so terribly grown-up, Henry, knowing so much.'

'I'm not grown-up, I'm frightened.'

'Is that why you brought Peg up here?'

'Yes. Somehow it's like that first night. Shall we take lots of sleeping pills?'

'Henry, you are tipsy.'

'No, frightened.'

Henry reached for the bottle of sleeping pills and handed it to Muriel. 'I've taken some already,' he said, and got into her bed and put his head under the bedclothes.

Muriel stood looking down at the boy, then round the room at the cat and her kittens, at the dogs, and then out of the window at the stars. She listened. The house was very quiet. She went to the door and opened it. She could hear nothing except the clock in the hall ticking. She wondered whether the girls were asleep and Mr Perdue and Mrs Luard. The clock downstairs struck one and the silence seemed more complete. Muriel shut her door, swallowed several pills and got into bed beside Henry. She put out her hand and touched him. He was alive and asleep. She wondered why he was afraid and where Paul was and Sam.

'I'm not asleep.'

'I thought you were.'

'I was pretending.'

'I was thinking.'

'We must explore, get further afield, Mrs Wake.'

'How?'

'Somehow we must get to London. Get to London and Paris. Mrs Luard wants to "get at the shops" as she calls it. Hatton Garden will do her for a start.'

'Or the Bank of England.' Muriel giggled.

'Yes, that will keep her occupied, but she told me she wanted to upholster all your chairs and things first before she goes off anywhere.'

'Will she come back?'

'She might. It depends.'

'I want Paul back and Sam.'

'Don't fuss. He'll come. My parents won't.'

'They only went to Spain.'

'Is that what they told you?'

'Of course.'

'They told me that too, but they were not going to Spain. I heard them planning. They said Germany and, "Push Russia and China into the Pacific, it's logical," my father said.'

'What on earth were they doing?'

'Planning to destroy and if it's not them it's someone else and whoever it is has succeeded.'

'But your parents must have been in the air, Henry, when it happened. It couldn't be them. You are imagining things.'

'No, I'm not. They were up to something. My father said, "What about Henry if we succeed?" and my mother said, "Oh, to hell with Henry, he's a bore." I heard them, Mrs Wake, through the keyhole absolutely clearly, and my father said, "Ah, well, good riddance," and they both laughed and I knew it was true because the next day before I left to come here I asked my mother for new shoes as I was growing out of my old ones. You know I've been borrowing Paul's since I was here?'

76

'No, I didn't.'

'Well, I told Paul not to tell you. The thing is, when I told my mother I needed shoes to grow into she said, "You won't need anything to grow into." So I put things together and now I know.'

'But they were in the air, Henry. They were flying.'

'Possibly, but they had the intention. That's enough.'

Henry seemed very small suddenly as he moved closer to her in the bed. 'Hold my hand.'

'Yes, I will. Don't worry, Henry.'

'Oh, I won't worry. I'm glad, glad, glad they are not my parents, or should I say were not?' Henry sighed and slept.

12

Muriel slept late the following morning and when she woke found Henry still asleep beside her. She lay still, not wishing to wake him. It had, after all, been about two or three when he had finally slept. She heard June and Ann moving about the house downstairs and once Mr Perdue call something and Mrs Luard's voice answer rather crossly.

Now, thought Muriel, I must get up, but she did not get up continuing to lie watching the sun trying to penetrate the curtains. She saw Charlie stir and jump up to the open window followed by her kittens. One after the other they went through the window and she heard their faint scrabbling descent as they climbed down the magnolia which spread across the front of the house to the ground. She heard Ann say, 'Here come the cats', and June remark, 'That poor dog must be bursting. I'll creep up and let her out'. Presently her door was gently opened and Peg went out followed in procession by all the puppies.

'June,' whispered Muriel.

June put her head round the door and smiled. 'I'll bring you some coffee.'

When she came back she entered silently, carrying a tray. 'I brought a cup for myself too.'

Muriel sat up carefully so as not to disturb Henry.

'Thank you, June. What's going on?'

'Old Ma Luard has started on your chairs. She won't let anyone near her.'

'What else?'

'Oh, nothing. Mr Perdue is tending the animals. What happened to you last night? We watched the summer lightning.'

'I saw none. I went and sat by the water. Henry joined me. We saw a pair of otters.'

'Can you think now? It was quite a party.'

'Yes, I can. June, what is going on? Why is it so wonderfully hot? Why are some of us alive and not others? Where is my Paul and my son Sam?'

'All those questions.' June sipped her coffee. 'No answers. Seems strange to us too. You saw coloured snow. We didn't.'

'I am sure we saw coloured snow.' Muriel was perplexed and stared at the girl.

'I should be worrying about my parents in Australia and all my relations and—'

'And what?'

'My fiancé. I was engaged but I don't feel engaged any more. Do you understand that feeling?'

'Yes.' Muriel put her cup back on the tray carefully. 'Henry said last night that I am suffering from shock. He may be right, but it feels more like release than shock.'

'It does to Ann and me too.'

'Release from everything except worrying about Paul and Sam.'

'It's hard for you. I'm sure Paul will come back. After all, what could have happened to him? Henry got back from Exeter.'

'Henry brought you, June, but Paul—' Muriel sighed, listening to June's voice, gentle and reassuring. Muriel noticed that she said Paul would get back but made no mention of Sam.

'When you were out last night old Perdue and Mrs Luard had another row.' June changed the subject.

'Oh Lord, what about? Not the sofa again?'

'Not exactly, but he wanted some of the velvet.'

'What for?'

'To line a casket. He said Henry had told him your little monk at the Abbey had put all the bits he could find in a tin and buried them in the cemetery.'

'He did.'

'Well, Mr Perdue wants to collect all he can find in the village and bury them in the grave you found him in, but he wants Mrs Luard to line the coffin with velvet.'

'She could I'm sure.'

'Yes, but she won't, or rather she said she wouldn't unless there was enough stuff left over from the curtains and covers.'

'Did Henry put this idea into his head?'

'Who else?'

June looked down at Henry's innocent sleeping face. 'Henry said that your monk said a Requiem Mass and had incense and that the tin was covered with a silken pall.'

'So it was.'

'Well, old Perdue is madly jealous and he is going to collect all the bits he can and bury them in a velvet lined coffin.'

'He won't hear of church unity.' Henry's sleepy voice came up to them from the pillow. 'Any coffee for me?'

'Of course. Really, Henry, I suspect you of making mischief.'

'Oh, no.' Henry sat up. 'I've offered to help him. He can't possibly do the whole village alone.'

'Henry, you are a macabre child.'

'Depends how you look at it. I shall toll the bell too as I did at the Abbey. For whom the bell tolls. Bells on her fingers and bells on her toes,' he sang.

'We must all go.' Muriel sat up angrily.

'Okay.'

'And if the poor man wants velvet he shall have it. But it isn't a joke, Henry.'

June laughed. 'Just imagine all those bits as you call them rising from the dead on the Day of Judgement.'

'You are as bad as Henry. I must go and see Mrs Luard.' Muriel got out of bed, put on her dressing-gown and went downstairs, hearing behind her June and Henry's laughter.

In the drawing-room she found Mrs Luard on hands and knees among the chairs and sofas, her mouth full of pins, a pair of scissors in her hand, snipping away at a great bolt of white velvet.

'Good morning, Mrs Luard.'

'Not one yard shall he have.'

'Please, Mrs Luard.'

'You're weak and who told you anyway?'

'June.'

'Ah, June. It's Henry who started it. If it hadn't been for him I should have been left in peace with my chairs.' Mrs Luard patted a small Victorian chair lovingly.

'I bought much more than enough and there is yellow and pink too.'

'He's not going to have any until I've cut out all the covers and the curtains.' Mrs Luard glared at Muriel who, recognising the look of the artist disturbed, retreated to the kitchen.

Mr Perdue was sitting on a chair by the Aga looking down at the little chicks and ducks.

'Good morning, Mr Perdue. How are they?'

''Ealthy. Much 'ealthier than they was. I'll get 'em out in the sun presently.'

'June and Henry tell me—'

'Ah yes, and that old woman won't give me a yard or two of velvet. She's an 'eathen.'

'I'll give you all the velvet you want. It is mine after all.'

'Not from the way she talks it isn't, nor them chairs.'

'She is an artist in her own line, just like you.'

'Trying to mollify me. Don't think I didn't hear that boy, I did.'

'When is the funeral?' Muriel hastily changed the subject.

'Tomorrow I thought.' Mr Perdue looked thoughtful. 'If you and those girls would help me we could make it tomorrow.'

'Then we must go down to the village now and start at once. We should have done this weeks ago, Mr Perdue.'

'Arr, time flies, but it won't matter.'

Muriel called Ann, June and Henry to her. 'Get boxes and baskets each of you.' Then, while they hurried to obey her, she went into the drawing-room, snatched the scissors from Mrs Luard, helped herself to at least four yards of white velvet while Mrs Luard watched her speechless, and said, 'You coming, Mrs Luard?'

'I don't hold with it,' Mrs Luard gasped, fat and furious.

'But I do.' Muriel swept up the velvet and went out to join the others. 'Here is your velvet, Mr Perdue. Come on all of you. It's shameful. We must clear the village.'

She led the way to the Landrover, jumped in, followed by Henry, and waited while Mr Perdue and the girls followed silently.

'I'm sorry we laughed,' June said gently.

'Well, none of us knows which to do, laugh or cry. It's quite natural.'

Muriel, having made a decision, felt better. She drove down to the village as fast as she could, not stopping until she reached the church. At the church the old man took over.

'You two girls collect,' he said, 'while Mrs Wake and I gets the coffin on to the Landrover and take it back to the churchyard.' Henry began tolling the bell which rang out slow and clear in the strong hot sun. Muriel walked round the village thoughtfully, leaving Mr Perdue to direct operations. When the bell stopped she went back to the churchyard. Mr Perdue, with Henry's help, had lowered the coffin into the grave where she had found Mr Perdue himself. The two girls had picked flowers which they threw in armfuls into the grave. The funeral was soon over and Mr Perdue looked relieved.

'Thank you for your help.' He looked round at them.

'We are all glad to help.'

'Not that fat old woman, she ain't decent.'

'She just has other interests,' said Henry. 'Shall we wind the clock while we are here?'

Henry and Mr Perdue went into the church.

'Let's go to the pub,' said Ann.

Muriel followed the two girls to the pub and sat on a stool by the bar with June while Ann poured them drinks.

'Is this going to be the pattern of our lives?'

'I think Mrs Luard will alter that.'

'She and old Perdue will make life unbearable. It's terribly kind of her to cover the chairs, but that occupation isn't going to last her for ever.' Muriel sipped her whisky.

'Young Henry will settle that. He has a plan.'

'Henry would have. That boy is resourceful. What is his plan?'

'I'm not sure yet. All I heard last night was something about "choosing the very finest of the period—collecting rare items" and something about "transport". After that they went into a huddle and whispered.'

'Oh.' Muriel looked at the girls thoughtfully. 'Are we really cut off from the rest of England?'

'Yes, there is a split right up what used to be the Exe valley and the sea has come in. You can't even see across.'

'Suppose the same has happened at Plymouth?'

'We think it's likely. June and I have been looking at maps.'

'I've been dreaming. I've only worried about Paul and Sam. I've only been thinking of myself.'

'It seemed natural to all of us.' Ann sounded reassuring.

'Well, it isn't. Another drink, please, Ann. Our lives can't go on like this, just looking after the animals, taking for granted we have no neighbours.'

'No, but it may take some time for us. Henry and Mrs Luard seem to be the only people planning anything. Mr Perdue is happy and busy with the farm animals. We have been very happy, thanks to you, and those two monks seem quite calm and very busy.'

'I think the trouble is,' June said thoughtfully, 'we don't know how to begin. We've done the obvious things like getting in stocks of food and clothes and you seem already to have had the idea of getting fuel.'

'That was my husband. He almost rebuilt the house too. He said we must. He must have had foresight.'

'Then you see we are all so used to the telephone, the post and communications of all sorts, we are paralysed without them. We have an enormous choice of cars, but we can't really get far. Our skates worked best.'

'We shall have to make expeditions to find out.'

'I must wait for Paul.' Muriel felt that she must no longer mention Sam. They all looked away when she did.

'Well, of course you must wait, but perhaps we shouldn't.'

'I'm perfectly happy to wait.' Ann sat down in a comfortable chair and put her feet up on another.

June laughed. 'You talk like the idle rich.'

'That's what I feel like, a sort of natural neutral beach-comber, happy and at peace with the world.'

'Old Perdue and Mrs Luard and Henry don't feel like that.'

'I would if—' Muriel sighed.

'If your sons came home, if your husband was not dead.' June spoke slightly impatiently, then said, 'Sorry. I wonder what's keeping those two so long. It doesn't take all afternoon to wind one clock.'

'You would, if you had found a mouse in it.' Henry came cheerfully into the pub.

'Henry, what entrances you make!'

'Well, I was listening outside the door for a suitable cue. Mr Perdue has one mouse, I have another.'

'Let's see.' The girls crowded close to him.

'Aren't you afraid?'

'Of course not.'

'Tut, tut. Old Perdue will be so disappointed. He said, "Arr, these'll make those girls get a move on and that old witch".' Henry imitated Mr Perdue's voice. 'He is planning to set them on Mrs Luard.'

'We mustn't let Charlie get them.' Muriel took the tiny mouse and held it in her hand, watching the briskly twitching whiskers and large shining eyes.

'What were they doing in the clock?'

'Heaven knows. Give it a peanut. It's terribly tame.'

'Let's put them in a tin. Hullo, Mr Perdue. What a find.'

'Nothing keeps vermin down.' The old man absently accepted a glass of beer held out to him by June.

''Ere's t'other.' He handed a second mouse to Muriel who passed it on to Henry. 'That Mrs Luard and these 'ere mice —'ere's to them that was.' He raised his glass and drank.

'Mrs Wake?'

'Yes, Henry.'

'Do you mind if I go off and do a little trip on my own?' Henry looked innocent and eager.

'What sort of trip?'

'Oh, just a short trip. I'll be back for supper. I can go in the doctor's wife's Mini. It's all ready.'

'So you have something planned?'

'Well, yes.'

'You don't want to tell me about it?'

'Not yet. The plan may be no good. It's a present for Mrs Luard.'

'You are up to no good.'

'What is good and what is bad? This is diplomatic.'

'All right, Henry. But be sure to come back.'

'I will.' Henry handed the mice to Muriel. 'They like milk,' he said to June and slipped out of the pub.

'I wonder what he is up to.' Muriel went to the pub window and watched Henry running down the empty village street.

'Another drink before we go home?' Ann collected glasses and poured out drinks. They sat in silence until they heard the engine of a small car start up and die away.

'There he goes.'

'Time we went back. We must do the milking and I must have another struggle with making bread.'

The girls laughed, since both of them and Muriel took it in turns to make rather unpalatable unleavened bread to eat with the tinned food and milk products they had at Brendon.

'How long before those chicks start laying, Mr Perdue?' Ann climbed into the Landrover.

'Six months, just about.'

'That will be the day.' June got in beside Muriel. 'I wonder whether any of us have lived so long without an egg.'

'It must have been done.' Muriel drove the Landrover on its winding way up the hill. 'You know, when the weather does change we shan't get even the Landrover down to the village. If you saw lightning that means rain.'

'If we could shift some of the tree trunks and old Bartlett's car we could use the road.'

'The breakdown truck in the garridge has a winch.' Mr Perdue spoke in superior tones.

'Then Ann and I can help you.'

'Of course.' Mr Perdue made a satisfied noise in his throat which Muriel and the girls recognised as purely male.

'You show us what to do and we will do it.' Ann spoke flatteringly. Muriel realised that the old man's vanity needed a bit of solace since the arrival of Mrs Luard.

'How do you imagine the mice got into the clock?' Muriel asked him.

'Climbed up to look at the view,' he said rudely. Muriel paid no attention but ploughed on.

'Climbed from where?'

'The crypt, of course. Boiling with mice the crypt used to be.'

'How clever you are, Mr Perdue.'

'Don't overdo it now. I can see what you women are up to.'

Muriel and the two girls laughed.

'It's that fat woman what's got no tact.'

'Here's old Mr Bartlett's car. Do you think if we all gave it a heave we could get it a bit more out of the way?' Muriel spoke hastily.

'Yes, we could. Not that he was old. He was two years younger than me.'

'I spoke with—' Muriel tried to think with what she had spoken—certainly not respect or affection.

'You spoke without thinking,' old Perdue snapped. 'Come on then, let's give it a heave. Not that I'm going to rupture myself, having just buried the doctor and the district nurse.'

84

'Quite a mild push should do it.'

They all got out and with a concerted heave levered the already lopsided car off the road.

'Now quite big things can get by.'

They stood looking at their handiwork with satisfaction before going on up the hill to the house.

Mrs Luard, surrounded by puppies and kittens, strolled to meet them. 'Had a nice time?' she enquired affably.

'That's one way of putting it.' Mr Perdue walked off calling, 'Muriel, Muriel, come on me beauty.'

'Muriel indeed! Where's Henry?' Mrs Luard was pettish.

'Gone exploring. It's for you he said.'

'Ah, he's a good boy. Reminds me of my old man, that boy.'

'Let's have tea.' Muriel smiled at the high praise given Henry. 'Shall we have it outdoors?'

June too was grinning. 'Yes, I like watching the evening sun.'

'You all smell like a pub.' Mrs Luard sounded in no way opprobious.

'I expect we do. Tea will steady us up. We've begun clearing the road to the village too.'

'I was thinking we would need that done.' Mrs Luard sat down beside Muriel and they waited for the girls to bring out trays of tea.

'We would be all right in the winter even if we did get cut off.'

'I shan't. I shall need the road.'

'Why?'

'To drive up and down, all being well.' Mrs Luard's mouth snapped shut.

Muriel poured out tea and handed round cups. 'What do you think of mice, Mrs Luard?'

'I love the little dears. It's one of the things I miss most just now, mice and men.'

'Henry and Mr Perdue found two.'

'Two mice? Lovely. Let's hope they aren't both female.'

'Mr Perdue will be disappointed.'

'Hoped I'd jump on one of my chairs and scream, did he?'

'Do it just to please him. We've got them in a tin.'

'Not me. I might break a spring, me being heavy.'

'Then he's doomed to disappointment.'

'Good.' Mrs Luard handed her cup to Muriel to be refilled.

'But you're not.'

June jumped to her feet. 'Look!'

They followed her pointing finger. Very high in the sky a tiny white object floated.

'A parachute!' shouted Ann. 'Where's the plane?'

'Not a sound of one—listen.'

The four women stood watching the tiny object grow slowly larger in the distance. Far away they heard a dull explosion, then silence.

'It's crashed.'

'Where is it going to land?'

'In the lake.' Muriel began to run.

'You're right.' The girls followed her, outpacing her with their long legs. The parachute, swinging slowly in the still air, grew larger rapidly until they could distinguish the human figure dangling.

'He's not much good at it,' Ann shouted.

'Or she.'

Muriel ran as she had not run for years, racing at an angle to the path the girls had taken, racing to where the boat old Perdue used for fishing was moored. As she reached the boat she heard the splash. She untied the mooring, grabbed the oars and rowed out into the lake with both Peg and Chap swimming strongly behind her. Glancing over her shoulder she could see the large, white parachute settling on the water like a jellyfish. She reached it and caught hold of it and pulled. Somewhere under the mass of silk was a human being. She pulled desperately at the silk and the boat tipped towards it suddenly, righting itself. She looked over her shoulder to see two hands gripping the side of the boat, followed by a brown face and a voice which said, 'Oh, thank you, thank you. I am not very good parachute.'

'Here, let me pull you.'

'Ah! Thank you, thank you. That is truly kind.'

Muriel leant back and pulled and got the speaker into the boat.

'Your dogs, kind lady, they want to come in too.'

Muriel caught each dog by the collar in turn and pulled them into the boat. They shook themselves, drenching her with spray, and stood balancing on their feet four square, wagging their tails.

'I am still tied to the parachute, lady.'

'So you are. Let me help.' Muriel helped the man off with the parachute harness. 'Where on earth do you come from?'

'From Afghanistan. This is Sweden I think?' The young man now sitting in the boat flashed her a brilliant smile. 'You speak very good English, almost as good as me.'

'This is England. I am English.'

'Oh! Then I am as bad pilot as parachute. The young ladies are signalling and calling.'

'So they are.' Muriel looked at Ann and June jumping and shouting on the shore.

'What do they want, those young ladies?'

'Oh, I expect they want to invite you to tea.'

'Tea, that would be nice.' The young man fainted against the gunwhale and Muriel rowed as hard as she could for the shore.

13

When three hours later Henry limped up the hill, nursing the bruises he had acquired when for a split second he had taken his eyes off the road and run into a tree, he found only Ann in the kitchen.

'Good heavens, Henry, you look a mess. What happened?'

'I saw a plane crashing and while I was looking I ran into a tree.'

'Sit down and let me look at you.'

'There was a parachute, Ann, I saw it.'

'So did we, it's here.'

'Oh, I missed it!'

'There was an Afghan hanging on it. Mrs Wake's taking care of him now.'

'Is he hurt?'

'No. Shocked I think.'

'Can I see him?'

'No,' said Muriel, coming into the room, 'not yet. He's asleep. Henry, what on earth has happened to you?'

'I ran into a tree when I saw the aeroplane.'

'Are you hurt?'

'Only bruised. I walked back. It's goodbye to that Mini though.'

'Oh dear, Mrs Lampson will be furious.'

'There isn't a Mrs Lampson any more.'

'Nor there is. Let me look at your bruises.'

'All right, but tell me about the Afghan.'

'We put him to bed.'

'I know, but where did he come from?'

'Afghanistan.'

'Are you being annoying on purpose, Ann?'

'Yes. Sorry, Henry. Drink this.'

'What is it?'

'Tea.'

'Treatment for shock—keep the patient warm and give him hot tea. It never said anywhere you must madden him with curiosity.'

'He comes from Kabul. He was flying to Sweden to see his sister who is or was studying there. He had never flown a plane so he got lost—'

'Almost a feat in itself these days.'

'Yes, and he had never used a parachute before either.'

'Seems like an intellectual!'

'He was on his way to Sweden because the Kabul Radio doesn't work any more nor their telephones or anything.'

'Any Afghans left?'

'He said quite a lot had disappeared in a disorderly way.'

'What does he mean—disorderly?'

'They left "bits" behind.'

'But there are some left alive?'

'He said some of the country people but not the townspeople, which accounts for him flying by himself.'

'It adds up.' Henry appeared satisfied. 'Will he be down for supper?'

'Not until tomorrow. I think he should sleep. I've given him a sedative.'

'How are the mice?'

'Fine. Mrs Luard says one of them is expecting. She put them down a mousehole to be safe from the cats.'

'Goodoh! Where is she now?'

'She's working on the chairs.'

'I've got good news for her.'

Henry put down his cup and left the kitchen, calling, 'Mrs Luard! Mrs Luard! It's all perfect.'

'Henry's bruises don't seem very bad.' Muriel picked up the empty cup.

'No, he's young. Running a Mini into a tree is nothing. I wonder how that Afghan got so far off course. As Henry says, it's almost impossible.'

'I'll go and see if he's asleep and if he isn't I'll ask him.' Muriel got up. 'I'll take him some tea.'

With Ann's help Muriel laid a small tray and carried it upstairs. She paused outside the room they had put their new visitor in and listened. Hearing movements in the bed she went in.

'Are you awake?'

'Yes, lady.'

'I've brought you some tea.'

'That is too much trouble for you.'

'Of course it isn't.' Muriel sat beside the bed and poured a cup of tea for the young man.

'Thank you,' he said, taking it. 'Thank you very much.'

'We were wondering just now how you got off course in your aeroplane.' Muriel smiled.

'My name is Akbar.' Akbar gave a little bow. 'I got off course, dear lady, because I have always had a pilot to fly me, dear lady, and when I noticed I had gone wrong there was no petrol left, so I baled out.'

'I see.'

'I am a professor of literature. I am not a practical man.'

'That explains it. Have some more tea. Does your head ache?'

'Oh no, I am very well. I am dry now and rested. I must find another plane to take me to Sweden.'

'That may be difficult, if not impossible.'

'Why so?'

'Well, here we are in a Nature Reserve and we are not allowed planes. Also things have happened.'

'What things?'

'Well, almost everybody but the people you have seen here have disappeared. We have no communications—'

'Not in Kabul either. Did you have snow, a lot of snow?'

'Yes, and terrible wind.'

'We too, a great storm.'

'And this part of England is cut off from the rest of the country by the sea. It's all very odd,' Muriel finished lamely, 'and the climate has gone mad,' she added.

'Tell me more if it is not too much trouble.'

Muriel told her new visitor all that had happened since that first night of fear, ending, 'I thought you might be able to tell me whether it's another war.'

'Oh no, not war, an accident of some kind.'

'That's what Father Richard says. He seems quite calm.'

'I, too, feel calm. Let us enjoy what has come to us.'

'Akbar—may I call you Akbar?—what has happened to us?'

'I do not know, lady. Maybe in Sweden they will know. They are very progressive.'

'Not if there are no Swedes left. It is over four weeks since we had our storm and everyone blew away.'

'Then maybe my sister she has blown away too.'

'Yes.' Too progressive, Muriel thought wryly.

'But here it is nice: nice house, nice climate, plenty to eat, pretty girls, why do you worry? I am here now. I will help you.'

'Thank you.'

'What is to be done first?'

'We thought we would clear the road to the village. Cut the trees away. There are not many across the road.'

'And make logs to burn?'

'Yes.'

'I would like that. I did that in my holidays as a boy.'

'We have saws and old Perdue says there is a winch at the garage in the village. We could begin at the bottom of the hill and work upwards.' Muriel felt enthusiastic with the prospect of something concrete to do.

'May I come in?' Henry came in, knocking as he did so. 'I am Henry.' Henry and Akbar shook hands.

'We were talking of clearing the road to the village. Mrs Luard is very keen on it too.'

'I can hardly see Mrs Luard as a lumberjack,' said Henry.

'No, but while we clear the road she can get on with covering the chairs and it will keep her and old Perdue apart. Then in the evening we can swim in the lake. What was the water like, Akbar?'

'Oh, warm, quite nice. Good for the health.'

'Are you a doctor?'

'Alas, no. I am a professor of literature.'

'There's a lovely library in this house.'

'Then I have fallen well.' Akbar seemed pleased. 'Two pretty girls, a kind lady and a library.'

'I think you should get some sleep and tomorrow, if you are well enough, we will all begin clearing the road.' Muriel looked thoughtfully at her new visitor, rose and went downstairs to join the girls.

'How is the Afghan?'

'Much better. He is pleased because there are two pretty girls.'

'We shall toss up for him,' Ann laughed. 'No sharing.'

'Hobson's choice.' June grinned.

Muriel felt irritable. All her visitors were so individual. Cross old Perdue, determined Mrs Luard, Henry full of secrets, the two girls so friendly and flippant. She went to the telephone and lifted the receiver. Nothing. She dialled 123. Nothing. She dialled 999. Nothing. She dialled all the numbers by which she had been able to get anything from the weather report to music. Nothing. She went out into the evening light and walked slowly round the house. The sun was setting and the sweet smell of flowers was all round her. Below her in the meadow the cows grazed and out on the moor she could see the sheep and ponies. In the farmyard Perdue was feeding the chicks, who were growing out of the attractive stage and beginning to look like miniature ostriches. She went up to the old man.

'How many hens and how many cockerels?' she asked.

'Three cockerels, the others hens I reckon, and three drakes among the ducks. We can eat two of the cockerels.'

'Are you happy, Mr Perdue?'

'I'm all right.'

Muriel went in to supper.

'Where's Henry?'

'He went out. He took sandwiches and said we were not to wait up for him.'

'Then I shan't.' Muriel ate and helped clear the table and then followed Mrs Luard into the drawing-room. There she sat down and watched the older woman resume her clever cutting and stitching.

'You have nearly finished.'

'Yes, soon be done now.'

'What will you do then?'

'The curtains, and when the road is cleared—ah well, I shall have plenty to do and no interference.'

'No, none. I rang 999.'

91

'What d'you want to do that for?' Mrs Luard was angry.

'Only to see if the telephone worked and it didn't.'

'No. Good job too. Wish my dad and my old man was alive, they'd have a laugh.'

'I suppose they would.'

'Take the salt out of it a bit though.'

'Why?'

'Well, not much fun in the profession when there's nobody to stop you, is there? They weren't like me and that boy Henry now were they?'

'No, I daresay not. But how are you and Henry alike?' Muriel stroked the velvet chair Mrs Luard was finishing.

'Ah, Henry and me we have higher interests, not that they are the same, mind you.'

'Henry has gone out.'

'Yes, I asked him to find me something I wanted.'

'What was that?'

'You'll know soon enough. Now you go to bed. I can see you're tired.'

'That Afghan—'

'Oh, the girls and I will manage him. You go to bed.'

'Mrs Luard, will you try and be nice to Mr Perdue?'

'I see no cause to be.' Mrs Luard looked obstinate.

Muriel sighed and left the room.

'I really felt happier alone with the boys,' she muttered to herself. She went upstairs, looked in on the sleeping Afghan, stood undecided for a moment on the landing watched by the dogs, and then went into her room and slowly went to bed. Lying stiffly in her bed, she heard the noises in the house. The girls talking to old Perdue and, what seemed very much later, all three of them going to bed. Somebody had a bath. The clock in the hall and the cuckoo clock in the kitchen struck midnight in unison. Far away she heard the village clock chime twelve, followed by the Abbey down in the valley tolling midnight too. Slowly she relaxed. The dogs sighed in their sleep and the puppies made snuffling noises. The night was so still she could hear the rasp of the cat's tongue as she licked a kitten.

14

'Mum, Mum, wake up.'

Muriel woke soggily. Paul was climbing onto her bed and hugging her. Both the dogs and an avalanche of puppies were greeting him. It was very dark and above the dogs' whimpers of joy she could hear a hiss and disturbances from the cats' chair.

'Oh, Paul! Oh, Paul! Are you safe?'

'Yes, of course I am. Has Peg had all these puppies? Let's have a light. Oh goodness! Charlie's here too.' Paul switched on his mother's bedside lamp. 'What a collection!'

'Paul, thank God you are back!' Muriel clung to him. 'I thought you had gone for ever.'

'Sorry, Mum.' Paul was stroking the dogs and the cat. 'Can I get in with you. I'm rather tired.'

'Of course.'

Paul pulled off his shirt and jeans and got in beside her. The dogs and the cat retired to their beds. The cat gathered her kittens into a bunch and turned her back on the light, and the dogs with their noses on their paws gazed ecstatically at Paul.

'I left John at the Abbey. Father Richard wanted me to stay the night but I thought you might be lonely.'

'Are you hungry?'

'Only sleepy. Father Richard said Henry was back and something about two girls.' Paul breathed deeply adding, 'We walked from Plymouth.'

'All those miles!'

'Father Richard and Peter fed us.'

Not wishing to show too much emotion, Muriel remained silent.

'Mum, you're crying.'

'Only because I'm glad you are back.'

Paul laughed and almost immediately fell asleep. Muriel listened to his breathing for a while, curled up beside him, and fell asleep again. She did not notice the dogs move uneasily and walk to the window listening. Chap stood alert by the window for the rest of the night while the bitch and the cat listened suspiciously by their broods. Muriel slept the dreamless sleep of profound relief.

When the Angelus sounded in the valley, Muriel stirred, looked at Paul still asleep beside her, slipped out of bed and, followed by the dogs, crept into the passage. She listened for a moment to the stillness broken by Henry's rhythmic snoring, Mrs Luard's loud breathing and an occasional abrupt snort from behind the door leading to Mr Perdue's bachelor wing. The dogs trotted down the stairs and stood by the front door looking up at her. Muriel crept back into her room, took an armful of clothes, dressed hurriedly and went downstairs. She opened the front door very quietly and slipped out after the dogs. It was dawn and she watched them throw up their heads and sniff, then begin to run north up the yard and on to the moor. Muriel followed, waiting until she got out of earshot of the house before she whistled. She did not want to wake her household so early.

Up on the moor in the increasing light she saw the dogs far ahead of her running with their heads up, already out of earshot. She saw their figures silhouetted against the sky for a second, and then disappear. Whistling at intervals, Muriel followed up the hill to the top from where she could see for miles around the moor. A long way off she heard the dogs barking. She shaded her eyes, and standing at the top of the hill looked westward to where the sound of the dogs seemed to come from. Advancing towards her from the direction of the holiday camp came a long line of tracked vehicles led by a ferret car flying a pennant.

Muriel stood in complete disbelief until the small vehicle drew up beside her. From beside the driver stepped down a trim figure in naval uniform who saluted.

'I am Commander James,' said the man, holding out his hand. 'Paul told you about us I take it, Mrs Wake?'

'Not a word,' said Muriel, taking the outstretched hand. 'He arrived exhausted. He is still asleep.'

'Wanted to surprise you I expect.' Commander James spoke easily. 'Paul and that monk fellow said there were people in the Abbey. I brought this lot across the moor. Navigation is easier. We spent the night in the holiday camp by the prison.'

Muriel looked at the calm young man and at a motley collection of people getting out of the tanks, jeeps and other army vehicles now stopped in a long line across the moor.

'Are you all from Plymouth?'

'Well, I am, and Petty Officer Coke here, and those people over there are from the marine farm off Fowey. We found them in Cornwall and I brought them over.'

'Over what?'

'Over the water. Cornwall is two islands now. It's split up the Tamar and at the far western end by Hayle. The Petty Officer and I were doing an underwater test when this thing blew up. It was pure luck your boy found us.'

'Paul found you?'

'Yes, he shouted down the blower from the ship and we shouted back. We'd been down twelve hours too long anyway.'

'We got the bends fearful.' Petty Officer Coke spoke for the first time. 'Pretty good at first aid that monk fellow was.'

Muriel was bewildered. 'Who are the others?' she asked.

'A job lot of people we found in Plymouth. Those girls are mostly telephonists or from the hospitals. They want to get to London.'

'I don't understand anything.' Muriel felt exasperated. 'What's going on? What has happened?'

'We don't understand either.' The young Commander sat down beside her. 'None of us knows anything.'

'Is there another war?'

'I don't think so. There's no enemy. It's a great big accident I think.'

'Father Richard said that.'

'Ah yes, they talked of him.'

'Are there a lot of people in Plymouth?'

'No, just this job lot. We thought we'd visit you on our way to London.'

'The bright lights,' said the Petty Officer, as though this explained everything.

'I doubt if you will find those. Nobody answers the telephone and there is no television or radio. There have been no planes.'

'We noticed that too.'

'Have you had breakfast?' Muriel looked at the crowd of some forty people.

'Oh yes, we ate before we started.'

'Why didn't Paul come back for all these weeks?' Muriel was suddenly angry.

'I'm sorry, Mrs Wake. He came out in a ship with the Petty Officer and me. He was a great help.'

'I thought he was dead.'

'He said it would be all right. Of course we were longer than we meant to be.'

'What about the monk?'

'He was helping to search the city. It takes time you know.'

'I think everything will take time now.'

'Do us good perhaps.' An oldish man stepped up to her from the little crowd. 'Don't worry, you have him back now.'

'We should be getting on.' A woman spoke up sharply.

'Won't you stay?' Muriel pleaded. There was a pause and uncertainty.

'I should like to.' The young Commander spoke quietly. 'There's nobody in Plymouth now.'

'I'll stay with you, sir.' The Petty Officer smiled at Muriel. 'Could make myself useful to you I've no doubt.'

'We should get back at once to the underwater station,' an oldish man in baggy trousers and a torn tweed coat said courteously. 'If we don't all our experiments of years may come to nothing, and with this curious upheaval there will be so much to record.'

'I'm afraid I rather insisted, sir.'

'Oh, not at all, that's all right. Just get us connected on the telephone when you have time. There are boats to get across the water.'

'We'll do that, sir.'

'Then we will go back at once. There's no point in waiting.'

'Will you be all right?' Muriel looked at the small group round the older man, three men and two girls.

'Yes, yes, of course. It's been a pleasure to meet you but we must get back.'

The little group smiled, waved, climbed into their vehicle and turned back the way they had come.

'Scientists!' said the Petty Officer.

'Even so they must have families or something.'

'They are wedded to fish. We were mad to have brought them. They have been very fretful.'

Muriel watched the departing scientists and laughed. 'We can visit them I suppose.'

'They look upon all this as a great opportunity to be left in peace. There was someone called Harbuckel at the Ministry of Agriculture and Fisheries who was always breathing down their necks. Now he can't.'

'Poor things.'

'They hope he is dead very fervently.'

'Do they?'

'Well, dead to their outfit. They say he visits them and wastes their time with red tape.'

'We want to go on.' An aggressive voice spoke from the crowd.

'Me too,' chorused the rest.

'How will you get to England?'

'Plenty of boats. I will see they get there.' A large man spoke up from the group. 'We are only down here on our holidays. I've got to get back to my office. There have been too many delays already.'

A chorus of approval met this statement.

'Will you take command, sir?' the young Commander asked the large man.

'Command, command? I'll lead them. Get them across the water and that sort of thing.'

'Then let's go.' The woman who had spoken first spoke again. 'I've got to get back to my shop. It will go to ruin unless I get back.'

The group dissolved, climbing back into their vehicles.

'Goodbye,' shouted the large man.

'Can't we stop them? Don't they realise?' Muriel appealed to the young naval officer beside her.

'No. It's a free country. They are fed up already. They won't believe until they see for themselves that there is probably nothing left.'

Muriel and the two men watched the column of vehicles move away jerkily, heading east.

'Better without them if you ask me,' said the Petty Officer. 'You and me going to run Plymouth, sir?'

'More or less.' The young man smiled, adding thoughtfully, 'I suppose.'

'Come to my house first.'

'Thank you, we would like to. Then we must go to this Abbey of yours and see whether they are all right.'

'I know they are because Paul got out to me in the middle of the night.'

'So he did. Wouldn't you like to come aboard?' Muriel climbed into the ferret car.

'Some of those people rather frightened me   she said.

'Me too.' Petty Officer Coke started the engine. 'And I'm not easily frightened. Which way?'

Muriel pointed and with the dogs running alongside they drove down across the moor to Brendon.

'Those people seemed evil,' she said.

The sailors looked at her sidelong, saying nothing.

15

Only Mrs Luard seemed indifferent to the new arrivals. Muriel and the girls cooked a large breakfast while Petty Officer Coke told them all about Plymouth. His officer seemed tired and quite content to let him describe the events in Plymouth as they had seen them. He winced when Coke described the long wait in the underwater tank fathoms down in Plymouth Sound.

'We didn't get no response from the blower not for hours and we was just conking out, our oxygen run out, see, when a little voice came down the blower shouting, "Anybody there? Anybody there?" You should have seen the Commander wake up. "There certainly is," he said in his most prissy voice, "Heave us up."'

'Mum, it was very weird,' Paul broke in. 'We hauled them up and they collapsed at once, but we knew roughly what to do.'

'And that was roughly what they did.' Commander James spoke up. 'Saved our lives really.'

'Then what did you do?' Ann leant across the table towards Commander James.

'Do call me James, please.' He looked round.

'All right, what did you do then, James?'

'We couldn't believe what Paul and that monk fellow told us about the storm, the snow, everybody vanished and so on. We thought they were pulling our legs. We made a thorough search, but they were right. Everyone was gone.'

'No police?' Muriel questioned.

'The coppers! Hah! They was gone with the rest.'

'But who else?'

'Well, that big chap who took command so to speak and led the blooming lot we did find off across the moor, he was in the hold of a pub as you might say.'

'In a cellar?'

'Yes. Troublesome fellow that, uppish.'

'The people you saw,' James said slowly, 'came out of the ground like rats.'

'Will they get across to England?'

'I think so, but one of us should go and see that they do.'

'I'll go on my skates.' Paul spoke eagerly.

'Skates?'

'Yes. The roads are so difficult we can only skate or walk.'

'I'll go with you.' June got up. 'The sooner we go the better.'

'What's the hurry?' Mr Perdue asked.

'Those people. Well, those people are dangerous. I hope I'm not exaggerating.'

Muriel looked at James finishing his second breakfast.

'No, you are right. They are dangerous. They are frightened.'

Paul and June were getting ready.

'Get back as soon as you can, Paul. You only came home last night.'

'Okay, Mum, I will.'

'What do you two think?' Muriel asked her visitors.

'We think we are due for a spot of leave.'

'No joking. What do you really think?'

'What can anyone think? None of us knows more than anyone else. Akbar here says it's much the same in his country. We found nobody in Cornwall except the scientists in the Fish Farm, and as soon as they found they had plenty to eat for years they went down underwater again, except the ones you saw.'

'That was cool,' said Henry admiringly.

'Yes, they said they were seeing a lot of fish which don't belong in these waters and were making notes.'

'Who for?'

'For their own satisfaction I suppose. I don't think any of them thinks there will be anyone left to read them.'

'There may be in other places.' Muriel tried to sound hopeful. The two sailors said nothing but passed their cups to Ann who poured out more coffee.

'When will people come and look for us?' Akbar enquired.

'I don't know. I take it we must reconnoitre.'

Akbar sighed. 'Here it is so nice. Nice climate, nice people.'

'We are ready now.' Paul and June came in. 'We ought to go and we won't be long.'

'Don't let those people see you,' Petty Officer Coke whispered in June's ear.

'Why not?'

'Because it's better not.'

'We ought to go over to your Abbey.' James stood up.

'I'll come with you and show you the way.'

'Can we walk?'

'Yes,' said Muriel. 'Coming, Henry?'

'If you don't mind I think I won't.'

'I'll get on with my chairs then.' Mrs Luard was helping Ann clear. 'You go, dear.'

'All right, but will you be all right on your own with Mr Perdue?'

'That Mr Perdue can see to the animate objects while I see to my chairs.'

Ann and James walked on either side of Muriel along the track leading down the valley. The Petty Officer and Akbar strolled slowly behind them.

'Mrs Luard doesn't seem to fit in with the scenery somehow.' James looked across the rolling moor.

'Her family were all professional thieves and we found her on a sentimental visit to the holiday camp to be near the prison.'

'Well, it's funny, the extreme tidiness of the place. Did she tidy up the bits by the way?'

'Yes, she told me she did. Why,' Muriel continued, 'did you go off taking Paul in a ship? I was worried to death.'

'I'm sorry. Paul said you wouldn't be expecting him back at once. The monk was busy looking for survivors, so we took Paul along with us. We went in an Air-Sea Rescue launch and I'm sorry to say we got stuck.'

'Stuck! I thought you were sailors.'

'We are, but no chart is any good any more, not round the coast of Cornwall anyway. We got stuck on a bar which has been thrown up at the mouth of the Fal. We took three days to get off it but after that we went more carefully.'

'Where did you go?'

'All round the coast. We landed at every port. Your son has a horrid way of chanting, "Anybody there? Anybody there?" by the way.'

'I've heard him. Gives you the willies. But what else can you do?'

'I used an old-fashioned loud hailer.'

'Was there anybody there?'

'No. Only the fishery people. They are a nice lot, but dedicated scientists only interested in fish. They can use the launch. We have several at Plymouth.'

'Did you go inland at all?'

'Oh yes, we went inland wherever we landed, pinched cars and so on and shouted, but it was useless. Not a sausage, not unless you count the bits.'

'Funny,' said Muriel, 'the way we all say bits, not pieces or remains or any other word.'

'We found,' went on James, 'that Cornwall is now two islands. We went right out to the Scillies. They have disappeared. They were very low. There's only a tip of rock where Bryher was and a tiny bit of Tresco.'

'Oh dear, they were so lovely.'

'They was my home,' Petty Officer Coke called out from behind them.

'There's the Abbey,' Ann pointed, 'down there among the trees.'

'Father Richard will be glad to have both his novices back.'

They walked down the valley to the Abbey in the sun. The silence was absolute.

'Where can they be?' Muriel began to hurry.

By the Abbey gate stood a motor scooter. 'I see he had to abandon his transport,' said James. 'He left Plymouth in a tank.'

'The roads are completely cluttered.' Ann spoke slowly as she watched Akbar at the Abbey door removing his shoes. He smiled at her.

'Atavistic,' he said. 'It's a holy place.'

Petty Officer Coke coughed and went in, crossing himself and genuflecting.

'What's *he* up to? He's a Methodist,' whispered James to Muriel.

They went in to the Abbey. A ceremony was just finishing. The two novices Peter and John were walking in procession. Father Richard followed. The monks disappeared into the Abbey and Muriel stood waiting with her companions.

'What's going on?' asked the Petty Officer.

'Haven't a clue,' said James.

'I have been ordaining the novices as priests.' Father Richard appeared beside them.

'But surely,' Muriel spoke hesitantly, 'only a Bishop can do that.'

'There *is* no Bishop.'

'In times of stress it is quite correct,' said Akbar, 'for a priest to ordain. I am a student of history as well as a professor of literature.'

'Yes,' Father Richard smiled. 'In Japan the faith was carried on for several hundred years.'

'Look! Look!' One of the new priests was pointing at the sky. High above them a vast flock of birds flew across the sky.

'Birds!' cried Muriel and fell silent.

They stood in a group watching as every minute or so a great flock of birds blotted out the light of the sun. James had a pair of binoculars slung round his neck and put them to his eyes. 'Swallows,' he said, 'martins, swifts, finches of some sort. These are duck.' His running commentary was the only sound as they gazed upward. 'And listen, here come the geese.' From a long way off and very high in the sky came the rhythmic honking which swelled and grew as a vast gaggle of geese flew down from the north, their wings seeming to ruffle the still air until they gradually disappeared into the south.

'If that isn't a sign now!' The Petty Officer was jumping from one foot to the other in his excitement.

'We have always been on the migratory course.' Father Richard spoke calmly. 'There, Father, you have the birds you so missed.'

The newly-ordained priest was standing murmuring to himself, his eyes filled with tears.

'What next!' exclaimed Muriel.

'Oh, lunch I think,' said Father Richard.

16

Long into the afternoon James and Petty Officer Coke and the priests conferred. Muriel wandered on a tour of the Abbey church, the grounds, the lake and the farm until they came out to join her.

'Made any decisions?' she asked.

'Yes. We think we will stay with you, if you will have us, and see you through the winter. Coke and I can get supplies from Plymouth.'

'What do you mean, winter? It's so hot.' Muriel looked at James.

'It may be now, but the birds have migrated. You saw for yourself.'

'Yes, that's true.'

'Coke and I can help you clear your way to the village and see you through the winter.'

'What about Plymouth?'

'Plymouth must wait.'

'What about all those other people? They frightened me.'

'I think there will be room for all wherever they go,' Father Richard said dryly.

'That's settled then. We clear the road to the village, we establish communications with you and the Fisheries and we divide up the livestock. After the winter we can spread our wings further.'

'Winter, winter, we never get much more than a few days at a time here,' Muriel snapped.

'This winter after this tremendously hot summer we shall, Mrs Wake. Coke and I are going into Plymouth as soon as we can to get skis and toboggans.'

'I think you are crazy.'

'Not if you work out what has happened.'

'I can't work out anything. I want Sam my son.'

'Naturally you do.'

'We have much to be thankful for,' Ann remarked parsonically.

'Oh, Ann!' Muriel could not help laughing. 'Henry pinched our village parson's glass eye.'

'Time we went back. Thank you for all you have done. Coke and I will connect you and Brendon up as soon as we can.'

James took Muriel by the arm and led her up the hill. Akbar, Ann and Petty Officer Coke followed.

'What do you mean, connect up?' Muriel knew she sounded querulous.

'Coke and I are going to set up radio communications between Brendon and the Abbey. We just have to get over to Plymouth for the equipment. We can fix up the Fisheries in Cornwall too.'

'Mrs Luard won't like that.'

'What's she got against the Fisheries?'

'Nothing. She likes privacy that's all.'

'She may be glad of them some day.'

'That would indeed be a miracle.'

'I'm glad we are here.' James looked round him at the beautiful country lying so peacefully in the sun. 'We thought we were going to die.'

'So am I, and glad to have you here. But this is my home. Won't you pine for yours?'

'I have no home. The Navy was my home and that doesn't exist any more as far as I can see.'

'What about the rest of the world?'

'We decided this afternoon and I honestly think we are right, not just selfish, to make your house and the Abbey a solid nucleus and then work outwards. We are all sure of it.'

'There must be masses of people cut off all over the place,' said Muriel.

'We don't know.'

'What about all those millions in skyscrapers in the States and South America? What about China? What about everyone everywhere?' Ann's voice broke in.

'Last news was plague and pestilence,' said James.

'There are lots of Afghans,' said Muriel.

'Yes. Anyway I am sure we shall find out sooner or later.' James sounded tired.

'Bed for you when we get back.'

'You put everyone to bed,' Ann said.

'Well, they need it. I shall sit up and wait for Paul and June.'

'Henry is out somewhere too.'

'Oh Lord, so he is. I don't think somehow that Henry is up to much good.'

'But good may come of it.'

'That's true.'

'Yoohoo! Typhoo!' Boys' voices called from the hill.

'Henry and Paul!' said Muriel.

'And June,' said Ann.

'They've been damn quick.'

'That ancient family joke—' Muriel began to hurry towards the three figures running down the hill towards them. 'How did you get back so soon?' she shouted. They shouted something unintelligible.

'Sounds like June found a car.'

Petty Officer Coke cupped his hands and shouted up the valley, 'Found a car?' in tones of brass.

The wind brought laughter faintly down the slope and they saw Henry turning somersaults.

17

'What happened?'

'A terrible lot of things. You tell, June.'

'Well.' June looked at the little group. 'First, Paul and I got as far as the main road in his Mini. Then after a hundred yards or so it's blocked by two container lorries which have crashed head on so we left the Mini and walked. Then we found a Landrover and a clear road. We fuelled the thing at a garage and I drove it to Exeter.'

'What happened then?'

'We hid it in some trees near the university because Coke had said to be careful of those people. Then we walked on to where the river used to be and where it's now sea and we saw all those people from Plymouth. It was horrible. They were quarrelling and fighting.'

'Why?'

'It looked as though they were drunk and that very big man was throwing his weight about and shouting. They had two

105

boats, one towing the other, and they set off to cross to England.'

'Yes?'

'Well, there was a terrific tide running and the boat which was being towed capsized and everyone fell in the water.'

'Oh, my God! Were they drowned?'

'We think so.'

'Then what happened?'

'The people in the other boat started fighting again and it blew up.'

'Blew up?'

'Yes,' said Paul. 'Sky high and nobody was left, we could see that. Then just some heads bobbing and then nothing more.'

'How horrible!'

'I should not have let them go alone.' James sounded remorseful.

'Sounds a good riddance to me.'

'Henry, you are too truthful.' Ann was looking at him. 'They were human.'

'Not very,' James said quietly. 'There wasn't one among them who wouldn't have cut your throat.'

'Well, that's all,' said June rather too brightly. 'We drove back and when we saw Henry at the house we came on to meet you.'

They reached the top of the hill and walked down into the dip to Brendon. In front of the house, with Mrs Luard at the wheel, stood an outsize maroon Phantom Rolls.

'My present to Mrs Luard.' Henry waved a careless hand.

18

Autumn began to colour the moor almost overnight. All the men, led by James, began the task of clearing the road to the village of fallen trees. The valley, lately so quiet, echoed with the harsh scream of chain saws and the creaking of the trunks as they were winched to the side of the road. Muriel and the girls cooked for the hungry men. Mrs Luard stitched at the velvet chairs. James seemed always to have his eye on the sky and one evening told Paul to take the sheep and one cow down the moor to the Abbey.

'Why so soon?' asked Ann.

'Winter may come any day now.'

'Since Henry drove the Rolls up here we are all used to strange things.'

'I'm not having me Rolls risked again.' Mrs Luard was firm. 'He might have broken an axle bringing it up over the moor.'

'We could keep it in the garage.'

'Not all winter. I want to drive it down to the village and—'

'And what?' Paul had taken to teasing Mrs Luard.

'That's my secret and Henry's.'

'You must do as you please.'

'I shall. Just as soon as I've finished the chairs I'm off.'

'Oh, Mrs Luard!' Muriel was hurt.

'You can't see me and Mr Perdue holed up together in one house for the whole of a winter now can you.'

Muriel acknowledged the strong feeling between Mrs Luard and Mr Perdue with a nod. It was undeniable.

Two days running James and June used the Landrover to go to Plymouth. On the first day they came back with many more stores and another Landrover.

'The problem is where to keep them all,' said Akbar.

'Why? They are all right in front of the house.' Mrs Luard liked to wake in the mornings and go out and inspect them, smiling at the glossy Rolls among the Landrovers.

'They won't be all right in the winter.'

'Garn, we don't get much winter,' said Perdue.

'We shall.'

'One could be kept in the Dutch barn,' said Paul.

'What about the other?'

'I think the monks should have it. Father Richard can use it. They have a Dutch barn.'

'Okay, then we'll take them one tomorrow when we finish fixing their radio.'

Muriel and Paul listened to this talk without comment. Paul was tired from his wood-cutting and Muriel had reached a stage of sad bewilderment when nothing surprised her. All the activity disturbed her, though the young people and Mrs Luard seemed happy enough. Old Perdue, when not gazing in rapture at the Rolls, cherished the ducks and chickens which he now kept in what had once been the farmhouse kitchen. Muriel visited it on his insistence and found the once scrupulously clean kitchen covered with deep litter, a ramp leading up to the bathroom and perches fixed one above the other facing the now dead television set.

'If there is a winter like them chaps says there will be, then me ducks can get to the bathroom and me chickens can roost in comfort.'

Muriel inspected the curious arrangement and agreed that it was indeed comfortable. She sat down on a chair.

'Mr Perdue, what are Henry and Mrs Luard up to?'

'That boy, he's deep. He comes and goes when we are wood-cutting and he takes the Landrover and he's gone for hours but he don't say nothing.'

'Does Paul know what he's doing?'

'No. Just Mrs Luard. That old cow!' Mr Perdue spat.

'I can understand clearing the road so that we can get to the village and cutting wood and getting in stores, but I can't understand Henry.'

'Henry is getting in stores too.'

'Well, I'm glad he's a help. I thought you said he went off though.'

'So he does, and it's not here he brings the stores nor the wood nor the coal.'

'Then where is it?'

'I don't know and I can't find out. He's a sneaky boy.'

'Oh, no!' Muriel felt obliged to defend Henry, but within herself agreed that sneaky was just what Henry was.

'He steals,' said Mr Perdue.

'We all steal.'

'Not caviar nor Rolls Royces. We steal what's necessary.'

'What about the Landrovers?'

'They'm necessary.'

'I suppose they are.'

'Why,' said Mr Perdue standing up, suddenly belligerent, 'does Henry keep an armalite rifle under his bed?'

Muriel made no answer but left the farmhouse and went straight back into her own house. Upstairs in Henry's room she knelt down and peered under the bed. There indeed, clean and gleaming, was an armalite rifle and beside it quite a number of boxes of ammunition. I must, thought Muriel, have a showdown with Henry. But other things happened to put

Henry and his mysteries out of her head. As she went downstairs to lay the table for supper the telephone started ringing.

19

'Hullo? Hullo? Who is it? Who's there? Hullo? Hullo?'

Muriel held the dull dead telephone in her hand. She could hear the Landrover bringing back the men and boys from clearing the road.

'What are you doing with the telephone, Mum?' Paul looked at her with curiosity.

'It rang.'

'It can't have. James and Coke say we won't get the radio connected with the Abbey for three more days and Plymouth is going to take a week.'

'It rang I tell you.' Muriel stood holding the dumb instrument in her hand.

'And answer came there none.' Henry strolled up to her, took the receiver from her hand, smiled sweetly, listened, and put it back in its cradle.

'You must have imagined it.' He looked at her slyly.

'It rang I tell you.'

'I don't really think it can have.' James took up the receiver and dialled idly. 'No. Dead until we get the wavelength right. Imagination plays funny tricks.'

'Oh, hell!'

'Well, let's have supper.' June took Muriel's arm. 'We must ring the changes with the tinned soups. Ann and I thought mushroom would be nice tonight.'

'All right.' Muriel felt defeated by their common sense.

'Mrs Luard has finished the chairs.'

'How marvellous.'

'Come and look.'

They all trooped into the drawing-room where Mrs Luard stood alone in triumph among white, pink and yellow button chairs.

'Mrs Luard, they look wonderful.' James bowed.

'Very handsome I'm sure.' Mr Perdue spoke in neutral tones.

'This calls for a celebration. Got any champagne, Mum?'

'Of course. You and James get it.'

Muriel took Mrs Luard's hand and bent to kiss her fat face. 'My husband would have been so thrilled. You have made it just as he wanted it to be.'

'Let's all drink to Mrs Luard.' Paul was excited as he hurried up from the cellar followed by James.

'A party, a party!' Ann seized Mr Perdue round the waist and waltzed him round the room.

'Yes, yes, a party!' several voices exclaimed at once.

'And just look at the curtains!'

'Let's draw the curtains and switch on the lights.'

They drew the curtains, Coke switched on the lights and Muriel stood looking round her at the transformed room.

'It's gorgeous! How can I thank you enough?'

'Well, I enjoyed doing them.' Mrs Luard accepted a glass of champagne. 'Here's to you, Mr Perdue,' she said unexpectedly. Mr Perdue blushed, cleared his throat and drank.

'Supper's ready,' June called and they all trooped into the kitchen to eat.

As they were finishing their meal Muriel whispered to Paul who shook his head vigorously, so she turned to Henry who nodded and jumping up on a chair shouted, 'To Mrs Luard who has brightened our lives, I propose a toast.'

They all raised their glasses and drank. Mrs Luard bowed, raised her glass in turn and stood up.

'And I drink to you all,' she said, 'may you all live happy and free. And now that my work here is over I must leave you. I shall leave you with regret but I have my own house to care for and I hope that one day soon you will all come and dine with me there. I am going now since our naval gentlemen here tell me that the road is clear and I can drive down it. I have much to do settling into my own home before the winter sets in.' She paused and sipped her champagne. 'You will all,' she said, her eyes sweeping round the assembly, 'be more than welcome when I am ready. My thanks, my grateful thanks for all your kind hospitality here.' She bowed to Muriel. 'And help,' here she bowed to Henry. 'It was you who brought me car up here but it is I who shall drive it away.'

Mrs Luard rose, smiled once more round the table, and

started walking with great dignity for one so fat towards the front door.

They watched Paul open the front door for her. They watched Henry hold open the door of the huge maroon Rolls, piled high, Muriel noticed suddenly, with her luggage. They saw her grip the wheel in her fat hands and, with a final bow and wave, drive away from them into the dusk, the engine of the Rolls inaudible.

'I saw *that*,' said Muriel.

'Of course you did,' they chorused, anxious to assuage her, and she knew then that they thought she had imagined the ringing of the telephone.

Henry was collapsed with laughter on the newly covered sofa.

'Henry! Where has she gone?'

'I gave her Willoughby,' he gasped.

'But it's a National Trust monument.'

'Not now. It belongs to Mrs Luard. Mrs Luard of Willoughby!'

'Mrs Luard with four sets of eighteenth century gold plate,' said Paul, awestruck.

'Mrs Luard in the finest example of seventeenth century architecture with a garden designed by Capability Brown,' crowed Henry.

'Those pictures,' Muriel whispered, 'a whole room full of Zoffanys.'

'That furniture,' murmured Paul.

'And the glass, the porcelain, the gold.'

'Henry, what made you think of it?'

'I think it's a very fine setting for Mrs Luard,' Henry spoke complacently.

'The old cow!'

'Now, now, Mr Perdue.'

'Has she anything to eat there?'

'Oh yes, I've stocked her up with all she needs. It was fun!'

Muriel drew James to one side. 'Henry has an armalite rifle under his bed.'

'Has he now? I'll go and look.' James slipped out of the room.

'More champagne cried the girls. 'Come on, Mr Perdue, she's out of your hair.'

'Thief!'

'Oh *no*, she is taking over for posterity.'

And where did you find the Rolls then?'

'By chance in a side-road, quite unhurt.'

James came back into the room holding out his glass to be refilled. 'You must have imagined it,' he whispered.

'But Mr Perdue saw it too.'

'Oh, he wouldn't know the difference between a broken motor scooter and a gun.'

'But I would.'

'Have another drink.' James took Muriel's arm. 'It's getting quite autumnal. Come near the fire.'

Muriel gave in. 'I wonder how soon it would be decent to call,' she said.

'Give her a week.'

'We must fix her up on the blower, too.'

'I bet she would like one of the kittens and one of the puppies.'

'She said not until they are house trained because of the Aubusson carpets.'

'Henry, you know everything.'

'Well, it was fun. She wants Ringo, if it's okay by you and one of the tom cats.'

'You seem to have discussed it all with her.'

'I had to.'

'Will she be all right alone?' Ann sounded doubtful.

'She says she will. She has only one fear. She's afraid of burglars.' Again Henry began to laugh with helpless unrestraint. 'Burglars,' he giggled. 'Thieves breaking in! Burglars! Oh, Mrs Luard!'

20

'We thought you would like breakfast in bed.'

Muriel sat up and ran a comb through her hair and thanked the girls as they puffed the pillows behind her back and brought her tray, laying it across her knees. The smell of toast and coffee was delicious.

'Sit and talk to me.' Muriel looked at the girls who looked so young and cheerful. 'What is going on?'

'Well, James and Coke want to go to Plymouth to do whatever the final thing is to connect up the radio telephone with the Fisheries. They want June and Akbar to be here to answer it.'

'I don't want to be here when it first rings,' Muriel said violently, remembering the evening before.

'No need to be.' Ann looked out of the window. 'Lovely colours, the autumn really is here.'

'I think I shall go out with the boys.' Muriel buttered her toast.

'The boys went out very early. They left a note saying: "Expect us when you see us":'

'Where have they gone?'

'Gone to see Mrs Luard I expect.'

'I daresay. After last night they must be pining to see her installed. Where did Henry really find that Rolls?'

'He won't say. All he did say was that it was in perfect condition when he found it *and* it had a ginger moustache on the driver's seat.'

'That boy!'

'Yes.'

'I shall go alone then. Does anyone need me for anything?'

'What will you do, Ann?'

'Oh, potter about with Perdue, go for a swim, sleep in the sun.'

'Then you two, Akbar and Perdue will be here?'

'Yes.'

'Then I will take a day off. Do you think anyone wants me for anything?'

'No.' June put her arm round Muriel and kissed her.

'Right.' Muriel finished her breakfast, pushed the tray aside and got up. Half an hour later she was riding over the moor alone.

She rode first to the holiday camp and, leaving her pony in the yard, walked round it on foot. The swimming pool with the tables and cheerful umbrellas lay alone. The trim flower beds, still full of asters, were beginning to have a sprinkling of weeds among the flowers. Otherwise there was no sign of change of any sort, no breeze whispered in the passages, no doors opened, everything was still. Muriel picked up the telephone on the manager's desk and listened to nothing. 'Nothing, nothing,' she said to herself and went back the way she had come, mounted her pony and cantered over the brow of the hill towards the south. Far away she could see James and Coke in their Landrover dipping down towards Plymouth. She reached the Abbey about noon.

The priest who had been to Exeter was polishing the Abbey doorbell.

'Good morning. Can you tell me where Father Richard is?'

'He is seeing to the beehives though they are empty.'

Muriel walked back to where the beehives stood in rows by the orchard gates. 'What are you doing? There are no bees.'

'No, but there will be.' Father Richard shook her hand.

'How do you know?'

'That young man from Kabul told me that there are plenty of insects in Afghanistan. We shall get new bees from somewhere.'

'Father, do you think I am mad?'

'Dear me, no.'

'I heard our telephone ring and all the others say I didn't.'

'Perhaps they didn't hear it.'

'Do you think I heard it?'

'Naturally, if you say you did.'

'There's another thing. Perdue said Henry had an armalite rifle under his bed and when I looked there was, but when I told James and he looked he said I was mistaken and it was an old motor scooter. I am sure it was a rifle.'

'Then it was.'

'Henry has stolen a house too.'

'How comical.'

'Comical?'

'Well, you can't hide a house under your bed.'

'Then you think it *was* an armalite rifle?'

'I don't see why not. Henry is a collector.'

'He's a thief.'

'Has he stolen anything anyone wants?'

'No.'

'What about the house?'

'He gave it to Mrs Luard. He gave her Willoughby and a Rolls Royce.'

'Then he has set her up in style. Is she afraid of burglars?'

'Yes, she is, and Henry laughed his head off.'

'Well, it is funny.' Father Richard finished cleaning out the last hive and straightened up.

114

'You don't seem to take Henry seriously.'

'Oh, yes I do. I think Henry should be taken seriously.'

'In what way?'

'Loved.'

'Oh.' Muriel stood silent. 'I don't love him, he rather frightens me. After all, Henry is only thirteen, too young for all this—'

'His very youth may save him.'

'Do you think I am old?'

'No, but you were accustomed to matters as they were.'

'Matters? What matters? That priest is polishing your doorbell. Are you expecting visitors?' Muriel spoke crossly, feeling no wave of sympathy from Father Richard.

'We always expect visitors and he likes polishing.'

'James and Coke are going to connect you by radio to us and the Fisheries. They will have to connect Mrs Luard at Willoughby too.'

'If she wants to be.' Father Richard smiled.

'I'm going off for the day by myself, nobody seems to need me.'

Father Richard's face was impassive.

'I haven't been alone since the great storm. It seems silly when there are so few people.'

'It will do you good.'

'Can I look for anything for you?'

'No, thank you very much.'

'May I leave my pony here?'

'Of course.'

'Then I'll go, goodbye.'

Muriel unsaddled the pony and took off its bridle and turned her loose in the Abbey orchard. Up at the farm she could hear the priests Peter and John talking. She walked down to the main road and stood undecided. The huge dual carriageway stretched east and west, the wrecked lorries, vans and cars strewn along it. It looked sad and depressing. Muriel crossed the road, followed by her dog, and walked south downhill towards the sea. Chap ran cheerfully ahead of her sniffing the air, and Muriel's spirits rose as she walked on. She wondered a little about Paul and Henry and imagined to herself the pleasure they must be having at Willoughby with Mrs Luard. After a while she saw the long, low roof of a house she knew well lying in a dip by the river. She wondered what had become of old Mr and Mrs Bellew who had lived there. They had been kind to Sam when he was a child and taught him to fish. Muriel walked down to the house. There was no sign of life and all the windows and doors of the ground floor were shut.

Following what had become routine to her, Muriel searched until she found a ladder and carried it to the front of the house where she saw Mrs Bellew's window open. She climbed up and in at the window. The twin beds were slightly ruffled and a book lay open on one. She quickly collected the hair from the pillows and one set of teeth—Mrs Bellew had had her own — wrapped them in a face towel and walked round the house. As she had expected, there was nothing. The old couple had locked up and gone to bed. In the kitchen Muriel added a heap of Pekinese fur to her bundle and stood wondering what to do with it. Hitherto, with old Perdue's eye on her, she had buried what she had found in the nearest churchyard, or at very least in the garden, but at that moment she felt mutinous. 'Oh hell,' she muttered and shoved the bundle into a kitchen drawer. 'There,' she said, went upstairs, climbed out of the window, shut it behind her and went down the ladder. Chap was lying in the sun.

'Come on boy, old Bellew's boat.' She ran down to the river and there, as she expected, was Mr Bellew's boat moored to a little jetty. Muriel jumped in, followed by Chap, and rowed into midstream to be carried fast and quietly down to the sea. The river ran fast and Muriel soon left the oars to sit in the stern and steer. This river, the Mecca of fishermen, ran smoothly here, unlike its rough turbulence where, smaller and more violent, it began its life on the moors. All along the banks prosperous meadows, once filled with cattle or sheep, slid down the valley to the water. Now the meadows were empty. Several times Muriel passed over a shoal of salmon swimming upstream to spawn, several times she saw otters in pairs or alone watching her from the bank without fear and her heart rejoiced. When the river swung round a bend through the great oak woods which stretched for miles across country, Muriel noticed how brown the leaves were already and how silent the woods and empty. Chap, usually so alert, came and lay at her feet and went to sleep.

The river joined the sea at what Julian had called The Sink of Iniquity, a large seaside town of blocks of skyscrapers, flats, bars, circuses, bowling alleys, shops and huge luxury hotels

116

along the sea front. Muriel steered the boat to a stop in the crowded marina and tied it up. She got out with the dog and walked about the town. For the first time she was not jostled by busy shopping crowds nor deafened by the loud talk of holiday-makers or the noise of traffic. The streets were almost empty, here and there cars had run into one another and crashed, but all around her was silence. The shops were shut, the corners filled with drifts of hair, human, feline or canine. False teeth champed alone in doorways. It was her own village again but on a larger scale. Muriel felt in need of a drink. She looked in the toolbox of a car and finding a large spanner walked quickly to the largest of the hotels. Here in the dead season in February her husband had brought her many times to lunch and look out at the sea from the restaurant windows. Here was an excellent bar. Muriel headed for it. She was slightly puzzled at finding no need for the spanner. The hotel doors opened with a swish as she went in. Chap began to sniff, his nose down and his tail up, but Muriel headed straight for the bar, went behind it and poured herself a large whisky. It was when she had drunk half her drink that she noticed an odd smell and that Chap had gone. It was not the smell of the rich and scented which she was used to in this place, the mixture of women's scents, freshly varnished nails and make-up; it was not the smell of men's hair oil and tobacco, the clinging smell of cigars, nor was it drink or rich food.

'Chap,' Muriel called, 'Chap.' From the stool at the bar Muriel looked out at the empty sea, remembering the mass of blue, red, yellow and brown sails among the white which had delighted her in the summer. Uneasily she called again, 'Chap! Chap!'

Her voice became more urgent and questioning. That smell was in no way a luxury hotel smell. She got up, left the bar and went out into the hall.

'Who are you?'

A little girl was coming down the main stairs with Chap, her hand on his neck. 'Is this your dog?' The little girl stood looking at her.

'Yes, he is. Who are you?'

'My name is Patricia.'

'What are you doing here?'

'Taking care of the pigs.'

'Pigs!' Muriel now recognised the smell.

'Would you like to see them?' The child led the way to the stairs. 'This way,' she said.

Muriel and Chap followed her. The child ran upwards. Chap whined.

'He doesn't like hotels.' Muriel looked at the small girl.

'Oh, doesn't he? The pigs love them. This way.'

The child ran down the hotel passage to a door which she opened. The smell of pig grew stronger.

'Here they are,' she said proudly.

Muriel went into a large bedroom suite and stood rooted. Lying on a double bed were three young pigs who eyed her brightly from their small eyes.

'This is King of Copenhagen,' said the child, 'and these are Queen and Princess of Copenhagen.'

'What are you doing here?'

'Waiting.' The child suddenly looked anxious.

'Are you alone?'

'Oh yes. Except for King and Queen and Princess.'

'How did you get here?'

'We were here for the agricultural conference. My father brought me and them to the show.'

'Where is your father?'

'I don't know. I don't know where anyone is. We've been alone for so long.'

'We?'

'Me and them.'

Muriel looked at the pigs lying cosy and unconcerned on the bed. 'That explains the smell,' she said.

'What smell? They don't smell. They are terribly clean.' The child was indignant. 'They never foul the beds. They always go to the bathroom.'

'I'm sure they do.' Muriel looked at the child, small, pretty, determined.

'How old are you?'

'Eight.'

'Shall we go down and you can tell me all about it?'

'All right.' The child addressed the pigs. 'Like to come?'

The pigs jumped down from the bed. Muriel walked down the corridor with the child and the pigs.

'We only came to this floor yesterday,' said Patricia. 'We have lived on several floors but this one is quite nice.' She stood waiting for Muriel who was looking in and out of bedrooms as she walked towards the stairs. In each were drifts of dusty hair. The pigs trotted along, followed by Muriel, Chap and Patricia. When they reached the ground floor they sat down in the hotel lounge. The pigs wandered about before settling down to rest.

'Can you tell me what happened?' Muriel felt rather diffident.

'My father brought me down for a half-term treat with the pigs. He was going to show them at the show. Of course they are far too intelligent to make bacon from.'

'All pigs are.' Muriel looked at the three humorous faces.

'They love me.'

'I expect they do. Go on with your story.'

'Oh well,' Patricia seemed tired suddenly. 'My father had to go to this big dinner, the agricultural association or something, and I got bored in bed and went down to the underground garage where the hotel people had let my father put the pigs for the night in the trailer.'

'Go on.'

'Well, I got into the trailer with them and slept and in the morning there was nothing, nobody, just me and the pigs. We looked everywhere but everyone had gone.'

'Yes, I understand.'

'Do you?'

'Yes, it's happened in lots of places.'

'Has it?'

'Yes. What have you fed the pigs on? They look terribly well.'

'Oh, cereals from the store cupboards and I've raided the refrigerators, but things are going bad in them now.'

'I bet they are.'

'Can you get me home?'

'Where is home?'

'London.'

'Oh, I don't know.'

'There's a helicopter station near here. Could you pilot one?'

'No, and I think London is, well I think London is like this.'

'Have you been?'

'No, but there's no telephone or radio or post or television.'

'I want to go. Please take me.'

'Honestly, Patricia, don't you think it would be better to come home with me? The pigs can be gloriously happy on a real farm. There's lot to eat and there are other people.'

'No, I want to go to London. I want my Mummy.' Patricia began to cry.

'Oh Lord! Don't cry.'

'This is the first time.'

'Then have a good one.' Muriel pulled a handkerchief from her pocket and put an arm round the child. Chap put his head on the child's knee and the three pigs came closer, their twinkling eyes growing grave. After what seemed a long time, Patricia stopped sobbing, handed a very wet handkerchief to Muriel and said, 'I'm sorry.'

'Where do, I mean did, the pigs live?'

'Norfolk.'

'We can't leave them here.'

'Then you'll take me?'

'Yes, but we ought to go at once.'

'Let's go early tomorrow and arrive for breakfast.'

'Why?'

'Well, if we go now it will be dark when we arrive. I hate the dark. There's a frightening searchlight.'

'All right, Patricia. Let's get ready and start early. We haven't seen a searchlight.'

'Lovely, and you can tell me your story too.'

'I will. Let's have tea.'

Muriel and the child found tinned milk and biscuits in the hotel kitchens. Muriel and Chap waded through empty packet after empty packet of breakfast cereals.

'The pigs eat here,' said Patricia unnecessarily. 'And I've been taking them for walks. Shall we take our tea outside?'

Muriel put the milk and biscuits on a tray and followed the child and the pigs to an arbour in the garden. The pigs began rooting contentedly in the garden and Muriel observed without making any comment that they had already ploughed and furrowed up the once trim lawns.

'Wouldn't it be much better if we took them to my home?'

'Perhaps.'

Muriel wandered round the side of the hotel looking for signs of life but found none. When she went back to Patricia she found her watching the pigs rooting through a flowerbed.

120

'The pigs will have to walk.'

'Must they? Oh, all right. Come on, time for your baths.'

Patricia galloped along a path towards the hotel swimming pool and the pigs followed her. At the pool they drank and then stood in the children's paddling pool while Patricia scrubbed each pig in turn with an enormous loofah.

'I found this in a bathroom. There's no water in the hotel now.'

'No light either, I suppose?'

'Oh no.'

'Then let's go to bed.'

They went to bed on the fifth floor, the pigs in one room and Patricia with Muriel and Chap in another.

'This is nicer than sleeping with the pigs really. They kick and snore a bit. Tell me all about you.'

As the light faded Muriel held the child in her arms and told her all she could remember of what had happened to herself and those at the Abbey and Paul and Henry.

'Where have Paul and Henry gone today?'

'I don't know, but they will be back now with the others.'

'I'd like to meet them one day.'

You shall, Muriel thought, poor child. It's tomorrow you will meet them, but she said nothing of the plan she was making to take Patricia and her pigs straight to Brendon.

21

Patricia shook Muriel. 'Wake up, please wake up.'

Muriel looked sleepily round the room and remembered. She yawned. 'There's no hurry.'

'Yes, yes there is. There is a hurry. If we start now we can get a long way.'

Muriel yawned again and caught sight of Chap who was outstaring the King of Copenhagen.

'If King tries to get on the bed Chap might bite him,' she said.

'Oh, Chap, you wouldn't.' Patricia flung her arms round the dog who, without taking his eyes off the pig, gave a little moan.

'Oh, do hurry.' Patricia was all eagerness. 'I've fed Chap and the pigs, we are all ready. Mummy will be so thrilled. We must get to her.'

Chap growled faintly at the pig's twitching snout so near his nose. The pig turned and walked away into the next room, switching his haunches to and fro.

'Patricia, I've been thinking. They will think I am lost at home. I think we'd better go there first and then one of the boys can come on to London with us. They will be anxious about me.'

'What about my mother? Isn't she anxious? You promised. You did promise. Besides, if we go now you can leave me with Mummy and you can come home again.'

'Did you say you were only eight?'

'Yes.'

'You are pushing me around.'

'You promised me.' Patricia's eyes filled with tears.

'No.' Muriel was suddenly firm. 'Before I take you home I must tell my people what I am doing otherwise they will be worried stiff.'

Patricia opened her mouth to speak but closed it again in defeat.

'We must start now. We have a long way to go.' Muriel grasped her advantage over the child. 'Yesterday I drifted down in a boat but today we have to get back by road unless you want your pigs to walk.'

Muriel left the child with her pigs, calling over her shoulder, 'I'll be back soon,' and hurried out of the hotel with Chap at her heels. It did not take her long to find an empty Mini van parked in the street. Fastidiously she brushed the seat free of some rather greasy black hair, checked the fuel and drove back to the hotel. Patricia stood on the steps flanked by the pigs who twitched their mobile snouts to and fro and blinked their little eyes maliciously.

'Can you make them get into the van?'

'They won't like it if they have no view,' the child said petulantly.

'It can't be helped.' Muriel was determined to keep the upper hand.

'Oh, all right.' Patricia went to the back of the van and waved the pigs in. Much to Muriel's surprise they leapt in one after another while Patricia's face assumed a smug expression.

'Every time we find the road blocked we shall have to walk or change cars.' Muriel put the car into gear and started off.

'They won't mind,' said Patricia.

Muriel drove uphill away from the sea along the main street of the town, dodging in and out among silent stationary cars. Sometimes she drove the wrong side of a traffic island and was amused at the pleasure it gave her to break the law. They had to get out and walk five or six times, changing cars, before they got free of the town, and Muriel choked down her impatience each time the child and the pigs got in or out of fresh vans or cars. At last, on the outskirts of the town near the railway station, she found what she wanted, a Landrover. Here the pigs had to be heaved into the back and quite failed to co-operate, kicking Muriel, squealing and generally making the whole operation as difficult as they could. Muriel was pleased to see Patricia lose patience and smack one of the pigs with quite a spiteful hand.

Once packed into the Landrover, Muriel drove doggedly inland along the road which led eventually to the Abbey. Patricia and Chap sat beside her and the three pigs kept up a commentary of squeals and grunts rising and falling in intensity as she drove along the flat road or took to the verge to avoid obstacles or, as on several occasions, she had to bump through fields. The distance was not very great, but great enough to exasperate, and when she finally came to a halt at the trunk road she was glad to get out and lead a silent Patricia through the piled up traffic to the woods surrounding the Abbey and find a path which led them in blessed silence to the doors of the church.

'Stay here,' Muriel said to the tired child. 'I can get us help and food before we go on.'

Patricia looked at her sulkily from under heavy eyelashes as she went round to the door of the Abbey and rang the bell.

Father Richard answered the door, opening it wide when he saw her and smiling.

'Father, I have found a child and three pigs in the town by the sea.'

'Gadarene swine?' Father Richard grinned.

'Far from it. Very civilised.' Muriel told the priest how she had found Patricia the day before. 'I must take them to Brendon,' she said.

'We must feed you all first, then one of us can drive you up over the moor.'

'I don't want to trouble you.' Muriel hesitated before leading the priest round the corner of the church.

'But they are gone!' she exclaimed. 'I left them here.'

'They can't have gone far,' said Father Richard with his eye on the church door. 'Sightseeing I expect. Your dog seems to think so.' His eyes followed Chap who was sniffing at the church door.

'Not in the church surely,' exclaimed Muriel.

Father Richard pushed open the door with one hand and, reaching out with the other to dip his fingers in the holy water, crossed himself as he genuflected like a duck dipping its head under water. Muriel did the same and stood looking up the aisle.

In the distance stood Patricia looking curiously about her while the three pigs meandered on delicate feet twitching their tails and snouts.

'Patricia, bring them out,' Muriel called in a low voice.

The child turned and came towards them slowly, followed by the pigs.

Father Richard suppressed a smile. 'So like,' he murmured.

'So like what?' asked Muriel crossly.

'So like the summer visitors,' Father Richard smiled. 'Visitors in shorts and tops who think us a rare species, but more like the wonderful man who gave us the mosaic flooring.'

'Was he like a pig?' Muriel found herself laughing.

'He was a tycoon. Those pigs bear a strange similarity.'

Muriel introduced Patricia and Father Richard smiled at the child. 'We will give you something to eat and drink and I will drive you up to Mrs Wake's house.'

'Thank you. I have to get to my mother in London.' Patricia looked up at the monk.

'So Mrs Wake says. Would it not be better to wait a bit?'

'We've done nothing but wait.' Tears began to gather in the child's eyes.

'Tea, I think,' said the priest. 'Then you must decide. I cannot decide for you, but I would advise leaving your pigs at Brendon. They could not walk or swim two hundred miles or more could they?'

'Oh,' Patricia's eyes wavered towards the pigs. 'I hadn't thought of that.'

'Well then, tea first and then I will drive you over the hill.'

Father Richard was as good as his word, and after feeding Muriel and the child drove them in his Landrover up the track on to the moor and across to Brendon.

Old Perdue, pottering about in the farmyard, was the first to greet them. 'Pigs!' he cried. 'Pigs! Why, they are worth a month of anxiety. Ah, the beauties! Let me help now. Ah, what proper beauties!'

June came running out of the house exclaiming, 'Gosh! We've been anxious. We thought you'd had an accident. We were going to send out search parties, and here you are.'

James and Coke followed by Akbar and Ann joined them from the garage, exclaiming and extending greetings.

'Father, won't you come in?' Muriel said to the little priest.

'Thank you, but I must get back. You are safe home now and can rest.' He turned the car and drove away. Muriel stood watching the Landrover disappear over the moor and then let herself be drawn into the house.

'Listen, you must listen before you tell us anything. Coke has been seeing things.' Ann held Muriel's arm.

'Seeing what?' Muriel felt very tired.

'Coloured streaks in the sky.'

'Cloud effects,' said Muriel.

'That's what I said,' James agreed with her. 'Or lightning.'

'They weren't no cloud effects,' said Coke firmly. 'Streaks they was. Quite a lot of them too.'

'Tell us what happened to you,' said James firmly, pushing Muriel into a comfortable chair in the library and handing her a drink.

Muriel took the drink and sipped it, watching Patricia and the pigs settle themselves by the fire. She told them of her adventure, the discovery of Patricia and their return.

'The boys will be thrilled,' said June.

Muriel looked round her, suddenly noticing their absence. 'Where are the boys?'

'They went for a ride, that's all,' said James comfortably. 'They went off this morning.'

'But it's nearly dark.' Muriel felt the acid of fear racing through her veins. 'Where have they gone?'

'Nobody knows. To see Mrs Luard perhaps as they did yesterday. To look for you? They will come.' June looked at Muriel's worried face. 'Patricia and her pigs and Coke seeing streaks in the sky are much more exciting than the boys going for a ride. We can telephone Mrs Luard now. I'll do that if you are worried. That child should go to bed, she looks done in.'

125

'Oh dear.' Muriel looked at Patricia. 'Of course. Come on.' She led Patricia up the stairs followed by the pigs.

'Surely the pigs—' Akbar began to speak.

'Oh, shut up,' said Muriel. 'We can sort that out tomorrow.' And she set to work settling the child in bed and giving her what solace she could. Everyone else seemed to be going to bed, running baths and calling goodnight to each other, so that when she went downstairs to the deserted library she found herself alone with her dogs, listening.

Much later, it seemed to her, she heard the sound of horses' hooves and running to the door saw Paul riding up to the house leading another pony.

'Paul!' Muriel gave a little cry and ran to meet him. 'Paul!'

'Hullo, Mum. Where did you go? We were anxious.'

'I'll tell you. Come in. Were you at Mrs Luard's?' She walked beside the ponies and helped Paul take off their saddles and bridles.

'No.' Paul pulled the bridle over his pony's head. 'No, we weren't.'

'Then where?' Muriel questioned.

'Mum,' said Paul, watching the ponies move slowly away into the field. 'Henry has gone.' He tried to see his mother's face in the dusk.

'Where?' Muriel's voice came in a harsh whisper.

'To London.' Paul spoke flatly. 'To London to find things out. We found a sailing dinghy and I sailed him across to the other side. It's miles, Mum and the hell of a tide. That's why I'm so late getting home.'

'Go to bed, darling,' Muriel said absently. 'Go to bed now and so will I.' She crept up the stairs to her room and unthinkingly undressed and got into bed. 'Gone,' she muttered. 'Pigs, streaks in the sky and Henry is gone.' She felt as though the life had drained out of her, quite spent.

22

'Paul.' Muriel went into her son's room at dawn and woke him up. 'Paul, if Henry has gone to London, where in London has he gone?'

Paul looked at his mother sleepily and buried his face in the pillow without answering.

'Paul,' said Muriel sharply, 'answer me. Where has Henry gone? How was he going to get there?'

'He would go to his parents' house, wouldn't he?' Paul sounded unconvincing.

'No,' said Muriel, 'he might visit it but he wouldn't stay there.'

'Ask Mrs Luard or Father Richard.' Paul snuggled down in his bed and slept again. Muriel bent over and kissed his forehead and then left him to go back to her room, get into bed and lie thinking.

Later during the day she questioned the girls, James, Coke and Akbar and gradually became aware that none of them minded Henry's absence. Henry had made them uncomfortable. Mr Perdue openly rejoiced. 'Gone and good riddance, Mrs Wake. Sneaky boy, I told you. Not our kind. Let him go to London. We is happier without that Mrs Luard woman, now we'll be happier without 'im, you'll see.'

Muriel felt no happier, indeed less happy, if happy she had ever been since her husband's death, since the storm, since the disappearance of all her neighbours and the terrible loss of Sam. Restlessly she prowled round the house that day, looking askance at Paul who she suspected of knowing Henry's whereabouts, noticing a sudden intense friendship grow up between Patricia and Perdue so that Patricia quite stopped any reference to her mother or her past and slipped into a complete companionship with the old man and the pigs to the exclusion of everyone else.

At meals Muriel's eyes observed for the first time that June and Ann had paired off with James and Akbar and were behaving like engaged couples of long standing, treating her in her own house with bare politeness. Coke tinkered happily with the telephone, ringing up the Fisheries, the Abbey and Mrs Luard on the flimsiest of excuses just as though, Muriel thought, he had himself invented the telephone. A glorious toy.

'Coke,' Muriel suddenly addressed him. 'The telephone rang before you connected that radio telephone of yours.'

Coke raised his eyebrows and laughed. 'They said there was a great storm and coloured snow too. The Commander and I was under-water. Old Perdue didn't see no coloured snow.'

'He was drunk,' said Muriel.

'Them monks didn't see no coloured snow.' Coke spoke politely.

'They were underground. How could they have seen it?' Muriel resented Coke.

'Mrs Luard didn't see none either,' Coke went on.

'She was underground too, wasn't she?' Muriel walked out of the house into the yard loathing Coke and conscious of her unreason. She caught herself feeling lost and decided that a talk with Mrs Luard would help her unease. As she drove down the hill to the village she wondered how Mrs Luard would be faring all alone in Willoughby and whether she would be lonely by now. She left the Landrover in the village and walked across the fields to the large house, followed by her dog.

A puff of smoke rose from one of the chimneys as she drew near, followed by a wavering line in the faint breeze. Muriel banged on the door and waited, looking at the gardens formerly so well-kept and now growing weedy.

Mrs Luard opened the door suddenly and Muriel jumped nervously.

'Oh, it's you.' Mrs Luard did not sound particularly welcoming.

'I'll go away if you are busy,' Muriel said hastily.

'What's the matter?' Mrs Luard peered into Muriel's face. 'Come in and tell me.' She led Muriel into a room off the great hall and made her sit down by a glowing log fire.

'Mrs Luard, Henry has gone. Paul says he's gone to London.'

'Ah.' Mrs Luard looked infinitely sympathetic and wise. 'Tell me about it,' she said.

Muriel told her of her expedition to the sea, of her finding Patricia and the pigs and of the present situation at Brendon. 'Paul knows something I'm sure but none of the others cares.

Perdue is pleased. The young men and girls sit gazing into each other's eyes and Coke is in love with the telephone and, Mrs Luard, he doesn't believe there was coloured snow or a storm, or he thinks I am exaggerating. He—' Muriel stopped.

'He doesn't know,' said Mrs Luard, staring into the fire. 'He doesn't know half what that boy knows, not half.'

'What am I to do?' Muriel asked the older woman.

'Let me show you something neither Coke nor those others know, but I do and Henry does. Come along.' Mrs Luard took Muriel's hand and led her out of the room. 'I love that boy,' she said. 'He and I have a lot in common, more in common than you would think.' Leading Muriel by the hand she waddled down the hall.

'This is something Henry hasn't told anyone but me. This is one of the reasons I am here.' Mrs Luard stood by a table in the hall loaded with drinks and glasses, looking at Muriel with speculative eyes. 'Henry can keep his trap shut,' she said.

'Of course he can. In fact Henry's the most secretive person I know. I never know what he's going to do next. I don't know whether I love him or hate him. I simply don't know Henry,' Muriel burst out passionately.

'No need to abuse the poor boy.'

'I'm not abusing him.'

'It sounded like it. Have a drink.' Mrs Luard waddled across to the table. 'Or would you prefer something hot?'

'Something hot I think. I'm sorry, Mrs Luard.'

'Nerves.' Mrs Luard took her hand. 'Come along and you can meet them.'

'Meet who?'

'Oh, some visitors.'

'What visitors? More pigs?'

'No, this lot are human. Henry found them and brought them here.'

Mrs Luard led the way followed by Muriel and the dog. The corridor was dark and long and Muriel remembered it led to the kitchens of the old house. At the end of the corridor a light shone under a door.

'Here they are.' Mrs Luard opened the door. 'Studying, poor things. Can't speak a word of English.'

Muriel walked into the old kitchen. Round a bare wooden table sat three men and three girls, their heads bent over books and a pile of foolscap on which they were making notes. These people stood up and looked at Mrs Luard questioningly. Mrs Luard raised her voice and said to Muriel, 'You 'ave to shout at them. Henry says they are Albanian but that may be Henry's little joke.'

'Where do you come from?' Muriel held out her hand in greeting.

'They are spies,' Mrs Luard remarked complacently.

'No. Submarine.' One of the young men held out a dictionary open at a page which said 'Submarine. Underwater vessel. Gerundive—submersible.'

'Oh dear, they won't get very far with that!' Muriel exclaimed.

23

Sitting drinking cocoa with the crew of the submarine, Muriel gathered the gist of their story from Mrs Luard. Henry, driving his Landrover on one of his foraging expeditions in the late summer, had found them encamped sadly by the river up which they had walked from the sea. 'Or so he says,' Mrs Luard remarked.

Henry had taken them to Willoughby, taught them how to use the electric pump and light machine, installed them with plenty of food and come home to tell Mrs Luard. Mrs Luard's aversion to the law, and indeed to any form of uniform, had not made her anxious to tell James and Coke. Henry had installed Mrs Luard at Willoughby on condition she kept the whereabouts of the crew secret.

'But why the secrecy?'

'We thought the others would be nosy.'

'I daresay, but they all look very nice. Have they told you anything?'

'No, how could they?'

Muriel turned to the man who appeared to be the leader of the party and he produced a pile of drawings. The first was a rough sketch of a submarine. There followed a brilliant drawing of the ship sinking and the crew swimming ashore, a sketch map of England with a dotted line trail leading up the river inland from the sea, and a good likeness of Henry.

'Is there an atlas in the house?' Muriel asked Mrs Luard.

'No dear.'

'Then what's the idea?'

'Henry said I was to teach them English.'

'You don't seem to have got very far.'

'No, that's why I want Henry back, just as you do.'

'It all seems very improbable.'

'Oh, it is.'

'How did you hide them from Coke?'

'Coke doesn't demean himself enough to go into the kitchens and he isn't snoopy.'

'What next then?'

'Oh, we shall all be very happy living here for the winter, and they can keep me company.'

'I must talk to Father Richard.'

'Do by all means. He told Henry the laws of hospitality came first with monks.'

'Why do you call them spies?'

'Well, a submarine crew. Stands to reason doesn't it?'

'There is no reason anywhere.'

'Well, they all seem quite happy.' Mrs Luard looked round the room. 'Warm and happy. They talk to each other.'

'In what language?'

'I don't know. Look, they write like this.' Mrs Luard reached for a piece of paper.

'Kyrillic script,' said Muriel. 'I can't read it. I must get over to the Abbey. Father Richard will tell me what to do.'

'Ah, he said to leave them in peace. They came in peace. I telephoned to him.'

'Did you? But they might know something. Here they are, coming from a foreign country which may be full of people—'

'I hadn't thought of that.'

'Well, Akbar says Afghanistan is full of people.'

'He doesn't want to go back there.'

'I daresay not. He's in love with June. I'll get these people a dictionary. Look, Mrs Luard, you only have Modern English Usage here for them. That's no good.'

'That's all Henry could find. They didn't understand the French or German he brought them so he took them away again. Well, dear, do your best.'

'Patricia could come over and teach them.'

'That child you found?'

'Why not? She's very bright.'

'It means telling another person.'

'I think Patricia and Paul ought to know. You can't keep six people a secret can you?'

'I did when those two naval chaps connected me with the radio telephone.'

'I don't understand the secrecy.'

'It's just a feeling.' Mrs Luard looked round at the six calm friendly faces. 'Just a feeling.'

'But Father Richard knows.'

'He's a priest.'

'I thought you were anti-papist.'

'I'm not against that lot at the Abbey, not against them at all.'

'All right, Mrs Luard, but I'm going to tell Patricia and Paul. They won't tell anyone else. You know children, they won't give anything away.'

Mrs Luard nodded. 'Very well, you tell the children, but nobody else, and if Coke comes over this lot keep out of his way, and I will not'—here Mrs Luard thumped the table with her fist—'I will not have that old man know.'

Muriel got up. 'I think I will go now,' she said.

'Won't you stay the night?'

'No, thank you. I'm restless. And if Patricia comes over she can bring you a pair of kittens and a puppy.'

'Very well.' Mrs Luard watched Muriel shake hands with the crew of the submarine and escorted her to the front door. The submarine crew stood beside her watching Muriel walk away.

She reached home late and went into the sleeping house and quietly to Paul's room.

'Paul.'

'Yes.'

'Paul, will you come and talk to me or are you too sleepy?'

'No, I'd love to.'

'Will you wake Patricia. I want to talk to her too.'

'Of course.'

Muriel waited for the children in her room and soon they slipped in quietly. Muriel hushed the dogs.

'What is it, Mother?' Paul and Patricia sat at the foot of her bed, their arms clasping their knees.

'Mrs Luard has a foreign submarine crew with her at Willoughby.'

'Where from?'

'I don't know. She says Henry found them and she has kept them secretly ever since she went there.'

'When did Henry find them?'

'Before Mrs Luard went there.'

'That's why she was in such a rush. That explains it.'

'Is nobody but us to know?' Patricia fondled a puppy.

'That's what she wants. For the present anyway.'

'Can I choose a puppy now?'

'Yes, of course.'

'Then I'll have this one. It came to me first.'

'That's George,' said Paul.

'Mrs Luard wants Ringo. Listen, Patricia, can you go over to Willoughby and teach that crew English?'

'Can't Mrs Luard?'

'No, she's hopeless.'

'I'd like that. When can I start?'

'Wait till after breakfast. I'm going to sleep a bit and then go to the Abbey. I want to see Father Richard.'

Paul lolled at her feet. 'What a skunk Henry is not to have told me.'

'Well, he's like that.'

'Let him wait till I get at him.'

'Paul, will you wake me early? And not a word, either of you.'

'As if we would.' Patricia kissed her and left the room.

Muriel fell asleep wondering about children who seemed to take everything for granted without fear or question.

24

'Here I am.' Father Richard came round a corner wearing gum-boots under his cassock. 'What can I do for you?'

'I want to tell you about Henry and the submarine crew and ask your help.'

'Certainly.'

'You know about the crew?'

'Yes. How did you find out?'

'Mrs Luard showed them to me. Patricia is going to teach them English.'

'That child you found? Give her something to do.'

'Yes. She's intelligent. Father, who are these people? Mrs Luard says they are spies and says Henry said they were Albanians. They use Kyrillic script.'

'So do several countries. They may be Russian.'

'Father, what do you think?'

'Well, I only speak English and Latin. None of them speaks either I gather.'

'Are they spies?'

'It doesn't matter now whether they are or not.'

'No, I suppose not.'

'What help do you want?'

'I want you to marry Akbar to June and Ann to James. They want to marry. You must talk to them.'

'I can do that. I will go and talk to them.'

'And, Father, I want to get to London.'

'Are you afraid?' The monk looked away from her.

'Yes. I am anxious about Henry.'

'One can understand that; he is young.'

'I think Paul could get me across the water to the mainland as he did Henry. Do you think I am being hysterical and over-anxious? Do you think, as Coke does, that I have imagined almost everything that has happened to us?'

'Those people are not Albanians,' the priest murmured to himself.

'My mind is not at rest,' exclaimed Muriel.

'Small wonder, after all.' Father Richard smiled a little. 'You do not like Henry, just as we do not like the truth.'

'The truth.' Muriel looked at him. 'They do not believe the truth. They do not believe what they cannot see. They do not believe the telephone rang and it did. I swear it did.'

'Then ring it did, and all of us who were underground or under very good cover like your cows and ponies have survived the storm and everyone else has blown away or, if you like, died.'

'Oh,' said Muriel, 'is it as simple as that? I had not reasoned.'

'The result is simple, but what began it? Henry has no doubt gone to find out and you would be right to follow him. He is too young to be alone.'

Muriel made her way up the hill towards her house. The appalling simplicity of survival so quietly mentioned had struck her dumb and she had left the Abbey with tears in her eyes. As she came up on to the moor she stopped and looked towards Brendon. Her son Paul was hopping and skipping along the track to meet her in company with the dogs. Seeing her he stopped and waved his arm skyward, and Muriel looking up saw flashes of light between the clouds, fleeting colours stabbing across the horizon from the east.

Paul reached her, calling as he ran, 'Do you see? Do you see?'

'Yes, I expect it is only the Aurora Borealis gone mad,' she said, and laughed at Paul's crestfallen expression.

'I don't believe it,' said Paul, 'one doesn't see the Aurora Borealis down here, only up north. The telephone rang again, Mum. Everyone was out. I answered and there was nobody. It was very strange and queer. Who can it be?'

'I expect Coke has made some mistake,' said Muriel sadly. 'We are limited to the Fisheries, the Abbey and Mrs Luard; that's the lot.'

'Well, anyway, there won't be a bill this quarter,' said Paul cheerfully. 'We can use it as much as we like. We can chat to Mrs Luard and the fish people, we can talk to the Abbey.'

'Yes.' Muriel looked at her son, thinking with amusement that he was still of an age when she could talk to him and be accepted. 'Thank God you are not adolescent,' she said.

'Why?' Paul looked surprised and then grinned in comprehension. 'Sam was pretty broody wasn't he?'

'Yes, and he had just grown out of it. Paul, I may have been

135

rather mad since your father died and since the storm, but I am grateful to you and Henry. You heard the telephone; it brings us closer. You and I have both seen streaks in the sky, so has Coke. It may mean nothing at all. Old Perdue said Henry had a rifle under his bed—' Muriel paused, seeing Paul flush.

'He took it with him,' said Paul. 'He said you had James and Coke and Akbar to look after you and Mrs Luard had her submarine crew, so he took it.'

'Where has he gone?' Muriel felt her moment of intimacy lost.

'To his parents' house I suppose.' From Paul's expression he was obviously lying.

'Darling, we must follow him. Can you get me across as you did him? We could take Chap with us.' Muriel looked at Paul's face, so like his father's.

'Of course we could get across.' Paul turned a radiant face to her. 'We can chase after him. He was going to follow the main road, not the motorway.'

'We will not tell anyone else,' said Muriel childishly, 'except Father Richard. He is the only person who would understand such an absurdity.'

'When shall we go?' Paul looked at his mother sideways.

'Tomorrow.' Muriel felt a rush of determination. 'I shall ring up Father Richard tonight.'

'Use the telephone?' Paul sounded taken aback.

'Yes, I am no longer afraid of it.'

25

'This means of locomotion is no longer currently fashionable,' Paul said to his mother as he pulled up the sail of the small dinghy and sat down beside her. The wind filled the sail and the little boat heeled over and began to move in the water.

'Your father only said that because he was always seasick.' Muriel steered, peering across the water to the distant shore. 'It's lucky that I taught you and Sam to sail a boat.'

'Henry was sick all the way across. It gets very choppy when we get away from the land.' Paul's eyes were watering from the cold wind.

'Even Henry has his weaknesses.' Muriel smiled at her son. 'Personally I'm terrified of this crossing. You came back quite alone after getting Henry across.' Paul shrugged his shoulders and settled low in the boat, making the dog lie down at their feet.

Without speaking they manoeuvred the boat, working in unison as they had so often done before. The tide was contrary to the wind and the little boat rocked wickedly so that both Muriel and the child sat tense in concentration. It seemed a very long time before they reached the other shore and beached absurdly in a field where the water had stopped rising.

'We are very cut off.' Muriel looked back across the water.

'We had better tie her up and find the main road before it gets too dark.'

Paul helped her drag the dinghy up the field a little way and then rammed the anchor into the ground, furled the sail and lowered the mast as his mother stood looking around her, shading her eyes and trying to make out where they were. Far away across the water from where they had come she saw the dogged towers of Exeter cathedral standing against the back-drop of the sun. The wind whistled and moaned a little but otherwise there was no sound.

The dog sniffed up the hedge and trotted a short way up the field.

'Those pylons cross the road near here,' Muriel said to Paul. 'Let's go to them.'

Walking with the dog in the dusk they made their way across country until after a mile or more they met the road.

'Just the same as our side.' Paul stopped and looked up and down the road at empty lopsided lorries lying on their sides where they had left the road, mangled cars lying at all angles, so that it was not possible to know in some cases whether they had been coming west or travelling east.

'We must find somewhere to sleep the night.' Muriel looked at the lifeless countryside dotted about with houses and farms.

'A pub or a hotel would be best,' said Paul.

Muriel agreed and they began walking along the road not bothering to look at the wrecked traffic until they found a small hotel standing empty with its sign 'The Travellers Rest' swinging gently in the breeze. Muriel felt no fear of breaking in

137

and was glad when they found an unused bedroom with the beds made up ready for the summer visitors who would never come.

'It's a double room. Shall we share?'

'Yes, please.' Paul looked much younger than he had during the past weeks.

In the storeroom of the hotel they found some tins and ate, feeding Chap at the same time.

'Now let's sleep and hurry on tomorrow.' Muriel led the way up to the bedroom, switching the light on automatically.

'Damn!' she said.

'It's okay, I found some matches and a packet of candles.' Paul produced them.

'Oh.' Muriel felt foolish. 'Don't light them, Paul. Let's sleep in our clothes.'

'Beds damp?' Paul's voice was even.

'It's because we don't know,' said Muriel. 'The other side of the water we did.'

'All right.' Paul got into bed fully dressed and lay watching his mother. 'I suppose those ponies will find their way home,' he said.

'Oh, yes.' Muriel remembered the two ponies they had ridden from Brendon to the sea dividing Exeter from the mainland, standing looking at them with vague astonishment when she and Paul had taken off their saddles and bridles and left them to sail away in the little boat. One pony had whinnied and then turned away to graze. 'They may take some days to get home,' she said to console her son, 'but they will be all right.' She listened to Paul's breathing and to the silence all round them and lay wondering how long it would take them to reach London before she fell asleep.

Waking at first light she sat up in fear seeing Paul's bed empty. 'Paul!' she shouted. 'Paul!' The boy's footsteps came running up the stairs.

'Look what I found.' In his hands he held two young rats who eyed Muriel with curiosity. 'These are so young they must have been born after the storm.' Paul put them on his mother's bed.

'Yes.' Muriel stroked the small creatures. 'Were they in the cellar?'

'No, the bar. But I heard more. Chap wanted to have a hunt. May I keep them?'

'Why not?' said Muriel. 'Any sign of life is glorious.'

26

During the days and nights which followed Muriel never lost the feeling that she must waste no time but hurry after Henry. She made no effort to define this feeling, but as they travelled it grew stronger rather than weaker and she felt a nagging fear. Their progress was jerky. Often they found a stretch of road which was empty and a car to travel along it. Now and again they found bicycles in villages or towns and used those. Sometimes they walked, always empty handed except for candles and matches and Paul's two rats which lived inside his windcheater becoming ever more tame. By day they raided shops for tinned food and public houses for drink. By night they found beds in hotels. There was never any sign of life along the road, just the grim silence of an abrupt stop to the machine age. Paul was on the whole rather silent and Muriel, setting her mind on her goal, managed not to let her thoughts wander to the many times she had driven up this road with her husband with gaiety and enjoyment and plans of what they would do together in London. It was only sometimes at the end of the day that she realised his death and then grimly she relived the accident in which he had died. Driving along a straight empty road his Siamese cat had leapt over her shoulder from the back of the car to land in her lap jerking the steering wheel from her hands so that the car careered into a tree. She remembered her foot pressing the brakes and the silence and seeing her husband dead and the cat.

Sometimes towards the end of the day on this journey with Paul she would brake suddenly if they were in a car and come to a halt. One evening she did this and Paul's face banged into the windscreen. Paul rubbed his head as she apologised and looked at her queerly.

'Mum, it was not your fault,' he said. 'Surely by now you know it was not your fault. Nobody ever blamed you, did they? We love you, you know.'

'We?' Muriel looked at the boy.

'Yes, we. Henry and I and all the people you have saved. We understand. We aren't idiots. We are old enough. You should talk to me about it. Tell me.'

'Tell you what?' Muriel drove on. 'Tell you that I loved your father? Tell you that I should have been more careful with the cat in the car? Oh, Paul.'

'Well, it's very silly now,' said Paul. 'It's very silly to go on about it. After all, Mum, by now you might just have his hair and nothing else left. He might be gone, blown away.'

'You speak like Henry,' said Muriel. 'Henry must be infectious.'

'It's funny that we've seen no sign of Henry yet.' Paul looked at his mother. 'And no more lights in the sky. Just this eternal junkyard.'

'Yes.' Muriel stopped the car where the road was completely blocked by an oil tanker in collision with a milk lorry.

'Out again,' she said, 'and walk. Thank God we haven't got Patricia and her pigs with us. Paul, when are you going to tell me where in London Henry has gone?' Paul blushed and grinned.

'When we get there.'

'London is so big.' Muriel hoped to trap some information.

'Yes, enormous,' Paul agreed.

Muriel sighed. 'We should reach it tomorrow. The last signpost said fifty miles and the roads get wider so travelling should be easier.'

'No need for signposts now.' Paul walked beside her. 'Does it irritate you that I look into the cars for bits and pieces? Does it worry you that I try telephones and televisions?'

'Oh no, of course it doesn't. It's a bit macabre that's all. I like to see you and Chap and the rats alive. I don't like dead telephones or a vanished population. I feel I am so alone. At home we had quite a collection of people and animals. This journey has been rather a journey of despair, hasn't it?'

'Let's stop at that hotel.' Paul changed the subject and began running ahead to break in. Muriel watched him run down the road with his hair flopping and she was sure the little rats zipped into his side pockets would be protesting.

Muriel knew the hotel well having often stopped there for a meal or a drink with Julian. She rather liked it. I must not think of Julian, she thought, but of the living, and she watched Paul go into the hotel with a loving eye. He came out almost as soon as he went in and he was laughing and calling to her. 'Come and look, quick, come and look.'

Muriel joined him and he took her hand and led her into the public bar and pointed, his eyes shining with amusement, at the blackboard by the dart-board.

'Look, Mum.'

Muriel looked and then stared at the board which, wiped clean, bore the cryptic message written in chalk:

'Henry was here.'

27

'Henry was here.' Muriel looked at Paul. 'He is not here now.' Wandering round the silent dusty bar, Paul looked away from his mother.

'It's near here there are those long miles of wired-in War Department installations with "Danger Keep Out" written in red on notice boards,' said Muriel, 'and air-strips which don't officially exist where they test prototype aircraft.'

'Tested,' corrected Paul.

'Ah, yes. Paul, I don't like this part of the world. Before it gets dark let's see whether we can find a car, shall we?'

Together they left the empty bar and began to search the garages of the hotel. After a while they found a Volkswagen with the keys still in the ignition and the petrol tank nearly full. Muriel tested the lights and started up the engine which, after a stutter or two, ran smoothly enough. By pushing and pulling they got cars parked outside the hotel out of the way and Muriel got the car out on to the road. A wind was blowing, whipping bits of paper and fluff about the yard.

'It's cold.' Paul climbed in beside his mother. 'We haven't driven at night yet,' he added.

'No. I'll go slowly.' Muriel drove into the dusk. 'The road looks pretty clear,' she said, 'clear enough for us anyway.' She looked at Paul sitting beside her, and felt comfort from her dog on the seat behind.

'For aught we know Henry may have left messages all the way up to London,' said Paul, 'and we just missed them.'

'I don't think so.' Muriel switched on the lights of the car. 'If he had wanted to leave messages he would have chalked on the road. That message didn't seem a joke to me but a warning.'

'Oh.' Paul was silent. 'Warning of what?' He added after a few minutes, 'I don't know.'

Muriel drove slowly, puzzled by the fact that although there were wrecked cars every so often the centre of the road was clear as though a bulldozer had pushed the empty cars aside to make room in the centre for a car. She mentioned this to Paul who didn't reply.

Through the night she drove, and always there was a clear way in the centre of the road.

'I don't like it,' said Muriel suddenly. 'This isn't natural, or what we have come to know as natural. What shall we do?'

'Go on until you feel too unsafe and then we will walk. Chap will let us know whether there is anyone about.'

'All right, I'll do that.' Muriel drove steadily on without speaking and Paul fell asleep beside her. All the way into London the centre of the road was clear and Muriel drove on in the dark. Somewhere in the neighbourhood of Earls Court she felt it unwise to go any further and turned the car at an angle to the road and stopped it. Paul was asleep but behind her Chap was alert. Muriel switched off the engine of the car and the lights and settled to wait until dawn, listening with the dog who sat alert behind her, ears pricked.

Now and again Muriel dozed, listening to Paul's even breathing. There was a full moon and it outlined the tall ugly buildings of the district. Muriel got quietly out of the car with the dog.

Apart from small rustlings of the wind the silence was absolute. The growl of the great city in its sleep was gone. Gone too the sound of the occasional passing car or heavy lorry that she associated with sleeping London. Gone the slow measured tread of a policeman on his rounds, the faraway sound of an ambulance or fire engine, the hoot of a ship going down river on the early tide. The silence was worse, far worse than the silence she had become accustomed to in the country where it was only comparative, since her house was occupied and sleepers turned in their beds or cried out and the few remaining animals moved on the moor, the mice found in the churchyard

142

settled in the wainscots and the streams tripped towards the big river and the sea.

Standing by the car in which her son slept Muriel remembered telephoning the monk at the Abbey to tell him that she and Paul were going off in pursuit of Henry, and suddenly his voice rang in her ears and the curious sentence of farewell, 'Yes, do go. You must. And when you get back, if you do, you can tell me.' Standing with her dog in the street in Earls Court, Muriel went white and shivered. Then she leant into the car and shook Paul.

'Paul, wake up.'

'Where are we?' Paul stretched cramped limbs.

'Earls Court. Paul, it's light enough now to go on. Will you lead me? We must keep away from the main streets.'

'Oh, why?' Paul climbed out of the car, stretching and yawning, showing brilliant white teeth in the dim light.

'I would feel safer,' Muriel answered lamely.

Paul moved into the middle of the street to get his whereabouts.

'We must remember where we left the car.' Muriel followed him. Together they memorized the name of the side street and then set off in single file. Both Paul and Muriel wore rubber-soled shoes and the dog made very little sound.

Paul moved fast and Muriel followed. Neither spoke. They passed great blocks of flats and houses with closed doors, stepped over scattered heaps of clothing, made circuits round cars, and always Paul led east. Now and again he put his hand in his pocket to stroke one of the rats, but otherwise he stayed silent, moving fast.

It was growing light when they realised that many of the buildings they were passing were empty shells.

'Burned out,' whispered Muriel. 'There must have been a lot of fires.'

'Yes, and there's a funny smell.'

Muriel said nothing. She, too, had noticed an unpleasant smell every now and again.

They reached Kensington Gardens and walked through long grass to Hyde Park Corner noting constant signs of fire. At Hyde Park Corner Paul led her across the tangled skein of wrecked cars and lorries into Green Park.

'Are we going to Whitehall?' Muriel whispered.

Paul nodded, and twenty minutes later they passed the Cenotaph and Paul turned abruptly into Downing Street and ran to the steps of No. 10. He pushed at the door and went in. Muriel followed. How obvious, how childish, she thought, closing the door behind her and followed her dog who was running after Paul.

'This will be the Cabinet room.' Paul spoke out loud for the first time and then he began to laugh. Round the table sat in eternal session the Prime Minister and the cabinet, sitting portentously in dignified silence as they had been cast in wax at Madame Tussaud's.

'I thought Henry was—' Paul began, grinning widely.

'I know Henry is truthful.' Muriel looked round the room in silence, at the waxworks.

28

Muriel and Paul explored the house, finding their way into the Prime Minister's flat which, compared with the desolate hotels they had been sleeping in, felt warm and lived in.

'It feels lived in.' Muriel was puzzled.

'It is. Look, unmade beds and in here unwashed dishes.' Paul darted from room to room. 'Oh, I'm so hungry.'

'Then have some breakfast.' Henry, materialising on silent feet stood behind them.

'Oh, Henry!' Muriel wondered whether she could conceal her relief and joy. 'Oh, Henry, we just followed and we never found any sign of you until we saw a message on a dart-board in a hotel bar.'

'That wasn't meant for you. Have you had anything to eat? There is plenty here. Did I leave the door open? That was a pity, except that you got in which is lucky. We use the back window.'

'We?' Muriel queried.

'Yes, a man I found. He is nice, an aerodynamics expert called Briggs. He was in the government deep shelter working on something when the storm hit London so he survived. He should be here soon, in fact that's him at the back window.' Henry left the room and Muriel and Paul heard him run down the stairs and voices talking.

'Why didn't you tell me where Henry had come?' Muriel said to Paul.

'He said not to.' Paul looked at his mother uneasily. 'He wanted it to be a secret, but when you were so lost without him I felt I had to bring you up to him. I am your son but it is Henry you love.' Paul spoke crossly but without any trace of jealousy.

Before Muriel could answer Henry came back into the room followed by a short fair man with a mild expression.

'This is Mr Briggs.' Henry waved an airy hand.

Muriel shook hands.

'Come on, let's have breakfast. Have you seen the Cabinet?' Henry appeared to be in high spirits.

'Yes,' said Muriel. 'A very bad taste joke.'

'But the truth.' Henry laughed. 'The truth is a waxwork. *You* should know.'

'I'm hungry,' said Muriel evasively, 'and tired, and so is Paul.'

'Well, we eat breakfast and sleep by day. There is a tremendous store of food here.'

Muriel followed Henry to the kitchen and soon she and Paul were eating round a table with Henry and Mr Briggs.

'Are you the only person left in London?' Paul asked.

'No,' Mr Briggs answered shortly.

'Who else is left?' Muriel enquired innocently.

Henry laughed. 'We are not sure of the numbers.'

'Oh.' Muriel looked from Henry to Mr Briggs, feeling puzzled.

'It is best not to meet them.' Mr Briggs looked at Muriel. 'We explore by night. I have been all over London since the storm. There were fires everywhere and since then— well.'

'Well what?' Muriel was impatient. 'I must go to Patricia's home and see what has happened there, and I have dozens of friends in London.'

'Have you?' Henry looked at her with an amused expression. 'I will take you to Patricia's flat. She gave me the key.'

'She what?'

'She gave me the key. She found it among her father's things.'

'And didn't tell me?' Muriel felt annoyed.

'Well,' said Henry comfortably, 'she saw me with my own latchkey so she gave me hers too. She thought you were a bit insensitive about the pigs.'

'But her parents were not pigs.'

'From what I hear Patricia has a parental feeling towards the pigs,' said Mr Briggs tactfully.

'Oh,' Muriel smiled, 'she has. She is very strong on the subject.'

'Well, the pigs are there and the parents are not.' Henry looked at Muriel. 'Come on and I'll show you.'

Mr Briggs raised an eyebrow. 'I'm going to sleep,' he said, 'and Paul should too. Come on and I'll find you a room.' He left the room followed by Paul.

Muriel rounded on Henry. 'Your parents,' she said.

'There's just the empty house. They had gone away. I've ransacked it. They left nothing of interest. Shall we go and see Patricia's flat if you must?'

'Yes,' said Muriel, 'I must.'

'Then follow me and do what I do.'

Henry led Muriel out of the window at the back of the house and then by devious routes through Westminster into Pimlico.

'It's getting bloody cold,' said Henry. 'We can't spend the winter here. We must get home, it's safe there.'

'Safe?' Muriel, walking beside Henry, decided that he was over-imaginative. 'Don't be silly,' she said.

Henry said nothing but walked on, keeping close to the area railings until they reached the block of flats Patricia's parents lived in.

'Upstairs, No. 303,' said Henry laconically, 'here's the key.'

They climbed the stairs to the third floor in silence and came to a stop outside the door numbered 303. Muriel paused.

'Go on,' Henry said roughly.

Muriel put the key in the lock and opened the door, calling softly, 'Anybody in? Anybody at home?' Henry sat down in the corridor with his back to the wall and waited.

Muriel walked into a quietly luxurious flat, noting good furniture and carpets, one or two good pictures on the walls and the light switches turned on, but there was no light.

'No light,' Muriel murmured to herself and opened a door which led her into a bedroom. The bed was slightly ruffled as though someone had been lying on it, and a mass of long fair

146

hair lay on the pillow, nothing else. Muriel left the flat and rejoined Henry, feeling sick.

'See?' said Henry.

'See what?' Muriel flared up in hatred of Henry.

'See the truth of course.' Henry laughed in her face and then ran away down the stairs leaving her alone to find her way back to Downing Street.

29

Muriel walked proudly across the park and down Whitehall towards the Cenotaph which she had passed that morning in the dawn without paying it much attention. Now later in the day she paused and stared at it with mounting horror. Besides the conventional wreaths of poppies there were piled against the foot of the monument shoes, hats, jewellery, a bicycle, long strands of hair, bowler hats, umbrellas and 'Oh God!' muttered Muriel, 'Teeth, teeth, teeth.' She broke into a run and did not stop until she reached the closed door of No. 10 Downing Street where she hammered like a child with her fists until Mr Briggs opened the door.

'The Cenotaph,' said Muriel breathlessly.

'Ah yes. We found it like that.' Mr Briggs looked concerned for her.

'Who did it?'

'Who knows? Come in, it's cold.' Muriel allowed herself to be led upstairs.

'Was it Henry?'

'No. I personally think people rushed there during the storm. If you go to any church which is open you will find much the same.'

Muriel felt calm slowly coming back as she climbed the stairs.

'We must get out of here,' said Mr Briggs, 'and the sooner the better. Ah, here comes Henry.'

Henry climbed the stairs after them. 'This is pretty, don't you think?' He held out a diamond tiara to Muriel.

'Where did you get it?' Mr Briggs looked surprised.

'Cartier has had its windows bashed in.' Henry exchanged an enigmatic look with the young man. 'I shall take it to Mrs Luard.'

'I must look round a bit more. I cannot believe no one I love is left. I cannot.'

'It's snowing,' exclaimed Henry, looking out of the window. 'And freezing too.'

'I must go out.' Muriel pushed past the man and the boy.

'Let her go,' said Mr Briggs. 'She must see for herself, then she will come.'

'Then I shall go and get some sleep because we ought to go tomorrow before we are found.'

Muriel walked rapidly through the streets of Petty France and on towards Chelsea. She walked through the streets of Chelsea where her friends had lived and across to South Kensington. Every street was the same, empty, quiet, lifeless and full of rubbish, paper bags and sweet papers, cigarette ends and hair, empty cars and taxis and dusty shops. As she got near Gloucester Road, where some of Julian's highbrow friends had remained poised in top flats converted from the servants' quarters of giant houses of the late Victorian era, she felt a cold sweat break between her shoulder blades and the feeling that she was being watched. She tried not to walk faster or to betray her awareness but her heart began to thump and her eyes to flail from side to side of the street. As she hesitated over which direction to take, a shot rang out and she felt a bullet whistle past her head. At the same time a hand caught her ankle and she fell on the pavement.

'Lie still,' said a voice she did not know. 'Lie absolutely still.' Another shot rang out and a third further away.

'Someone is drawing their fire. Now run.'

A man she had never seen before pulled her to her feet and she found herself racing beside him through side streets. Suddenly, just as she thought she could run no more, the man stopped by a taxi standing by the pavement and, opening the door, pushed her in.

'Sorry to be so abrupt,' said the man, 'but it was the only thing to do. I wonder who is drawing them off. They were after me.'

'Trying to kill us,' Muriel gasped indignantly.

'Well, yes. My name is Waterford. What is yours?'

'Muriel Wake. What's going on?'

'Lie still. You are perfectly safe here. Where do you come from?'

'Devonshire. I got to Downing Street this morning.'

Muriel's rescuer was laughing. 'Sorry to laugh but it's such a funny combination. What is going on in Downing Street, if it's not indiscreet to ask?'

Muriel told the man about Henry and Mr Briggs and Paul and he sat thoughtfully on the floor of the taxi listening.

'And they did not tell you that it was dangerous to walk about in daylight?'

'I would not have believed them,' said Muriel truthfully.

'I suppose they knew you very well.'

'Henry does,' admitted Muriel. 'Please tell me what's going on?'

'Well.' Mr Waterford arranged long legs more comfortably. 'After the storm in July which eliminated nearly everyone there were fires. You have probably seen the areas burned. Many people who lived below ground survived and they came out but, just as in the last war, they took shelter in the tubes because they were afraid. Others escaped—owners of gambling clubs, strip joints, the criminal fringe. They banded together under some clever fellow and they got a bulldozer and cleared the road west out of London. I hid and I watched. In my innocence I was glad because I thought those poor people hiding in the tubes would come out and we could live again.' He paused.

'We have lived again in Devon,' said Muriel. 'There was one very frightening lot who got drowned trying to get to London.' And Muriel told her new friend of her little community in the country. 'What happened to the people who cleared the road?'

'They came back,' said Mr Waterford gloomily, 'with some sort of gas and they have killed all the people who were in the tubes and anyone moving they shoot on sight. Of course it can't last long for any of us.'

'Why not?' said Muriel.

'Well, just think. Drains, typhus, plague and so on. The moment the weather gets warm all that will start.'

Muriel, sitting on the floor of the abandoned taxi, was silent.

'Lie still,' Muriel's new friend said suddenly and Muriel listened to the sound of soft footsteps approaching.

'Where is she, Chap? Find her.' Henry's cheerful voice spoke close by.

'Here,' said Muriel, standing up. 'Henry, I am here.'

Muriel and Mr Waterford got out of the taxi.

'I followed you,' said Henry. 'Who is this?'

'My name is Waterford.'

'Don't you think,' said Henry in conversational tones to Mr Waterford as he politely shook hands, 'that Mrs Wake should just peep into a tube station?'

'Why?'

Henry shifted the rifle he was carrying to his other arm. 'If she sees what's in the station she will believe and then we must all get out. That clot Paul has only just told me they came in as far as Earls Court by car. We can get out in it and old Briggs can fly us home. *He's* only just let on he can fly—that he actually holds a licence.'

'Tomorrow,' said Mr Waterford as they walked along.

'Yes, tomorrow,' said Henry. 'It wouldn't be safe at night. Here's a tube station, Mrs Wake. Just take a look for yourself.'

Mesmerised by Henry's casual manner, Muriel let herself be led down the staircase of a tube station.

'So that's the smell,' she said as she turned away and was sick until she could be sick no more.

'This is the gun old Perdue saw under my bed at Brendon,' said Henry, watching her with sad eyes as she walked slowly back to Downing Street. 'It's snowing,' he said cheerfully. 'The snow will keep them indoors.'

Later Muriel, lying on a sofa gulping hot tea, looked at her son and Henry and at Mr Briggs and Mr Waterford. 'Is there nobody else left?' she asked.

'We do not think so,' they said gently. 'We have searched very thoroughly. The time has come to go.'

30

Muriel listened listlessly to the men and boys planning their flight, for flight she fully realised it to be.

'If we can get unseen as far as London Airport we should be lucky enough to find a plane to fly us down to Devonshire.' Mr Briggs was quiet and unassuming.

'If not a plane a helicopter,' said Henry.

'I have never flown a helicopter. My experience is rather out of date anyway.' The young man spoke practically.

'Then we must walk,' Paul said cheerfully. 'Get back the way we came.'

'In this weather?' Henry's voice was flatly contemptuous. 'Look at it. Snowing and freezing. None of us would survive.'

'It may not last.' Paul looked at his mother lying resting on the sofa.

'It will. I can feel it in my bones,' said Henry. 'And while we wait all those dead people are fermenting in the tube.'

'Really, Henry,' Mr Waterford mildly protested.

'Well, I am right.' Henry stared out of the window at the falling snow. 'The sewage system will clog up. We did a paper on it once at school. All those bodies will be rotting away where they were killed. It's unhealthy, as old Perdue would say.'

Muriel got up and left the room to wander about the house in the grey light, opening and shutting doors as she went, knowing that never again would she see this house. In one room she stared blankly at a pile of pictures, portraits partially destroyed. She recognised past Prime Ministers in gold frames. Somebody had either slashed the canvases or put a foot through each. 'Henry, I suppose.' Muriel smiled in spite of herself.

The others moved briskly about the house talking in low voices. At a window commanding a view of the street Paul sat with Henry's gun watching the approach to the house.

Later in the evening Muriel made a meal of what she could find and they all ate in preoccupied silence.

At intervals during the evening the two men left her alone in the house with the boys.

'What are those two men doing?' she asked.

'Making sure we are not yet discovered, I think,' said Paul. 'We don't want to get ourselves shot or gassed do we?'

'No.' Muriel went and watched Henry playing idly with the telephone switchboard.

'Henry, Paul heard the telephone at home,' she said.

'So he told me.' Muriel felt a long divide between herself and the boy.

Late in the evening they all slept, though Muriel was aware that the two men took turns to keep watch. Outside in the silent city the snow fell steadily to cover the traces of human life.

At dawn Paul and Henry woke her. 'Come and fill some thermoses, Mum.'

Muriel boiled water and filled thermoses with tea and coffee and watched Paul feed his rats before zipping them into the pocket of his windcheater.

Mr Briggs cleared his throat. 'If you know where it is will you go with Henry to the car you left in Earls Court. The rest of us will follow if Paul will give us a lead.'

'Why can't we all go together?' Muriel asked.

'Oh Mum, you know whoever shot at you knows we are about. Don't be so dumb.' Henry laughed at Paul's rudeness.

'All right.'

Muriel with her dog at her heels slipped out of the house and set off, her feet crunching on the snow.

'Are you sure you don't mind me with you?' Henry spoke softly.

'No,' said Muriel, knowing that she was lying. 'No, I don't. I am afraid for the others.'

'They will go by different streets so that we don't leave a huge great trail to be followed.'

Muriel said nothing, hating the snow and the freezing wind, hating her fear.

'They are going to create diversions,' said Henry cheerfully. 'The first is the best.'

'What's that?'

'A gunpowder plot, a slow consuming fire in the Houses of Parliament. By the time it gets going we shall be gone.' Muriel looked at Henry unbelievingly.

'It's perfectly true,' said Henry, and hurried her on through the snow. 'If all Whitehall is on fire they will go there.'

'It seems mad,' Muriel said indignantly.

'But it's true.' Henry seemed in no way put out but led her as fast as she could walk on the long trail to Earls Court. When at last they reached it he said, 'Now, where's that car?'

Muriel cast about until she found the street and saw the car standing covered with snow in the side street.

'Now we wait,' said Henry.

'Henry, you know I hate waiting.'

'Maybe this is the last time.' Henry tried to cheer her. 'No, don't get into it, get into another and we will watch for the others.'

Together they got into an empty car and sat close together for warmth, listening. After a long time they heard far away the sound of an explosion and saw the sky grow red. Waiting, they watched the sky and the streets until at last, running as though they had run a long way, Paul appeared with the two men.

'Ah,' said Henry and slipped out of the car and stood waiting to meet them. Muriel joined him and looked anxiously at Paul who looked exhausted.

'No time to wait,' said Mr Waterford. 'Where's the car?'

Muriel pointed and the two men and the boys gathered round.

'Get in with the dog and we will push.'

Muriel obeyed, started the engine, and with the men and boys pushing the car through the snow, drove slowly out into the main road. Keeping in low gear through the snow, Muriel felt the draught of the door opening as one by one the boys and the men jumped into the car as it was moving.

'Whatever you do, don't stop.' Mr Briggs was sitting beside her, 'And keep it, if you can, in the middle of the road.'

Muriel drove slowly, turning on the windscreen wipers and the heater, her heart in her mouth. The snow falling heavily made driving difficult.

'It may be difficult,' said Henry from the back seat, 'but the harder the snow falls the quicker our tracks will be covered.'

Behind her, a long way away, Muriel heard explosions.

'Don't look back, look at where you are driving,' Mr Waterford said dryly.

'What's going on?' Muriel asked.

'We set fire to the gas which is still in the tubes and the pressure is making explosions.'

153

'Why?' said Muriel angrily. 'Why destroy London?'

'Because it will flush out the people who are hunting us and distract their attention. Please do not behave like Lot's wife.'

'All right, I won't.' Muriel drove on.

'Of course if she did look,' Henry's cheerful voice remarked, 'she would see at last.'

'See what?' Muriel drove on.

'See what you have never seen,' said Henry airily.

'Time enough when we are airborne,' Mr Waterford said. 'I think, Henry, it would be best for you to shut up.'

Henry laughed. 'Couldn't she bear it?' he said.

'Not just yet.' Mr Waterford answered quietly.

'Very well.' Henry spoke gently. 'Drive on, Mrs Wake. You are doing very well.'

31

Muriel drove on doggedly, her heart in her mouth. The snow fell steadily but she managed to keep the car more or less in the centre of the road. Beside her Mr Briggs sat silent and behind her the two boys, Mr Waterford and the dog huddled in the back seat.

'What did you do in real life?' Muriel heard Henry asking Mr Waterford.

'I was doing research into the habits of Eastern peoples. The storm caught me underground and I have been dodging "the wreckers", as I call them to myself, ever since.'

'Now we have done some wrecking.' Henry sounded pleased.

'We had to save our lives,' Paul said reasonably.

'We must do some more at London Airport or they will follow us.'

'I don't think there are many people left,' Mr Briggs remarked from the seat beside Muriel. 'I have been watching them fighting among themselves. What is more, they are the kind of people who are afraid of the country so they will stay in the town and die.'

As he spoke the windscreen shattered and Muriel heard Mr Briggs grunt in pain.

'Don't stop, for God's sake,' Henry said from the back. 'Are you all right, Mr Briggs?'

'Give me a handkerchief or something. I've been hit in the shoulder. Go on driving, Mrs Wake. It's our only chance.'

From the back seat Mr Waterford leant forward and opened Mr Briggs' coat. 'You won't be much use as a pilot,' he remarked. 'The bullet's gone right through you into the seat. All I can do is stop the blood.'

'Go on, Mum, don't stop.' Paul spoke urgently. 'You know the way. Go on.'

Muriel smelt the smell of fresh blood and glancing sideways saw her companion looking very white as from the back seat Mr Waterford plugged a wound in the man's shoulder and without asking her took the headscarf off her head and fixed it in a sling to support Mr Briggs' arm.

'I won't die,' Mr Briggs said between his teeth. 'Drive on, Mrs Wake, drive on.'

Muriel drove as though in a nightmare through the snow, the sweat pouring down the small of her back and clogging her armpits.

'When we find an aircraft you will have to tell Mrs Wake how to pilot it.' Henry's voice was hard and clear.

'I can do that.'

'I have learnt to fly a little in good conditions. My husband taught me.' Muriel spoke with terror at the prospect before her.

'Then that will have to do.' Mr Waterford finished tying the sling and they were all silent until they reached the airport.

Muriel never very clearly remembered what followed except that she and Mr Waterford helped Mr Briggs out of the car and into shelter as the snow stung their eyes and blanketed all the neighbourhood. In the airport lounge they laid Mr Briggs in a chair and Henry ran to look for brandy which he found in a bar and brought back a bottle and some glasses. He dosed Mr Briggs and then turned to Muriel.

'Wait with him, Mrs Wake, while we find a plane. Don't let him move.'

Muriel sat beside the young man feeling very helpless, seeing the other man and the two boys run off.

'Does it hurt much?' Muriel looked at the white face.

'Like hell.'

Time passed slowly and Muriel fretted at the agony of its pace. At last the two boys and the man came back.

'Come on,' Henry exclaimed. 'We have found a plane. We must get it away. Come on, Mr Briggs.'

Mr Waterford and Muriel helped Mr Briggs up and slowly followed the boys and the dog.

'I found some morphia and I will give you a shot once you have told Mrs Wake how to get us off the ground.' Mr Waterford spoke as though promising a packet of sweets to a child. The other man smiled wryly.

The aircraft was small and Muriel recognised it as of the make Julian had taught her to fly in. They hoisted the wounded man into the plane and put him in the seat beside the pilot's.

'Now, Mrs Wake—' Henry's voice roused Muriel's anger to the point of outrage, anger mixed with love. With a dreamlike determination she started the motor, hearing the boys and the dog settle behind her with Mr Waterford.

'Can you navigate?' she asked her wounded neighbour.

'I'll tell you the course to set once you get up,' the wounded man muttered. 'Just taxi off into the snow and I'll tell you what to do.'

The noise of the aircraft increased as Muriel taxied slowly along the runway. Then suddenly her confidence flowed back and they were airborne. She flew the aircraft as she had been taught long ago and circled the airfield. Below her she could hear explosions and see fires breaking out, but her mind was set on one thing only, to get home.

Mr Waterford came up from the back of the aircraft holding a syringe. 'Tell her what course to set, old boy, and then I'll put you out of pain.'

Mr Briggs began muttering and the other man interpreted to Muriel while she obeyed, setting the frail little aeroplane towards the west.

'Good. Keep her on that course. Now I'll jab the poor chap.'

Muriel, concentrating on the controls, felt her neighbour relax and sink in his seat.

'Nobody will follow us now,' said Henry's voice gaily.

'Nothing to follow in,' shouted Paul.

Checking her position Muriel saw from the cockpit, even through the snow, a great blaze behind and below them.

'It will all burn. Nothing like aviation petrol,' Henry shouted in her ear. 'Now you get us home, Mrs Wake, that's all you have to do.'

Simple, Muriel thought to herself as she flew into the sky full of falling snow. Behind her Henry was laughing and suddenly she knew fully and for the first time what she must tell Father Richard.

32

They soon lost sight of the ground and Muriel kept the nose of the plane pointing west as she flew it through the snowstorm. Beside her Mr Briggs, with the morphia beginning to work, lolled in silence like a corpse, his eyes shut. Behind her she heard her dog bark nervously and the two boys' voices raised high above the noise of the engine as they shouted at Mr Waterford.

Muriel wondered at Mr Waterford's calmness, the manner in which he had saved her life, his efficient way of dealing with Mr Briggs' wound and, smiling to herself, she remembered his very long legs like a spider which enabled him to bend from behind her as she sat in the cockpit and inject Mr Briggs with morphia. She heard Henry's voice shout above the engine, 'About two hundred and twenty miles', and Mr Waterford's head came between her and the unconscious Mr Briggs to look at the altimeter and the speedometer.

'Just keep on flying,' the young man's voice said in her ear.

'I say, care for a swig?' Henry's face replaced Mr Waterford's and she saw he was holding a paper cup of brandy.

Muriel nodded and drank as the boy held the cup to her lips.

'We are all getting plastered in the back,' his amiable voice said loud in her ear. 'Ever landed in snow?'

'No.' Muriel shook her head.

'First time for everything.' Henry still sounded cheerful.

'First time for death,' Muriel snapped and the boy grinned. She noticed that Paul and Mr Waterford each sat looking out on either side of the plane, seeing nothing she supposed but clouds and fleeting snow.

Either brandy or their desperate position exalted Muriel and she too glanced from time to time at the altimeter and tried to calculate how fast and far they were going.

'They call this "Going West".' Henry's voice was in her ear again. 'Paul and old Waterford are watching for the sea.'

'The sea?'

'Yes, we have passed Salisbury. Paul saw the tip of the spire. Keep it up, Mrs Wake.'

Muriel felt resentful that she should find herself in this ridiculous position, flying two children, two men, a dog and two rats through a snowstorm all because of Henry who had led them to the horrors of London. Glancing sideways she saw Henry sliding into the seat beside the unconscious man and begin to peer forwards through the clouds. He does not seem worried, she thought to herself, and then rebuked herself, thinking that he was only a child.

'You are not only a child,' she suddenly shouted at Henry. Henry nodded in agreement.

'Sea on the left,' Paul shouted in her ear. 'Mr Waterford says can you bear right a bit. We don't want to ditch in the sea.'

Henry laughed and looked at Muriel whose brows were knit in perplexity. She turned the aircraft slightly right and flew on.

'Will this ever end?' she said.

'Yes.' Henry seemed to have heard her.

'Fasten your seat belts, please.' Henry's voice was a dainty imitation of an air hostess. He fastened the seat belt round Mr Briggs who grunted in pain. Behind her she felt Paul and Mr Waterford securing themselves.

'There's the sea dividing Exeter from the mainland.' Henry pointed downwards through a gap in the clouds and Muriel saw angry sea horses chopping up the sea before the clouds cut off the sight of the sea which had once been the river Exe.

'Now watch out for the hills.' Muriel felt Henry's directions unnecessary as she peered through the clouds looking for the moor.

Now everyone was silent and Muriel knew that she and only she could bring down the aircraft. The clouds thickened and thinned giving her tantalizing glimpses of the ground below them. Each time she saw the earth she tried hard to recognise some land-mark. Suddenly, before she expected it, she saw the reservoir by Brendon below them and realised that she was overshooting her house. With the blood thumping in her head she banked the plane, hearing cries of protest from her passengers. She dropped height, the engine stuttered, the snow rushed up at them and before she could raise the nose of the plane it bumped, rose in the air, then bumped a second time to lie still in the snow, lopsided.

'Mum, you've done it.' Paul clambered up to her.

Muriel felt a great wave of relief followed by pain. Chap barked and she heard voices. The voices died away and surged back. She recognised Coke and James and the two girls chattering.

'Watch out, Mrs Wake is hurt, so is Briggs,' Mr Waterford was shouting.

'Get them out and clear before it catches fire.' Commander James's authority seemed to dominate.

'Patricia, get those damned pigs back to the house.'

Muriel felt herself lifted out, laid in the snow and then suddenly lifted again by Coke. 'It's all right, Mrs Wake, soon get you to the house.'

'Mr Briggs, Coke, Mr Briggs has been shot.'

'We'll take care of him.' Coke's boring reassuring voice answered. 'The Commander and the other chap's got him.'

Muriel fainted. Coming to she gasped, 'I'm terrified.'

'Too late to feel terrified now.' Henry, leaping through the snow with Paul beside him, kept up with Coke sedately carrying her.

'I can walk,' Muriel said crossly. 'I'm not a bride to be carried over the threshold.'

'You've broken a leg,' Henry's voice cried cheerfully. 'Watch out, there she goes!'

Behind them, lying wrecked in the snow, the little plane burst into flames with a staccato explosion.

'We have a surprise for you.' June's face loomed up beside her.

'Best get her to bed and get her leg set first,' said Coke.

Muriel felt sudden warmth as Coke carried her into the house.

'If you can get her into bed I'll set her leg and give her some morphia.' Mr Waterford, his hair full of snow and his nose bleeding, loped alongside.

'And who are you?' From beside the Aga old Mr Perdue rose with dignity as the cat jumped crossly off his lap her whiskers twitching.

'Waterford's the name. Can you get those girls to fill hot bottles for Mrs Wake and the other chap? He's been shot.'

'Arrh,' said the old man in disbelief.

Muriel, flinching with pain and half conscious, was carried up the stairs. June and Ann undressed her and listened to her muttering, 'My head, my head.'

'She's cracked her head,' said June to Mr Waterford.

'Has she? I'll give her a shot of morphia and see to the leg then I must see to poor Briggs.'

Muriel felt the prick of the syringe and great pain in her leg as the young man set it.

'She'll be all right. Get me something to make a splint. I expect she's got concussion too.'

'Lucky you know how to do all these things.' June's voice came through a dull haze. 'I wanted her to see her surprise.'

'It must wait. Let her sleep.'

Muriel felt pain, relief, the comfort of her own bed, and slept. Much later she woke and remembered the horrors of London, the terror of the flight. The watcher at her side took her hand and held it firmly as she cried out, sweating with fear.

'It's quite all right now. They are all safe and so are you. Don't worry any more.' The watcher leant over her and kissed her.

Muriel opened doped eyes and stared. 'My God,' she whispered.

'Yes, it's me. I'm sorry I couldn't get back sooner. I arrived the day you left.'

'Sam.'

'Yes, Mama. Sam. Go to sleep now.'

Somebody gave Muriel another injection, but the hand which held hers was the long-fingered hand of Sam. Her fingers relaxed and she slept.

Henry put his head round the door. 'Want to eat?' Sam nodded.

Muriel opened her eyes and saw Henry.

'I saw Sam.'

'You saw Sam. Go to sleep.' The child's face bore no expression as he watched her close her eyes and begin to breathe deeply.

33

Outside the house the wind sank to a whisper as the snow rose round the walls. June and Ann helped Coke shutter the windows, creeping silently round the house so that they would not disturb Muriel and Mr Briggs.

Mr Waterford lay in a chair by the library fire and stretched his long legs, relaxing for the first time for many weeks, comforted by the presence of a collection of puppies and kittens, made drowsy by the warmth.

Outside, struggling through the snow, James and the three children helped Mr Perdue feed and water the animals and shut up the poultry. They closed all the sheds and barns and made their way back to the house.

'How long will this go on?' one of the girls muttered.

'Winter, it's winter,' the old man said.

'Where is Akbar?' Henry asked suddenly. 'Jolly old Akbar.'

'In bed with a cold.'

Henry clapped his hand to his mouth and spluttered with laughter. June looked at him with disgust.

'Nothing funny,' she said.

'No, no, but so normal.' Henry's eyes filled with tears of laughter. 'In bed with a cold. How gorgeous.'

'It's the contrast,' said James dryly.

'He drops in on us from Afghanistan, marries you and catches a cold.'

'Well?' June bristled.

'Oh, nothing.' James looked at Ann affectionately, knowing that she too would find Akbar's cold funny. Ann smiled at him.

'I think it's nice and normal to have a cold,' she said firmly.

'I am going to have a small session on the blower,' said Henry and went off with Paul to the telephone where they spent an hour or more talking to Mrs Luard and then to the Abbey. On their return Henry remarked casually, 'Mrs Luard is okay and Father Richard is coming up with medicines as soon as he can.'

'Medicines?'

'Yes. He says not only Mrs Wake and Mr Briggs will need them but Sam too. He says Sam may have had some shock.'

'Haven't we all?' Paul glanced at his friend.

'Yes, indeed yes. He said mental as well as physical though.'

'Oh.' Paul looked thoughtful.

'And of course there is Akbar's cold,' Henry said cheerfully to June. 'He may not have an ordinary British cold but a fierce Afghan one.'

'Shut up,' said June, hating Henry.

'Shut up is what we shall all be in this weather. If it freezes hard enough we can go visiting.'

'It will freeze,' Mr Perdue said with conviction. 'Ah yes, it will freeze.'

'Suit Akbar then.' Henry looked at June who looked away.

'I believe most people catch cold on their honeymoon. It's a sign of love,' Henry said to June. 'I've heard it said often.'

'Rubbish,' said June and began to prepare a tray for Akbar's tea which she intended to share with him in their bedroom.

Watching her leave the room a few minutes later, old Mr Perdue turned to Henry and said bluntly, 'You are not to tease them as is newly married. They get touchy.'

'Oh,' said Henry, turning to Ann. 'Are you touchy, Ann?'

'No,' Ann answered, 'but I have a cold coming on. I think Akbar will give it to us all.'

'Sure to,' said James, 'since we are all cooped up together.'

'I should like,' said Ann, 'to find a house where we could live on our own, James.'

'June and Akbar want to do that too, but none of us can move in this weather.'

'I daresay Mrs Wake would like to be left alone now she has her son back. I'm going to move into the farm.' The old man spoke gruffly. 'And I'm not going to wait for the spring either.'

'I'll come and live with you,' Coke said slowly, 'company for me, company for you, see?'

'All right.' The old man looked at Coke. 'All right. We'll have a kitten and keep house together.'

James wandered away into the library and stood watching Mr Waterford asleep in a chair. He wondered vaguely how long the other man would sleep and how soon the monk would arrive from the Abbey with medical relief. Taking Ann with him, he climbed the stairs to look into the room they had put

Mr Briggs in and were met by feverish eyes staring at them from a flushed face.

'How are you feeling?' James asked.

'Pretty dim.'

'Medical supplies on their way,' said James. 'We all need them.'

'How is Mrs Wake?'

'Not too good, but her son is back.'

'Paul?'

'No, her older son Sam. He was abroad when the storm hit us. He turned up the day she went to London.'

'Poor London,' Mr Briggs muttered, 'burned, ravished, infected, blown up.'

'Why?' James got no answer but Ann tugged at his sleeve and pointed out of the window. Joining her he saw the figure of a monk, very small, coming through the snow and Henry and Paul running to meet him.

'The rescue team.' James and Ann left the room and went downstairs to find Father Richard shaking snow from his habit in the hall.

'How are they?' Father Richard enquired.

'They all look as if they had come out of hell,' said James. 'There is Briggs with a shot wound. Mrs Wake is semi-conscious and has a broken leg. Her son Sam is back.'

'Yes, I want to talk to him.'

'And we all have colds.'

Father Richard laughed. 'I had better see Mr Briggs first. His wound must not become infected.'

'Do you know any medicine?' Henry enquired at his elbow.

'Enough,' said the small monk and began climbing the stairs.

'I thought souls were your métier.' Henry's sophisticated voice followed Father Richard.

'Oh, drop dead,' said Father Richard amiably, remembering the parlance of the Youth Club of former days.

34

Mr Briggs submitted to the firm but gentle treatment administered to him and then lay back comfortably bandaged and rather drowsy.

'Waterford gave me morphia,' he said to the monk who was preparing a syringe.

'One more jab won't make you an addict,' Father Richard answered. 'You will sleep. Your fever will go and you will be up in a few days, but you must take it easy.'

'All right. You seem to know. But do you think we have brought any infection from London with us?'

'I'll ask Henry and that other man.' Father Richard smiled at the anxious face. 'It's a risk we have to take. We have no vaccines here, only common medicines. I shouldn't worry.'

'Spiritual infections.' Henry spoke from the doorway.

'I should call you a carrier,' said the monk tartly. 'Now I must see Mrs Wake. Good-bye and go to sleep.' He drew the bed-clothes up round Mr Briggs' chin.

'Akbar has a cold.' Henry, not to be subdued, accompanied the monk down the passage.

'Really. Now where is Mrs Wake?'

'Here, in here.' Henry led the way.

'Hullo, Sam, feeling better?' Father Richard went into Muriel's room.

'Yes, thanks. My mother is rambling a bit though. Wants to see you.'

'She's wanted to ever since the night of the storm,' Henry said cheerfully.

'Now buzz off for a bit. Give yourself a rest.' Father Richard put a hand on Muriel's forehead and took her wrist while Henry watched. After a moment Muriel opened her eyes and stared at the monk. 'I must—' she began.

'You must rest. Let your leg and head heal. Everything is all right now and there are plenty of people to attend to things. There is nothing you must do just at the moment.'

'Sam. Sam is back.'

'Yes, Sam is back and Paul and Henry are safe. You brought them back and two men. Everything is under control.'

'It isn't,' said Muriel. 'I am not.'

Father Richard gave her a shot of morphia and stood watching her with Sam and Paul and Henry. 'She must be kept very quiet,' he said gently, watching her drift into sleep. 'Come on, Sam. I want to hear more than you told me when you arrived. Let's go to the library.'

Sam and his brother followed Father Richard out of the room forgetting Henry who curled up in a chair by the bed and fell asleep with his lips slightly parted, his face white with exhaustion.

Downstairs in the library they all gathered round the fire, even Akbar in a dressing-gown sniffing and sneezing at intervals. Mr Waterford woke from his sleep in the armchair and stared at them as he rose stiffly.

'You are from London. Henry told me on the telephone what had happened there. Was he exaggerating?'

'No. Nobody could have exaggerated it. London became a combination of Dante's Inferno and Giotto's Hell.' Mr Waterford sat down again. 'Sorry. I feel a bit shaky on my legs. It's the relief of getting away. I never thought I would. Then those children and Mrs Wake appeared and we got away.'

'Could you not have got away before?' asked June.

'Perhaps I could, but all the time I felt there was something I could do to stop them. Stop the destruction. It was really the sight of Henry's waxwork arrangement which convinced me.'

'Children.' Sam spoke in a neutral voice. 'By the way, where is Henry?'

'Asleep in Mum's room. It's all right, he just feels safe there.' Paul looked at his elder brother. 'If she wakes up he will be there. She is *used* to him now.'

Sam laughed, looking round the group of faces. 'Nice,' he said and then, stretching his arms above his head, he remarked at random, 'Nice to find people alive and sane. Nice to find my mother and brother, my home and,' he hesitated, 'a house party.'

'We shan't stay for ever,' said James. 'Ann and I want to live within reach, so do June and Akbar. Old Perdue and Coke are setting up house together and the Abbey is still going, I take it. What about you, Waterford and Briggs?'

'I want to write a book and now I have the time. I can't answer for Briggs. He is the sort of man who will want to go and find out what's happened on the continent, when he is well again that is.'

'You can tell us about the continent, Sam. You were there after all.' Paul spoke with the envy of a younger brother.

'It is just the same as here,' Sam answered. 'Everybody is gone. Nothing left. I found my way home by boat from the Baltic coast. To be honest, I was so scared on land that I made my way to the sea and looked for a boat. When I found one I could sail I followed the coast until I got to Calais, then I crossed the channel on a quiet day and followed the coastline until I got home. Then I walked inland to the Abbey and found Father Richard and came home.'

'Did you see nobody? No planes, no ships?' James asked.

'Plenty of ships drifting, and many wrecks,' said Sam, as though the recollection were repellent to him.

'When the weather improves we shall have to go across the channel and see whether we can find any explanation,' said James.

'I think Henry knows some explanation but won't tell,' said Paul.

'Possibly,' said Sam. 'His parents were mixed up in something fishy.'

Paul got up and left the room to join Patricia who was lying on the floor in the drawing-room with her pigs round her, slowly scratching their stomachs with a small stick.

'What does Henry know that we don't know?' Paul lay down beside Patricia who just looked at him without answering.

In the library Father Richard was getting ready to leave. He gave June and Ann careful instructions on the nursing of Muriel and Mr Briggs. 'I must go now or I won't be back before Compline,' he said and left them to walk over the snow-covered moor and down through the woods into the valley.

James, seeing the total exhaustion on Mr Waterford's face, took him upstairs and found him a bedroom and, amused, watched him undress and get into the bed in what seemed one movement and fall immediately asleep.

With his new wife he looked in on Mr Briggs who, too, was sleeping quietly. They noticed Akbar and June vanish into their room, with Akbar suppressing a sneeze as he went, then they tip-toed towards Muriel's room and opened the door.

Muriel lay sleeping alone with her dog at her feet, her face white and expressionless.

'Look.' Ann pointed to Henry sprawled in a chair.

'Leave him,' said James.

'Should we?'

'Why not?'

'I don't know why not.' Ann flushed.

'Don't be silly then.' James turned to Sam and Paul coming towards them. 'It's all right, isn't it?' he asked the brothers, who looked in at their mother.

'Will she be all right if she wakes?' Paul whispered to his elder brother.

'Yes. God, I'm tired. I am going to bed. You should too.' Sam closed the door and led Paul away. 'Come and sleep. We can talk later.'

In her room Muriel heard them whispering and stirred in her sleep. Henry opened his eyes and got up to watch her. Then he moved to the window to look at the falling snow in the dusk and, going back to the armchair, fell asleep again.

35

Muriel lay in her bed and heard the noises of the house. Her fever made her acutely conscious. Clocks ticked and outside her window the wind rustled. She felt the pain in her leg. The pain of her head made it impossible to think. Once or twice during the night she cried out and Henry, rousing himself, came to her side.

'Henry, what happened?'

'You flew us home from London and crash-landed in the snow. You will be safe now.'

'Safe?'

'Well, London was not safe.'

'Why were we in London? I saw Sam, Henry. I saw Sam.'

'Yes,' Henry said patiently, 'you did. Sam is back. He is very tired. He is sleeping but he is quite all right.'

'Where's Julian?' Muriel felt the empty space beside her with her hand. 'Julian, Julian,' she muttered. 'There was a storm. Somebody shot at me in London. I must get home. I must get to Father Richard to talk to him.'

'Presently,' said Henry, pulling the bedclothes up to her face, watching her go off to sleep again. 'I hope you don't stay bonkers,' he muttered and went to rouse James.

'Someone should sit with her, nurse her.' Henry, standing sleepily in the doorway of James and Ann's room, roused them. 'She is wandering in her mind.'

'I'll go.' Ann got out of bed and put on a dressing-gown. 'Make some tea, sweetheart,' she said to James.

'Sweetheart.' Henry followed James and helped him make tea.

'I don't need you,' James said quite kindly. 'Go and sleep, Henry.' The boy said nothing, but James found him curled up in the armchair when he came up with a tray. They all drank tea, watching Muriel sleep. James and Ann stifled their yawns and exchanged glances.

'Somebody responsible must sit with her,' Ann whispered. James nodded and settled in a chair beside Muriel's bed.

Muriel startled them all by crying out suddenly, 'The cat.'

'The cat's all right,' Ann reassured her.

'No, he's dead, dead.'

Ann looked at James who shrugged his shoulders.

'We must make a rota, this may go on for days,' he murmured.

Very early he woke June and Akbar and together they went to visit Mr Briggs who greeted them cheerfully.

'Better, I'm much better.' Mr Briggs seemed to have lost his fever. 'How is Mrs Wake?'

'Rambling,' said James. 'We must sit with her in turns. I'm going to arrange it. She is alone at the moment with Henry.'

'Then she will be quite all right,' said Mr Briggs.

'Oh, is that your opinion? How odd. He's only a child. June and Ann and Sam and I can take turns to sit with her. I shouldn't think Henry would be of much use.'

'You lack imagination,' said Mr Briggs from his bed. 'She followed Henry all the way to London. Personally I am delighted she did, otherwise poor Waterford and I would have perished.'

'How?' James looked obtuse.

'Don't be a fool,' Mr Briggs snapped. 'London was bedlam.

People were terrified. The strong destroyed the weak. They took a lot of trouble. They cleared the road to the west and brought in gas and murdered people. They shot people. They ravaged and burned. They used chemicals and gas.'

'You make it sound like Belsen,' said James lightly. 'You have had a shock.'

'That's mild,' said Mr Briggs angrily. 'Ask Waterford, ask Henry.' James looked perplexed.

'Ordinary people don't behave like that,' James said.

'These were not ordinary people, they were terrified people, not dumb-bells like you who know how to behave.' James looked offended and Ann hurriedly broke in saying that arrangements must be made to nurse Muriel.

Muriel tossed and turned in her sleep and days, then weeks passed. Now and again she opened her eyes and saw Ann and James sitting beside her or Akbar and June sitting hand in hand on the window seat. She wondered who they were and where they came from and why her leg and head hurt so much.

Late one afternoon she opened her eyes and saw Mrs Luard sitting comfortably beside her, knitting.

'You are not wearing your tiara,' said Muriel with a flash of memory.

'No, dear,' Mrs Luard said reasonably. 'I'm keeping it for best.'

'What are you doing here?'

'Henry came to fetch me. Said you needed a sensible woman. Those girls are too preoccupied.'

'What girls?' Muriel remembered no girls.

'Ann and June. They are married now, you know.'

'Married? I don't understand anything.'

'I daresay not, but you will.' The older woman's presence was soothing. 'That child Patricia and your Paul are going to stay for a bit in my house and teach my crew some English.'

Muriel did not answer but lay still, trying to recollect.

'It will all come back.' Mrs Luard watched her face. 'My old man got a crack on the head once and he was out quite a long time. The pigs went too. Ever so funny they looked walking over the snow.' Mrs Luard laughed. 'Your Sam is a handsome boy,' she said, but Muriel's mind was far away and she was staring in horror at heaps of bodies piled up in grotesque positions in the tube.

'We must get out. Escape. I must tell Father Richard.'

Mrs Luard raised her eyebrows and went on knitting, her ear cocked to the sounds in the house, Akbar sneezing and that horrid old man talking to Coke in the yard. She was glad that nice Mr Waterford and Mrs Wake's older son had gone off more than an hour before to fetch the priest. Mrs Luard sat waiting beside Muriel, her knitting needles clicking with a soothing rhythm. Now and again she glanced at Muriel's dog who sat with his head pressed on the side of the bed watching Muriel's face, his ears laid back. Later Mrs Luard saw the dog's ears move and, hearing nothing, went to the window. Across the frozen snow walked Sam and Mr Waterford on either side of the little priest, slowing their long strides so that they should not outpace him. Mrs Luard and the dog listened to the three men come into the house and the sound of Henry's voice raised in greeting.

Father Richard came into the room with Henry and Mr Waterford. 'Let's see the leg. How is she, Mrs Luard?'

'Comes and goes,' said Mrs Luard lifting the bedclothes off Muriel's leg. 'If you ask me, the longer she's gone the better.'

'I'm not going anywhere,' said Muriel clearly. 'I have broken my leg and it will heal quickly. I always heal quickly. I have banged my head too.'

Father Richard grinned and examined the leg. 'It seems to be knitting all right.' He put back the bedclothes. 'How does your head feel?'

'Muzzy,' said Muriel.

'Well, that will clear. Your leg is mending but will keep you in bed for a while longer. I've brought you some tablets for your head. They can't do you any harm.'

'Got any tablets for her soul?' Henry stood looking at Muriel. Mr Waterford suppressed a smile.

'I'll take the tablets.' Muriel shut her eyes.

'She's wandering off again,' said Mrs Luard and left the room with the others to speak to them. 'Do you think she will be herself again?' she asked the priest abruptly.

'Who was she?' the priest murmured and went down the passage to visit Mr Briggs who was quite himself again.

36

By the time Christmas came Muriel was receiving visitors. Each time someone came to see her Henry slid out of the door. Sometimes he was gone for hours on end and Muriel wondered where he went.

One afternoon when Sam and Mr Waterford were sitting in her room she said to them, 'Where does Henry go when he disappears for hours on end?'

'Oh, he visits the submarine crew and Paul and Patricia. He visits the Abbey. Last week he was gone two days visiting the fish people.' Sam smiled at his mother, glad to find her lucid.

'Can they speak any English yet?' Muriel asked.

'Of a sort,' said Mr Briggs. 'The children are giving them a crash course in basic English. They teach very well. They come from Dubrovnik, charming people. I have visited them too.'

'I wish I could get about,' Muriel said petulantly. 'I am mewed in and surely there are things to be done.'

'Not until the spring,' said Sam. 'When the spring is come Briggs and I and James, Coke and Waterford are going to get a boat and cross the channel and explore. If people were left, as Akbar says they were in Afghanistan, there will be pockets of people like us all over the world who have survived. We just have to wait for the snow to go and the weather to be good.'

'Sam, the snow was coloured. I remember the radio announcer said so and we all saw it here.'

Sam laughed. 'I know. It was an experiment. You know the Americans, they will try anything. Their experiment got out of hand, or into other hands, we don't know.'

'And death to nearly everybody. Was that an experiment too?' Muriel was angry.

'Very likely, but shall we ever know? It was a monumental disappearance, not like the calculated deaths in London.'

'Did your American friend die?' Muriel asked Sam.

'He vanished,' said Sam shortly. 'I met no one until I got to the Abbey when I was staggered to find little Father Richard alive and kicking. He sent me on here as I've told you.'

'I don't think any of it matters,' Mr Briggs said surprisingly, 'nor does Waterford.'

'Mrs Luard was a great find, Mama.' Sam wished to distract his mother.

'Coke, Paul and I saw streaks, coloured streaks in the sky, before we went to London.' Muriel's memory revived again.

'I did too,' said Sam. 'The French have, or had a warning system. I tried to use it. I tried to ring you up, but though I heard the bell ringing I got no answer, so I took it for granted you were dead.'

'Coke and James had already been fiddling with the telephone,' said Mr Briggs, 'that was why you got no answer.'

'Your suggestions are too pat.' Muriel looked at Sam and Mr Briggs. 'What is more, until I have thought it over nobody is going to try and find out anything. Nobody is going to risk what we risked in London.'

Neither her son nor her guest answered but exchanged quick glances over her head.

'Noises off,' said Sam. 'Oho, here come Patricia and her pigs.' He looked out of the window.

'Send them up to me.' Muriel knew why she was tired of her son's company but could say nothing. She sat alone waiting with Chap beside her, waiting to hear the trot, scuffle, trot of the pigs coming along the passage with the child.

Patricia knocked and came in answer to her call, followed by the pigs, Paul and Henry.

'How are you?' Patricia asked formally.

'Better, thank you.' Muriel looked at the little girl's face glowing from the cold air outside and realised that she was beautiful.

'You look rather cross,' said Paul, kissing his mother. 'What has upset you?'

'Oh nothing,' Muriel answered evasively. 'How are the rats, darling?'

'Never mind the rats, what made you cross?' Henry stood beside the other children, staring at her. 'You should not be cross now. You are much better. You are in your right mind. You have Sam back. What's the fuss?'

172

'Don't be so governessy,' said Muriel laughing. 'Or so perceptive,' she added. All the children laughed.

'Now we no longer have television we watch faces,' said Paul. 'Something has annoyed you. Tell us.'

'It is just that Sam and Mr Briggs have been visiting me and they are so rational.'

'Ah.' All the children looked thoughtful. 'Mr Waterford isn't,' said Henry, 'nor is Mr Briggs as a rule.'

'They try to allay my fears,' said Muriel. 'It's the falsity I hate.'

'Rather silly.' Paul sat down on the floor. 'I'm very chuffed about everything that has happened.'

'Mrs Luard takes it all very calmly. She loves her house, her possessions, her visitors, her new mode of life,' said Henry. 'Is it the spirit of scientific enquiry which annoys you, or just that you can't get about and boss us around?'

'Not that.' Muriel stroked a pig between its eyes and watched Patricia rub each pig in turn until they lay flat on the floor, their tiny eyes swivelling in their heads, watching the children talking to Muriel.

'Out of the mouths of babes and sucklings. Are they still sucklings?' Henry teased Patricia who hit him without animosity.

'You children are getting no education,' Muriel murmured.

'Oh, we are,' said Paul with emphasis. 'You'd be surprised what we have learnt from Mrs Luard's submarine crew. What the sailors get up to is *nobody's* business.'

'Dear me,' said Muriel. 'And who else teaches you?'

'Akbar. We watch Akbar and June and James and Ann, but they aren't so amusing.'

'Old Perdue teaches us a lot too, and you, you most of all.' Patricia put her arms round Muriel and hugged her. 'You are better than the pigs,' she said.

The two boys laughed.

'I shall have to wear a mask.' Muriel laughed up at Paul, and then her laughter died as she caught sight of Henry's face which bore an expression of extraordinary sadness.

37

The day came when Muriel, with Sam supporting her, and using a stick, was able to leave her room and walk downstairs to sit by the library fire. Only Mr Waterford was in the room reading, and he stood up when she walked in.

'Don't go,' Muriel said to him as he moved towards the door. 'Please don't go.'

The man sat down again, smiling.

'One of my legs is shorter than the other now,' Muriel said conversationally.

'My fault for setting the broken leg badly.'

'No, I think you did it wonderfully well. I am lucky.' Muriel paused, looking from Sam to the other man. 'Isn't it time you told me what you know?' she asked.

'We know so little,' Sam answered her. 'We know that Henry's family were mixed up in some international plot which either never happened or went wrong. We know,' Sam flushed, 'that my father was too.'

'How?' asked Muriel. 'How did you guess?'

'Well, he made this house "warproof" didn't he? He almost rebuilt it. He laid in stores and supplies for years. It was a refuge. But then he got killed so it did not matter to him did it?'

'No,' said Muriel, 'it did not matter any more. But you, Sam, you guessed and I guessed too that he was up to something. Did you go to Germany to try and find out? Did you find anything?'

'Not a sausage,' said Sam.

'So,' Muriel looked at her son and her guest. 'So nothing that they planned happened, did it?'

'Oh, Mama,' Sam exclaimed impatiently, 'of course it did. I told you about the silly snow. I told you about the warning system in France. You must know that they were part of a conspiracy to destroy. To stop America, Russia and China destroying the whole world, they wanted World Government, you know they did. My father took precautions for his own family, he didn't want them involved. And Henry's family didn't care much about him. They just sent him down here to you. They were out to destroy.'

'Don't be so old hat,' said Muriel quietly. 'You are barking up the wrong tree, not seeing what's under your nose. What happened is much more old hat than that, older than time, older than anything you know about. You have experienced it and you will not see. You are stupid, my poor darling, stupid.' Muriel stopped, seeing Mr Waterford lying back in his chair with tears of laughter running down his cheeks. Sam angrily left the room, slamming the door.

'Fool,' said Muriel mildly. 'His father used to do that.'

Her guest, stretching his legs to the fire, laughed more than ever. 'Keep it up,' he said.

'I am quite sure there was no man-made catastrophe,' said Muriel.

'Maybe not. Mankind just added to it.' Mr Waterford watched Muriel's face with interest.

'For years,' said Muriel, 'we have lived under the threat of nuclear destruction. I see no sign of it. Destruction, yes, but nuclear no.'

'There were a lot of do-gooders plotting,' said Mr Waterford.

'Yes. My husband, Henry's family, scientists in America, in England, everywhere. But they didn't do good.'

'No, I can't say they did. A smart piece of work with coloured snow, and a new communications system of coloured streaks in the sky, that was all.'

'The storms, hurricanes, plagues and other pestilences were not started by man.' Muriel looked at her companion.

'No,' he said, staring into the fire. 'No, those lunatics in London added to the disasters, but they didn't create them. They were a very frightened lot of people. It was curious. I watched them and Briggs tells me he watched them too. They got a bulldozer and went out of London to the experimental station where the poison gas is made, clearing the road. Then they came back and poisoned the people taking shelter. Then they started fires, then they waited.'

'And you waited?' Muriel asked.

'I waited and hid until the day I met you.'

'Rescued me,' said Muriel.

'We are getting away from the point.' Mr Waterford got up and put a log on the fire. 'The point is that none of this that has happened to us and all over the world apparently is man-made. It's not just a natural phenomenon either.'

Muriel was silent for a long time. 'What is that book you are reading?' she asked.

'Science fiction. Ray Bradbury. He's very good.'

'Who gave it to you?' Muriel knew quite well that it was one of her personal books which she kept in her bedroom.

Mr Waterford laughed. 'Henry, of course. He has got Briggs rereading H. G. Wells and Briggs is furious because he is only interested in aerodynamics and has found some books he wants to read in the shelves here, and Jules Verne is positively whizzing from hand to hand. That is, when hands are not being held.'

'What do you mean?' Muriel said obtusely.

'I mean what we see. James and Ann. Akbar and June and Mrs Luard's submarine crew. The procreation of man.'

'Oh. Is it going on much?' Muriel laughed.

'Of course,' said Mr Waterford. 'Of course it is, and all egged on by Henry.'

'Poor old Perdue.' Muriel's mind wandered to the old man.

'Oh, he and Coke are getting down to it too.'

'What!' Muriel was shocked.

'No, no. They have taken charge of the animals.'

'Oh.' Muriel looked abashed. 'What about Patricia's pigs?' she asked.

'The time will come when they will desert her. It's only natural.'

'I cling,' said Muriel, 'to the natural.'

'Do you?' Henry appeared by her side. 'Do you?'

'You are right.' Muriel looked at Henry. 'I have not clung enough. I was just screwing myself up to the point of being natural when all this started.'

'Oh rot,' said Henry. 'You have always been natural, you know you have.'

Muriel did not answer but looked out of the window at the imprisoning snow.

38

Muriel's leg grew stronger as she spent the days limping about her house, wandering from room to room and climbing up and down the stairs. Sometimes she telephoned to Paul and Patricia at Willoughby and talked small talk to them as her eyes looked out of the window of her room on to the vast spaces of snow so strange with all the hills rounded and softened. The children sounded happy and told her about the Yugoslavs, how quick they were to learn, how hardworking, how happy.

'The children say your guests at Willoughby are cheerful,' Muriel said to Mrs Luard whom she found sitting reading by the library fire.

'Yes, they are a jolly lot,' Mrs Luard agreed, 'not like this. It's sad. That child Patricia must not read it.'

'What are you reading?' Muriel had seen Mrs Luard knit but never read.

'A book about pigs written by a chap called Orwell. It would upset Patricia.'

'I suppose Henry gave it to you,' Muriel said flatly. 'Henry is insidious; he is making everyone in the house read science fiction.'

'I'm not a great reader.' Mrs Luard laid the book down. 'Now you,' she said quietly to Muriel, 'you limp, but you have no need to. Your leg is perfectly all right. No need to limp at all.'

Muriel limped away, cherishing her lameness, followed by her dogs. She felt nearer to her dogs than her children or visitors. Her dogs neither spoke, hinted, nor laughed at her, as she felt Henry did.

Henry is the devil, Muriel thought angrily to herself as she let herself out of the house by the back door and limped along a well-trodden path to the farmhouse and the cow byres. She sniffed the agreeable smell of cows and ponies and heard in the stillness caused by the snow the quiet contented clucking of hens and a bird suddenly fluffing out its feathers as it preened itself.

She knocked and went into the warm farm kitchen. Coke and Mr Perdue sat on either side of a wood fire. They were playing cards. Both men rose to their feet in surprise.

'First time out,' said Coke cheerfully. 'Still a bit on the lame side.'

The old man looked at her rather nastily Muriel thought. 'Is your head all right?' His voice, Muriel thought, sounded sarcastic.

'Perfectly,' Muriel answered, sitting down in a chair Coke offered her.

'Young Henry was here. He offered us books.' Coke spoke politely.

'Oh, Henry. It's Henry's latest craze.' Muriel tried to keep her voice cheerful.

'Sneaky boy that. He wants something to happen.' The old man spoke gratingly. 'Something to happen, as though enough hadn't happened already.'

Muriel felt as though she had a hand on a doorknob which she could turn if she wished. 'I don't think my head is quite recovered,' she said. 'What do you think, Mr Perdue? Is my head all right?'

'As right as it ever was.' Mr Perdue showed his gums. 'No woman is right in the head. None.'

'Rubbish,' said Muriel, laughing. 'Oh, what rubbish you talk, Mr Perdue.'

Coke grinned and glanced at the cards he held in his hand, and Muriel saw that he was about to play a king to Mr Perdue's queen. 'I must go back now. It's been nice seeing you.' Muriel moved to the door and went out quickly, shutting it behind her.

'Hail!' Henry greeted her as she crossed the yard.

'Henry, you must not inflict all those books on everybody.'

'Oh, why not?' Henry walked beside her.

'You know perfectly well why not.' Muriel looked at the boy.

'Oh, well.' Henry looked deflated. 'I'm going to stay at the Abbey, Mrs Wake. I thought I'd better tell you.'

'Of course. I should worry otherwise.'

'I'll see you there then.' Henry began running away from her across the frozen snow and she stood watching his light figure trotting downhill, trotting so lightly that his feet left no imprint as he went over the moor and down the hills through the woods.

178

'Where will he see you?' Sam came up to her.

'At the Abbey,' Muriel said softly. 'I must get there when I can.'

'We could make you a sledge and tow you down if your leg isn't strong enough.'

'No, thank you. I shall go when I can walk there myself.'

'Very well. Come in out of the cold, Mama.' Sam took her arm.

'How well did you know your father?' Muriel asked him, limping beside him.

'As much as I wanted to.'

'What a funny answer.' Muriel was surprised. 'He was a strange man,' she said.

'Very,' said Sam.

39

Muriel went into the room Mr Perdue had slept in before he moved to the farm with Coke. One of the girls had cleaned it and left it unnaturally tidy. The furniture stood primly, the bed was made up but flat. Muriel went across to the writing table and opened a drawer. She was surprised to find it empty, freshly lined with clean paper. Her husband had always kept his papers in folders in this desk and files of letters ready to be answered. Now she found nothing. Puzzled, she went out into the passage and called Sam and Paul who came up the stairs together looking very alike.

'Your father's desk is empty.' Muriel looked at her sons.

'We emptied it,' said Sam. 'There was a lot of rubbish in it.'

'I don't believe you,' said Muriel.

'Oh.' Sam looked embarrassed.

'He had a life apart from you.' Paul took her hand. 'He didn't really mind about you.'

'He did not mind?'

'No. He was wrapped up in his pipe dream. His new world. His World Government. That came first.'

'But we had such fun together.' Muriel remembered the man who had been her husband, who had indeed been her life, as she looked at her two sons. Muriel closed her mind and left the room.

'You should not have said that,' Sam said to his younger brother.

'It is my association with Henry which makes me say these things. Henry has gone down to the Abbey and I don't think he will come back.'

'Good thing.' Sam looked thoughtful. 'Are you going back to the pigs?'

'Yes,' Paul said quickly. 'Yes, the pigs and Patricia and the submarine crew are good company. It's your turn here.'

Sam looked put out and went to join his mother who was in the library with James and Ann and June and Akbar.

'Where are the others?' said Sam.

'I don't know. They will come back. Sam, these two lots of young people want homes of their own. What houses near here do you suggest?'

Sam felt his mother was applying her mind to something which did not interest her in the least. 'The old Admiral's house would suit you, James. Everything in its place. I shouldn't think it would take you more than a few days to get it in order. Shall we go and see it? You can walk there.'

'Yes, I'd love to.' James was enthusiastic. 'Is it too far for Ann to go?'

'No.' Sam felt and could feel Muriel was feeling the same thing, that these people, strangers to him, wanted to leave. He resented them feeling this as his mother had done so much for them.

'And what house would you suggest for us?' June asked Muriel.

Muriel looked at the girl thoughtfully and then said, 'The vicarage in the village. That would suit you perfectly.'

'I suggest,' said James, 'that we get the houses ready and warm and clear of débris and then go as soon as possible.'

'Yes, you do that. Coke and old Perdue are settled. Why not you? It didn't take long for them.' Muriel watched the two young couples leave the room and sat thoughtfully by the fire.

Mrs Luard joined her half an hour later and sat down beside her. 'Funny, isn't it?' said the older woman.

'What's funny?' Muriel looked at Mrs Luard sideways.

'We all wants a home of our own, that what's funny. But there is something else.'

'What else?'

'You know, they know, we all know that you have to be alone. It isn't only that they want to be by themselves and set up house. Henry dropped a hint before he left.'

'What about Mr Waterford and Mr Briggs?' Muriel's resolve to be hospitable reasserted itself.

'They are going to see me home and bring back Paul and Patricia. Then I think they will stay with you.'

'That's nice,' said Muriel brightly. 'I couldn't bear only a household of children.'

'We can all visit,' Mrs Luard remarked.

'I am going to bed to think.' Muriel got up and limped up the stairs followed by her dogs. Getting into bed she lay quiet and tired, unable to think at all.

During the following days she heard Mrs Luard's departure and the return of Paul and Patricia. She listened, too, to comings and goings about the house as June and Ann made their preparations. Now and again Sam brought her food but as often as not he found his mother asleep.

Muriel dreamed and woke dreaming of the empty writing desk and the house which without her help emptied itself of visitors.

In the library Mr Waterford sat by the fire reading and Mr Briggs wrote the book he never had had time to write and which he supposed nobody would ever read.

Days passed and clocks ticked and Muriel lay waiting for the moment, the moment in time when she would act. Waiting for the courage which she needed.

40

The house buried in snow, gripped by the intense frost, was deathly quiet.

Visiting Muriel as she lay in bed, Sam, Paul and Patricia reported that June, Akbar, James and Ann were happy in their new homes, that although the village was mostly buried in snowdrifts, it was easy to visit Mrs Luard and the Yugoslavs walking on the hard snow, that everybody seemed happy. Muriel got the impression that her household and neighbours in their state of semi-hibernation were satisfied, content even. But she was not satisfied. She thought of her husband Julian, and faced the fact that he, Henry's parents and in all likelihood many other people, had plotted for power, that what they had wanted had been dangerous, insane; that their schemes, going dreadfully wrong, had led to the catastrophe which Father Richard charitably suggested might be an 'accident'.

She searched her mind as to whether, if she had not been blind and complacent, she might have been able to prevent some of the horrors which had taken place. Although she knew that worrying was useless, since the explanation of what had caused the end of the world as she had known it would remain a mystery, she still fretted.

She wondered resentfully whether Sam and Paul had not been high-handed in sweeping away all evidence of their father's activities. She was aware that it was something she should perhaps have done herself. In the event her sons had been right. It was useless to dwell on a life which was gone, never to return.

Not prepared to lapse into the contentment and ease of those about her, Muriel retreated more and more to her room to lie wakeful, listening to the absence of sound in this frozen world, waiting for she knew not what as days and weeks dragged by.

On a night of full moon she listened to the muted sounds of Sam, Paul and Patricia, Mr Waterford and Mr Briggs going to bed. Her dogs lay at her feet and Charlie crouched in the armchair. From the farm the occasional sound of a hen's cluck, a pony's stamp in the stable, sounded loud as pistol shots. As sleep settled over Brendon, the quiet was so intense she fancied she might have become deaf. Then at last in the unearthly stillness came the suspicion of a sound.

The dogs raised their heads, thumped their tails, the door opened and Henry slipped into the room.

'Mrs Wake.' He kissed her cheek. His face was icy.

'Henry.' She held his cold hands in hers.

'Are you ready?' he asked in an urgent whisper.

'I will get dressed.' She got up and started putting on her clothes. 'I am ready. I won't be long.'

As she dressed Henry talked in a low voice looking out of the window. 'We must remember all the good things. We must think of the people and animals who have survived. They are all good. They are all important.'

'Yes.' She was excited, she felt new life in her veins.

'Put on several jerseys, it is still very cold.'

'Yes.' She pulled on a third jersey. Henry took her hand. They went down the stairs in stockinged feet followed by the cat and the dogs.

In the back porch they put on gumboots. Henry picked up Charlie and put her inside his windcheater. They stepped out into the moonlit yard.

'Listen.' Henry held up his hand. 'It's coming alive, waking.'

Muriel heard as once before the drip of water from icicles hanging from the eaves, the gargle in the drainpipes. She watched Henry run lightly across the yard to open the doors of stables and byres, moving quickly in a haze of sweet smelling steam from cows and horses and restive sheep. One of the ponies whinnied softly.

'Come on.' Henry took her hand.

'What about the others?' Muriel whispered.

'They will come when they wake. They will see our tracks.' He was leading her onto the frozen moor. She saw as they walked across the moonlit world that their feet and those of the dogs charted the course for the others to follow.

They hurried over the brow of the hill and down into the valley, speeding over the crisp snow. The moon was setting as they came over the hill and into the woods and all about them the sleeping world came alive. The snow melted, icicles cracked, the streams, long frozen, chuckled and gurgled to rush down the hills to the river, to the sea, to the world beyond.

As she followed Henry, Muriel felt a rush of emotion which she tried to analyse.

'Henry, stop!' she cried, for he was outdistancing her.

'What is it, Mrs Wake?' In the curious light before dawn, when moonset gives way to sunrise, Henry looked larger, taller, stronger than she remembered.

'What is it?' he asked again.

She said, 'Don't laugh, Henry, but I feel hope.' She feared he would mock.

'At last,' said Henry, staring at her. 'You had lost it, hadn't you? Even when Sam came back he didn't bring hope.'

'No,' she said, smiling at Henry. 'I had to find it for myself.'

'Yes.' He was serious, concerned.

'But you helped me find it,' said Muriel.

Henry looked embarrassed and amused. 'Come on,' he said, and led her through the woods, noisy now with snow dropping in dollops off the trees, water dripping, a fox barking in the distance, a badger moving across their path so that Chap barked and his bark echoed loud down the valley.

'You are not lame any more,' said Henry.

'No,' said Muriel, surprised. 'I am healed.'

They walked out of the woods, across the fields to the Abbey, golden and rosy in the dawn light.

'I made a collection for you, an exhibition,' said Henry. 'For other people too. I thought it would amuse you.'

'Will *you* show me? What is this collection?'

'Oh,' cried Henry, 'it is not really amusing. I collected gold and jewels, bits of hair, a bull's nose ring, your parson's glass eye, false teeth, deaf aids, badges, bottles of pills and always money, money, money. I thought—'

'What?' Muriel stood still and looked at Henry.

'I thought they would serve as reminders,' said Henry, speaking lightly in his most offhand manner.

'I see,' said Muriel. 'We may need reminding.'

'There is Father Richard waiting for you. You want to talk to him.' Henry pointed to the Abbey porch where the monk stood waiting to greet them. 'Paul said you were ringing him up, trying to reach him the night of the great storm long ago.' Henry pushed her forward.

'So I was,' said Muriel, remembering that night.

'Go on then. You cannot put it off any longer. I will wait for you.' Henry gave her another push and she walked on to meet the monk, leaving Henry sitting on the Abbey steps with Charlie on his knee, a curiously lonely figure.

Father Richard took her hand. 'So Henry brought you.' He led her into the Abbey. 'It's about time.'

'Henry came to fetch me. He has changed in some way.'

'We all change when we grow up,' said the monk.

'So that's what has happened to him.'

'You did not come here to talk about Henry, you wanted to talk about yourself. We can talk about Henry later.'

'He reminded me that I needed to talk to you the night of the storm, before what you call the accident.'

Father Richard laughed. 'As well call it that as anything. What was the trouble?'

'I wanted to tell you about Julian. I suspected—no, to be truthful I had found out before he died in the car accident he was plotting something horrible with other people, with Henry's parents. They wanted to rule the world, they were putting the blame on other nations. I could have tried to prevent it, I should have.'

'Maybe.'

'I loved him. I did nothing.'

'He was a lovable man.'

'But wicked!' cried Muriel. 'I did nothing to stop it. When he had the crash which killed him I should have done something. I did nothing.' Muriel stared at the priest. 'Should you not give me some sort of spiritual jog?' she asked resentfully.

'I should think you have had enough of those. What about—' he paused.

'What?'

'I was going to suggest—er—looking forward, having a bit of hope.'

'Hope has come back. I realised that this morning.'

'Then stop blaming Julian. Remember you loved him.' Father Richard sat down in the choir. They had been walking towards the altar. 'There's an awful lot to be done,' he said thoughtfully, 'and if we have hope we can get on with it.'

'Oh.' Muriel was mystified. 'Don't you think—'

'I am not in a position to judge. I do know that whereas confession may be good for the soul, hope and looking forward to what's to come is much more important. Ask Henry.'

'Henry?'

'Henry represents the future. I know—' the priest held up a hand to quell her protest—'I know you do not altogether like him, but you trust him. Did you not follow him to London?'

'Yes.' Muriel remembered that long nightmare journey with Paul.

'And he brought you back. It seems to me—' Father Richard stood up and started walking towards the porch —'that you underestimate Henry. If you have rediscovered hope, have a bit of faith too.' He sounded quite tart, Muriel thought, as close to being reproachful as she had ever known him.

Henry's voice startled them.

'Here they come,' he shouted, loud in the empty Abbey.

When they reached the Abbey door Henry was running with the dogs to meet a crowd of people walking out from the woods, their voices carrying cheerfully in the cold clear air, mingling with the sound of rushing water.

Sam and Paul, Mrs Luard and the Yugoslavs, Coke and Perdue, James, Ann, Akbar, June, Mr Briggs and Mr Waterford, the people from the fish farm, Patricia dancing along among them, now talking to one group, now dashing to greet another.

'It's a carnival,' exclaimed Muriel.

'It is Easter,' said the monk. 'Spring.'

Muriel stood with Father Richard watching the people coming out of the dark woods into the sunshine.

A vast flock of starlings swooped from the east, momentarily blotting out the sun. They settled chattering and whistling on the Abbey roof drowning the sound of rushing water and human speech. As suddenly as they had come they flew off and the sound of their wings died away.

The people gathered in the sun looking up at Muriel, waiting for her to speak. She searched their faces, the faces of friends, strangers, her sons. She looked for Henry. He stood apart, almost, she thought, as if ready to take flight.

'It has been a very long winter,' she began. 'It is over now.'

'Until the next'—old Perdue's voice from the crowd.

Some people smiled at the interruption, some looked anxious, Paul laughed outright. Henry began to move away.

'Henry *wait*,' Muriel called to him, 'wait a minute.' She looked again at the crowd of people. 'There is no proper end to a new beginning,' she said, 'but we have to start as best we can with someone to lead us—'

'Oh,' cried the people, and 'Who?' they questioned. 'You?'

'No, no, I am too old, too tired. I suggest—' Muriel summoned up all her courage. 'I suggest,' she said, 'that we elect Henry.'

There was a stunned silence. Muriel saw that Henry, white-faced, was edging away. The crowd began to mutter, to grumble, to discuss. Then someone cheered and suddenly they all cheered and a girl from the fish farm ran out of the crowd and caught Henry by the arm and pulled him forward. She cried in a loud voice which carried authority, 'We have all been annoyed by Henry. We have all been irritated by him. He has made us *think* and that has been infuriating. That is what a leader is *for*. Everyone with any sense complains about their leader. I vote for—' her voice was drowned by cries of, 'Henry, Henry, Henry.'

Muriel ran down the steps and joined the crowd, thinking, This is what I have been waiting for in the frozen world of winter. And much later, walking home with Sam and Paul after a day of rejoicing, she said, 'There will be other Henrys in other countries,' and Paul answered, 'Henriettas also.'

They will be young enough not to be daunted, thought Muriel, remembering all the terrors they had experienced and that after the initial shocks Henry had shown very little fear and much wisdom.

'We shall have to keep our wits about us from now on with Henry in charge.' Paul sounded pleased with the prospect.

'It's a good thing everybody doesn't like him,' said Sam.

'Why?'

'We have seen what too much power can do,' said Sam. 'We need the unpredictable Henry represents.'

'We shan't collapse into contentment,' said Mr Waterford who had caught up with them. 'With that boy around we dare not be complacent.'

DATE DUE